control

CHARLOTTE STEIN

sourcebooks
casablanca

Published by Sourcebooks Casablanca, an imprint of Sourcebooks, Inc., in conjunction with Xcite Books.

P.O. Box 4410, Naperville, Illinois 60567-4410

(630) 961-3900

Fax: (630) 961-2168

www.sourcebooks.com

Originally published in 2010 in England by Xcite Books.

Library of Congress Cataloging-in-Publication data is on file with the publisher.

Printed and bound in the United States of America.

VP 10 9 8 7 6 5 4 3 2 1

Chapter One

THE FIRST APPLICANT FOR the assistant job is very promising indeed. He puts his head between my thighs with minimal supervision and almost no prompting.

The only problem is—I don't recall *creating* an oral presentation portion of the interview. Or, for that matter, a portion that requires the answer: *you know you want it.* To a question I don't remember asking.

But I guess I must have asked for something, or none of it would have happened. Maybe it was all the staring I did at the curling, many-colored tattoos all over his heavy-looking arms. Or the way I bristled beneath the weight of his deep blue gaze. I must have leaned forward and asked about his previous job experience in a way that suggested an underlying code.

Job meant sex. Experience meant now.

It was sharp of him, really, to understand. He got a cross in the interview attire column—such a thin, barely-there T-shirt!—but he got a big tick in the "takes initiative" and the "understands subtle instructions" columns.

I don't think I got any ticks in the "cool, calm, controlling boss" columns, unfortunately. But can't I be forgiven? He looked like liquid sex and I can't remember the last time I had anything even remotely resembling a drink. Or resembling a hard, solid body over mine. Or resembling the scent of someone besides myself all over me—the slick slide of a tongue against my skin.

It's probable that some of these needs showed on my face. And though I'm sure that some people are of the mind that women who wear neat little pleated skirts and boxy corduroy jackets— the uniform of bookstore owners and librarians everywhere—are bookish and quiet and quite dull, there's probably an equal amount who view said women as repressed cauldrons of lust.

I'm pretty sure he sensed my boiling cauldron.

I think he felt I was a certain type—the type who won't admit they want it, not even to themselves. But when he pressed me up against the door to the back and then shoved me through, I didn't deny anything. My insides shimmied to think of this big handsome man having me up against something. Just doing it, without columns or questions or things neatly arranged.

Even better than that, it had come to me in a sudden flash that he might be fucking me to get the job. Of course, such an idea could have put a damper on things—what a terrible person I am! How awful, how seedy! Such a shame that thinking the word *seedy* only made the whole thing sweeter—perhaps *because* the job is so nothing, so pathetic. It's a sales assistant job. It requires all the skill and ability of a tomato.

But I'm a sucker for a tomato that lies on the casting couch for me, apparently.

When he had bent me over my kitchen table, I don't mind admitting that I moaned aloud. I moaned and pushed my hand into my knickers before he even got there, skirt shoved rudely up, finger firm on my clit.

I was as swollen as anything, just swimming in cream and buzzing to the touch, while in my head I had imagined the casting couch version of him asking what it would take. Would I give him the job for a nice hard fuck? What about if he let me fuck him? His rough stubbled face would twist into a grin on that one.

The expression he didn't make makes me wet, just thinking about it.

Back in reality, he had just kicked my legs apart. Grunted something like *oh yeah, you really need it, huh*? While the same thought sung in my mind and my clit fluttered and pulsed to feel my knickers being wrenched down my legs.

There's nothing like a horny boy, and he was very horny indeed. He had bent me over the kitchen table and knelt between my legs, thrusting his tongue roughly into my pussy and all through my slit, juicing me up for his prick.

He needn't have made the effort, however. And I felt it was only perfunctory anyway—a little flourish to show what a clever stud he was, before the main event.

The main event was glorious. As I sit here, going over the whole thing, I can almost feel the rough wood of my kitchen table, drawing against my cheek. The way the edge had bitten into my fingers as I held onto it, and the sound of latex snapping and my own trembling breaths rubbing through my aching body.

His grunts turned me on more, though. His urgent grunts, sawing back and forth as he jolted against me. And then his bruising grip on my hips and my bare arse, while his thick cock stretched and fucked into me.

I remember what he had said, shortly before he shot inside me. I remember because it almost made me giggle:

"You want it, you slutty little bookworm."

But the giggle was cut short by the sudden realization that my feet were no longer touching the floor, prompting a fresh burst of arousal that turned into something more when, quite suddenly, he smacked one big rough hand down on my bare arse.

I had called out in twisting mixtures of pain and pleasure, feeling my pussy spasm around his jerking cock, gasping with relief when it became a tense and roughly unfolding orgasm.

And then even better, I had turned my head on the table and seen the person standing in the doorway—a person who could have been standing there for who knows how long and judging by the flush on his cheeks probably had been.

A very uptight and nervous sort of fellow, who ran when I caught him looking.

Of course I can't hire him. When would we ever get any work done? I'm rocking in my seat right now simply thinking about him—anything more would be a complete disaster. Not to mention the travesty it would make of me, trying to give him an order. Clearly, he was not the type to obey commands without a whisper.

And that's what I need. I need to be able to trust someone to follow my meticulous plans for my shop, whether I am here or not. The whole point of hiring an assistant is so that I can have a day off, a weekend off, a good night's sleep. Maybe find some time to develop a torrid affair *outside* of work, instead of giving in to the voracious need to bonk potential assistants.

I have the whole thing laid out, and the lay out does not include rough sex in my kitchen.

Unfortunately, the second applicant does not turn up. And the third is just as wholly unsuitable as the first—a gum-chewing girl in an outfit I barely understand. Despite the fact that we're not five years apart in age.

I'm ancient at twenty-eight, it seems.

By the time I turn the open sign to closed and check and re-check the locks three times and climb the stairs to my flat, I'm close to sure that it's better to simply do everything yourself. I can rely on myself. I am trustworthy. Just look at the wonderful job I do of re-wording the advert for an assistant:

RELIABLE, HARD-WORKING, NON-HORNY ASSISTANT REQUIRED. MUST HAVE A THOROUGH UNDERSTANDING OF

ALPHABETICAL FILING. EXPERIENCE WORKING IN EITHER A
BOOKSTORE OR LIBRARY DESIRABLE, BUT NOT ESSENTIAL.

Perhaps I should take out the word desirable. It just gives people
the wrong idea, apparently. It gives them the idea to put their hand
over mine, and then their hand on my thigh, and then they say
things and suddenly we're in the back of my store.

Later on, when I'm lying in bed pretending to myself that I'm
watching *The Office*, I think about his tattoo. The one high up on his
left bicep. It had been some sort of twisted artistic thing, something
that I've got no idea about—but the blues and greens had drawn my
eye. I like a man with tattoos.

Or at least, I think I do. It's been a long time since I really
thought about what I like, if at all. There was Greg, who beguiled
me with his urgent forceful manner and his weird business-speak: all
those alien words that I felt free to invent dirty meanings for.

When he rapped into his mobile that he needed to draw a line
underneath all forward planning, my head had filled up with images
of intricately constructed foreplay games and a big red S for slut
stamped on my arse.

Sadly, I had been mistaken.

I was mistaken in Kevin, too. Kevin liked to speed walk. He
went for power runs. I had high hopes for our bedroom adventures,
but sadly his can-do up up up attitude did not extend to sex.

I think I may just be too difficult to please. Even today's en-
counter, on reflection, doesn't seem that exciting. Despite the fact
that just remembering the wood against my cheek and the sound
of harsh breathing in the tiny downstairs kitchen sets me off again.

I stop pretending completely that the television is holding my
attention and play him back in my head, instead. The couple in the
flat next door to mine—they own the pet store next door, too—are
going at it, and it makes for a good soundtrack. Headboard banging

against the wall, lots of grunts and sighs…they usually don't make much of a fuss, but this time I definitely hear Jeanette, crying out with something that could possibly be real pleasure. It makes me wonder if I sound the same when I'm with someone.

It makes me wonder what I'm missing out on, if timid Jeanette's getting better sex than me.

I press my finger against my still aching clit and sigh, just to hear my own voice. Then louder when I rub, gently, then louder yet to think of someone over me. The first applicant, with his sinewy arms and his tattoos and his narrow sly face, all rough with stubble. I imagine said stubble scraping against my sensitive places—my tight nipples and the soft expanse of my thighs and my clit—oh God rub my clit.

I'm wet before I know it and clutching at the pillow, the first applicant turning quickly into the usual suspects: that hottie from my latest favorite movie, that waiter from Delmonicos with the weird manner and then weirder yet…oh Lord, I always go weirder yet when I'm this close, body tensing and mind homing in on things I didn't even know I wanted.

Like that guy, staring at us from the doorway.

I try to switch the channel back to the first applicant, to being pushed down over the kitchen table and shafted hard, but it's too late now. My clit is jumping against my busy fingers and my juices are running between the crease of my arse cheeks, and I couldn't stop even if the couple next door banged on the wall and told me to knock it off.

In fact, I think I'd quite like them to do that. There's nothing like being caught in the act, it seems, even if the act is solo. I have a secret streak of needing-to-be-spied-on, and my mind won't stop going there. To him, and his too-thick glasses and his tweediness and those hunched shoulders and Jesus, that's a good image. Oh, that's so good. I bet we really shocked him—I bet he couldn't walk straight all the way home.

I bet when he got home he did just what I'm doing right now.

The thought is enough to send me right over the edge, so fiercely that it shocks me. All the sounds I wanted to cry out catch and stutter in my throat and I arch up off the bed, wanting more. I want a cock in my pussy and someone else's fingers on my clit and when we're through, I want to start all over again.

As I lie on the bed still shaking and dazed, I realize what I must want: someone to watch. I want to be watched, right now. Or else I want to watch someone else, someone tweedy and uptight. Is that it? I just don't know. I own a smutty bookstore, and I've got no idea.

Could somebody tell me, please?

Jeanette from next door brings me a pie and I have to wonder: Did she hear me the night before last? It's a possibility. But then again, she often brings me things. I think her and Derek believe that I'm lonely or too young to be running a bookstore or some such.

They're nice people. She stays and has a chat with me during the before-lunch lull. We sit in the general romance section where I've got my comfy chairs and my little antique table so that people can pretend they're in one of the big chains while they shop for porn.

Of course, I don't sell erotica alone. But truth be told, that's why people come to me. The big boys are terrified of being anything but family-friendly, so my store continues to make money. And I feel that I *am* family-friendly, anyway.

Families are born, after all, because of some of the things I sell. I've wanted to do the thing that makes babies plenty of times, after reading something from the erotic romance and erotica sections. Hell, sometimes the paranormal romance section gets me going, too. Sometimes just standing in front of shelves and shelves of reds and purples and flaming silvers gets me going.

I do love my store. Occasionally I'll take my shoes off, just so that I can wriggle my toes into the thick crimson carpeting.

Jeanette seems to appreciate it, too. She keeps pushing her plain white trainers into the pile and she has that look on her face—the one she always gets when she's in here. A kind of wonderment, I think, despite her sure and certain knowledge that I am a lonely spinster. She giggles every time she has to say the name of my store: Wicked Words.

Though at least she gets the intention. I honestly didn't think people could miss it, what with the red lettering on black and all the glossiness, but I get a lot of disappointed Goths and Wiccans, too. Some who are expecting handcuffs, some who aren't.

Not that I mind. In truth, I thought it would alienate far more people than it actually ended up doing, in such a bustling but twee city as York. And I honestly didn't think that so many romance fans would be attracted, but I get more romance customers than any other. They like me, because I get in a lot of the big American names that take seventeen years to filter down to us. I get the smaller ones, too, that never appear on these shores.

I fill a niche with my Wicked Words.

"Did you manage to hire anyone yet?" Jeanette asks, just as I'm busy trying to think about books.

At least I can answer no, thank God.

"Really? That chap who came by yesterday looked…interesting."

I think about his mouth, crushing mine. The wood against my cheek.

"Him? Oh, he was awful. No good at all. Couldn't hire him."

"That's a surprise. He looked just the sort to fit right in here."

She glances around as she says this—it's pretty obvious what she means. Big, liquid-sex Andy Yarrow, surrounded by books that feature men just like him, doing plenty of randy things. Yes, I'm sure he'd fit right in amidst all the sex and the horny shopkeepers.

"He didn't know the first thing about books," I say, which is perfectly true. He did have plenty of firsthand experience of the kinds of things that go on in my books, however—though of course I don't say this.

"That's odd. Maybe he was just nervous."

As Andy appeared about as inclined to nerves as a robot programmed to kill, I have to start wondering if Jeanette knows him somehow. Perhaps this is some sort of defense of him, which will then be followed by her persuading me to hire him. I can't imagine why she keeps banging on about him, otherwise.

"I don't think he was the nervous type," I say, at which she laughs.

"What, that little mouse? I think we've got our wires crossed, Maddie. He was the most nervous I've ever seen such a tall man be! He could hardly ask me if you would make a nice boss. I told him yes, of course—"

"Who on earth are you talking about?" I ask, but of course I know the moment the words are out of my mouth.

The nervy guy. The one who watched.

"The chap with the dark hair and the glasses! Didn't you interview him? Perhaps he took a fright and ran off..."

Of course, of course—he wasn't some spying customer at all! He was my second candidate.

Chapter Two

IT'S ODD, SHOWING HIM the ins and outs of the place. I can feel his eyes on me all the way around my store, as though they're checking me for specks of seediness. My wicked ways are going to rub off on him—poor, sweet, nervous candidate number two.

His name's Gabriel Kauffman. Gabe, he tells me, but he doesn't sound convinced about this shortening of his name. Clearly he prefers Gabriel, but that's a bit too formal for someone who's probably seen most of my tits and at least some of my pussy.

Or maybe he doesn't look convinced about the shortening because he'd like things to stay formal—something I can well believe when looking at him. He's even more tweedy and well put-together than the glimpse had suggested.

He has side-parted his hair so perfectly, I could use the white stripe of his scalp to rule a line under *Bargains!* on the sign in the window. It's made even whiter and straighter looking by the perfect coal black of his hair.

I think it should be weirder that I immediately think *Snow White*, but somehow it doesn't seem weird at all. The perfect pale skin, the dark hair, the probable fear that seven dwarves are going to do dirty things to him…it's all there.

Snow White was pretty nervous and unaware of her own beauty too, after all. And she likely thought all sorts of things, before the dwarves reassured her that they just wanted her to keep house.

I tell him his duties in a clear, direct sort of way. No sexual subtext.

He seems to respond well to boundaries. Restrictions. He's as obedient as a dog, his tongue curling up to his teeth whenever I lay out another rule or duty for him. I explain that the shelves need dusting every Wednesday, that I like the little recommendation cards to lie flush to the wood, that the book of the week stand should be perpendicular to the shelf behind it.

I like right angles, I tell him, and his tongue touches his upper teeth. He has neat little pointed incisors, I note—that should seem vampiric, but don't.

Eventually, he manages to work up the nerve to ask questions, though they're not exactly the questions I expect. If Andy asked them, I'd be nervous. They're the questions of a thief, a meddler, a pain in the arse.

"So, while I'm working in the shop, where will you be? Will you be here with me?"

He looks away while he says it, too. I'd think he was planning something, if he wasn't so wound tight and reined in. He probably just wants to make sure he doesn't fuck everything up.

"At first, I'll be with you. There'll be a short training period, and then you'll be on your own for three mornings and two afternoons of the week. Maybe less at first, if you're not quite ready."

He turns and flashes me the first smile of this entire interview and hiring process. It makes his face different—much less somber, obviously, but it gives him a boyish air, too. His application told me he's thirty, and he looks it until he smiles. It's the heavy eyebrows, I think, and the tweed.

"I think I'll be fine. Everything seems really straightforward," he says, and then there's a moment. It's not exactly the kind of moment that tells me he's going to use what he saw against me in some way, but it's definitely one that gives the impression that he hasn't forgotten. The whole thing hasn't just slipped out of his head, as his behavior until now had almost suggested.

I think the event embarrassed him. But not enough to make him block it from his mind.

I stick out my hand, and he hesitates before shaking it. As though maybe sex is coating my palm, or girl cooties, or something similarly nerve-firing. It's weird enough that I imagine, for a second, that he's never actually shaken a woman's hand before.

But then he steels himself, and grabs ahold of me, and shakes until my teeth rattle.

I need to get Gabriel on his own as soon as possible. I know this, because while we're in the store together, stuff happens. Stuff that isn't within the boundaries and restrictions and rules. And it's entirely my fault and it's nothing to do with him, it really isn't.

It's just that I keep thinking: *watch me.*

I keep bending over, right when I shouldn't. In much shorter skirts than I'd usually wear for work. And stockings with seams, that I absolutely *never* wear for work. It's much too delicious and addictive when he reacts as predictably as a puppet whose strings have just been pulled.

He gets flustered. Blushes are really obvious on his face, because his complexion is that perfect milk-pale—he can sometimes compose himself by the time I turn around, but he's never able to hide that flush high up on his cheeks. Sometimes it even gets him around the throat and at the tips of his ears, and then I just want to lick it off him.

By the end of the fourth day, I'm beginning to suspect that hiring him was as much a mistake as hiring Andy would have been. Apparently I'm not allowed to hire any men at all, because I'm a sex maniac.

Not that he knows it. I mean, obviously he knows I have sex with men in my kitchen. But I don't think he has any idea that I'm delighting in driving him up the wall. He tells me that he was largely homeschooled. That until a year or so ago, he still lived with his parents. When I ask him if he has a girlfriend, he goes even redder than he did for my shirt with one too many buttons undone.

"No," he says, but it's after a long, long, putting-books-on-the-shelf pause.

I'm absolutely dying to ask if he's ever had a girlfriend. The urge to run my hand down the strange arch of his back is more overwhelming, however. I settle for a pat, but even that startles him. I'm not sure he knew I was directly behind him, and now he hurriedly stuffs the book in his hand onto the shelf—as though he's been caught reading something he shouldn't.

Which is odd, because he was only looking at the back cover. What's wrong with the back cover of *Temptress in Time*?

For the first time I wonder: What on earth is a man like him doing in a shop that sells erotica and erotic romance novels? They must be like alien spaceships to him.

"You know, you get a twenty percent discount on anything in the store," I say, half-laughing. His expression stops me from taking it to the full laugh.

It's a perfect mixture of both utter terror and starving hungry eagerness. I've never seen a man look so famished—not even Andy. Not even carb-free-dieting Kevin. It makes me do something very odd, indeed.

As he's watching, I lift my hand and sort of place it casually on my chest. High up—not in a suggestive way at all. But then…then I guess it becomes suggestive. More suggestive than I was with Andy. More than I've ever been with anyone, as though his reserved nature somehow permits me an excess of freedom.

He's not going to say anything, after all. He's not going to do anything. He just watches as I slide my hand down over my plump left breast, tugging my shirt just ever so slightly as I do, so that a curving upswell of flesh is revealed. And when I get to my nipple—stiff beneath the lace clasp of my bra—such a surge of tingling sensation rolls through me that I go weak in the knees.

I think I come very close to sitting down suddenly, on the floor. My heart is vibrating its beats through my body. I can't stop staring him down—I want to live in those big chocolate eyes of his. I want him to look at me forever, watch me touching myself like such a dirty, wicked girl. He seems paralyzed, but that's fine by me. I want him perfectly still and taking me in, every nuance and shudder, and is he holding his breath?

I think he is.

"Is there something you want to ask me, Gabriel?" I say, though I know he couldn't ask if he was forced to with hot pokers. I shiver just thinking about his restraint. I shiver thinking about Andy, who would have grabbed me and fucked me up against the bookcase ten steps before this moment.

I don't know which is better—this exquisite tension, this waiting, this teasing. Or just getting.

"I…" he begins, but he doesn't really seem to have the necessary breath for it. "I think that…"

I'm holding my breath, now. The lids have drooped down over his eyes. You could almost mistake it for sleepiness, if it were not for his hoarse voice and the fact that my hand is fondling my tit.

"I think that…" he says again, and this time I lean right in. *I'm* the eager one, now.

But he just finishes with:

"…we should keep the Regency romances in a separate section to general historicals. Don't you?"

Of course, by the time Andy comes sniffing around my patch again, I'm ravenous. I'm as hungry as Gabriel probably doesn't know he is. A week of talking to him about clockwork toys (it was the family business, until his parents died), the books of Charlotte Bronte, and exactly what I'd like for lunch, right down to the kind of pepper and how many times I'd like my coffee stirred—and all as I'm dressing too sexy and being very inappropriate, employer/employee-wise—would be enough to drive anyone bonkers.

And I'm not anyone. I'm someone that, for the last five years, has been living largely in a sex drought. While managing a sex book shop.

Anyway, it's raining when he turns up on my doorstep. We're closed, but I have to let him in. He'll catch his death. His clothes will get soaked and then he'll put on a wet T-shirt competition through the glass of my shop door.

When he steps inside, I think of Gabriel, staring at me. I try to hold on to that power.

"So—you hired that other guy, huh?" he says, as he shakes the rain out of his hair—all over my shop! Does he think he looks sexy doing that?

Because fuck, he does.

"I hardly think you'd have been appropriate, Mr. Yarrow," I say, but he just grins.

"Because of all the sexual harassment that would have gone on in the workplace?"

There's already sexual harassment going on in the workplace.

"Because…" I say, but I don't get any further.

"Because…"

Because I can't control myself around someone like you.

"What is it about you?" he asks. I know he's not really asking, however. And he proves me right by tugging me suddenly to him, without waiting for my answer.

I lose a little of my breath along the way. My inappropriate heels stutter through the carpet.

"Have you fucked that little pansy yet?"

Something like defiance stings its way through me, to hear him use the word *pansy*. Unfortunately he chooses that moment to rip my shirt open, so the defiance gets left somewhat by the wayside.

"Have you been spying on me, pervert?" is about all I can manage. It bounces off him as though made of nothing stronger than paper.

"He doesn't look like he'd be willing to give you what you need."

"What do you know about the things I need?" I ask, but it sounds weak and ridiculous when I'm standing here with my shirt hanging open, not bothering to cover myself and certainly not stepping away from him.

The aching thrum between my legs won't allow me to do either.

"Just stop me when I'm wrong," he says, then reaches down for the hem of my skirt.

As he rucks the material up, slow, slow, he leans down to kiss me. Not rough or sudden at all but deliberate. His tongue eases into my mouth when my lips part for him. His fingers waltz over my prickling thighs.

I'm already shaking. It doesn't take long for things to splurge. His hands go into my hair and then my hands are in his hair and when I press forward, I can feel his thick erection through his jeans.

Not like Gabriel, who probably straps himself down. Andy just ruts up against me, roughly, forces me back until my arse hits the polished edge of my shop counter. It's little more than a desk, really, with a till and a few advertising knickknacks. There's plenty of room for him to bend me over it, should he so choose.

Though I don't think I really want to give him the choice.

"Fuck me like you did before," I tell him, but it comes out so much more brutish than simple words can suggest. I bite his leaning-into-me throat on that last *before*, and he responds with some force of his own in kind.

He lifts me—right up off the ground!—and sits me abruptly

down onto my counter, spells out for me that it's not going to be like before. He's going to do what he wants and I have to squirm and agonize.

When he shoves my legs apart, I agonize all right. I let out a little sharp sound which gets even louder when he tightens his fist in my hair and yanks my head back, to lick shivering stripes over my curving throat.

On the last lick he bites, and I moan unashamedly. I go for the front facing hooks on my bra, and fumble myself free.

The air is almost unbearable against my swollen nipples. His tongue is far, far worse, however. He makes these lovely quick, tight circles, before catching the tip with just the barest hint of his teeth— first one, then the other. I can't sit still for it, not at all, and I buck my hips, spread my legs wider.

I'm not wearing any knickers. I didn't wear them, for Gabriel. I was hoping he'd catch a glimpse of something—a flash of glistening pink, perhaps—but now it's serving an even lovelier purpose.

It means I get to be fucked, quick. It means that when I manage to get my skirt all the way up my thighs, he can see my bare pussy and no longer wants to wait. His fingers part my slick folds easily, too easily, and then I'm caught between a tongue against my stiff nipples and a rough rub against my clit and that sound—the sound of a zipper being tugged down.

He straightens but keeps his fingers busy between my legs, face lust-slackened, wicked eyes gleaming.

"God, you want it so bad," he says in a voice as roughened as my own, and the juicy sounds my pussy is making don't deny it.

But I think of Gabriel, not Andy. I think of Gabriel, staring at me, ravenously, and my clit jumps beneath Andy's rough touch. A little *ah* flutters out of me, and he rubs at me more firmly.

I'm going to come, any second. Any second now.

"Suck me off," he says.

I moan and grow slicker to hear the words, but they're still frustrating. He takes his hands away and I'm mortified to find myself reduced to whining, even as the thought of his cock in my mouth stirs me further.

I slide off the desk and down onto my knees with very little fuss at all. I make even less fuss when I come face to face with his prick, as solid and thick as it had seemed in me, pushing out from the parted wings of his jeans like a club.

The urge to touch myself grows very strong indeed, to see this evidence of his arousal. Of course I knew he was excited, but somehow it isn't real until I can lick the fine trail of pre-come from the tip of his bursting cock, until I'm allowed to palm his tightly drawn up balls and feel his choked groan buzzing through his entire body.

"Go on," he tells me. "Go on, slutty little bookworm."

His hand is in my hair but he doesn't force me. He just waits for me to force myself.

Though when I part my lips and swallow the length of him down, it doesn't feel like I'm forcing anything. It feels like I'm hungry for cock, a slutty bookworm who needs teaching some sort of lesson—how could I torment that poor man in such a way?

Maybe Gabriel will walk in, right now, and he can punish me, too. They can take turns in my mouth, Andy urging Gabe on, ordering him to hold my head and fuck my face. He won't do it, at first, but as things get more urgent and slippery, and all that hunger inside him comes bubbling to the surface and oh God, Gabe, I want to make you surface, God—

I suck greedily, now mindless with dirty thoughts I never know I want to think until they're right there. But it's only when I get my hand around the base of him, and jerk him off as I lick and nibble and swirl my tongue just so, that his legs start to tremble. He grunts for me in a way that clasps my whole body, close to orgasm but not quite going over.

My clit is aching, just aching, and I can't deny it any longer. I have to touch myself—I don't care how much of a slutty bookworm it makes me.

My finger skids in all the wetness soaking my slit, prompting a frustrated sob from me that apparently goes directly to his cock. Every sound I make forces him to buck forward, so it's no surprise that when I finally find my clit and press just once, lightly, my long moan of delight triggers his orgasm.

I'm still shocked, however. He cries out and spurts thickly into my mouth as I frantically rub at myself, but it's not the sweet-salt taste or the swell of him or his cry of pleasure that wrenches out my climax. It's him pulling away from me, mid-spurt, to stripe my face with the last of his come.

Chapter Three

I CAN TELL HE'S seen. It could be that I meant for him to. I'm no longer sure of myself or what I might do at any given moment, and letting Gabriel see my ass-print on that glossy countertop is no exception to this problem.

I'm only surprised that the countertop held the print so well. I thought it might fade overnight, but when I come back onto the shop floor with morning cups of coffee and he's polishing the top as though devils possess him, it's fairly obvious that the fading didn't happen.

I wonder if he knows. His blushing face tells me he does.

Though exactly what that restrained little brain of his is conjuring up, I've no idea. Me flashing a customer with some ankle, and accidentally riding up a little bit too much skirt so that an arse-print gets left? Maybe he imagines that my arse cheeks got a little hot, and I felt the best way to cool them down would be to plant them on the glossy wood.

It can't be sex. He might be as horny as a horn-riddled dinosaur, but I don't think he's capable of processing real, actual, dirty thoughts. He's probably still stuck on bra straps and snogging as sexual fantasies.

I have a brief flash of delicious pleasure as I leave him to take care of the shop, thinking of him trying to make sense of an arse-print in his innocent pigtailed mind. Imagine if he'd forgotten something yesterday and came back just at the wrong moment! Then seen me and Andy doing terrible things through the inch of glass not covered by posters and sheltered by bookstands.

Poor, innocent Gabriel. I just want to hug him, and make it all better. And maybe when I hug him, I'll let my hand stray to his neat little backside.

I buy the collected Poirot and a sensible winter coat to calm my fevered brain, and then enjoy a delicious nonsexual lunch at a restaurant that doesn't have a hot waiter to further my progress. Of course, the whole time I know I'm just delaying my return to the shop. I mean, that was the purpose of hiring Gabe—so that I could have more time to myself. So that I could shop for things I need, and sleep, and suss out the competition.

I didn't hire someone so that I could spend my time harassing him. Especially when it's someone who's likely only going to be confused by that sort of attention. He needs a nice girlfriend, someone who is patient and sweet and as unknowledgeable about sex as he probably is. They can fumble under the sheets together, in the dark. She'll be vaguely unhappy for the rest of her life, but become an expert at baking pies. He'll start stashing gay porn in the toilet cistern.

I'll fuck Andy until I die of exhaustion. It will all work out for everybody.

Or at least, that's what I think until I catch him reading *Sins of the Flesh*.

I think I give him an out. And by that I mean—I bustle into the shop overloaded with bags, get a little tangled, and give him the perfect opportunity to pretend he wasn't reading anything at all. He stands up from his seat behind the counter, with absolutely nothing in his hands and no book anywhere to be seen in front of him.

But I know that's what he was doing. I can feel a smile pulling at the corners of my mouth even as I play along with his total innocence, that little pink flash of book cover I saw through the glass playing over and over in my mind. I guess his secret porn stash in the cistern is actually my book shop.

The smile pulls at my mouth harder, but I get it under control.

"Hello, Gabe," I say, and, as with all guilty people, he seems to find it hard to make perfectly articulated words. He says something that *sounds* like hi, but could reasonably be anything. His hands go into his pockets—as they often do when he's having to do something awkward, like make casual conversation.

The problem is that I actually *want* to make casual conversation with Gabriel. I want to chat about the weather! When is he going to talk to me about the weather?

Instead he helps me with my bags, and I spend my time guessing about him. Did his mother make him like this? Some spank-happy teacher, at the Enid Blyton School for Unruly Boys? Nothing at all but his own strange need to be so self-contained? He's not irretrievably weird, exactly, but you have to be a certain sort of man to feel you have to hide your need to read naughty novels from naughty novel store owners.

God, I'm dying to know if it really was *Sins of the Flesh* he was reading. It's right there on the stand by the counter, and it's got a hot pink cover, and it is absolutely unabashedly filthy. It's just the kind of book you'd read if your draconian parents stopped you from looking at girls' breasts until the age of thirty.

I stop just short of saying to him—as he puts the teabags away, in the almost-too-high-for-me-to-reach kitchen cupboard—that he can read any book he wants, whenever it's not busy. I could tell him it's a good advertisement—that customers often ask about the books they see we're reading.

But then he turns around, and there's this look on his face. His eyes are big and sweet and clearly the sort that are easy to wound, but there's a furtive smile there, too. His mouth is curling—the way I suspected mine was doing, when I first walked in.

It makes me not want to spoil his secret. I doubt he's been en-titled to many in his strange little life.

"I shelved the books that came in this morning, and watered the plants. Oh, and I got that big cobweb out of the top right corner," he says. It's where we're stuck—in boring work exchanges.

I never thought I'd be concerned about too much attention-to-detail talk when I imagined hiring an assistant. And he's so good at the attention to detail! He polished the little lip of non-carpeted stuff on the step up to the second tier of the shop, for God's sake! He cleaned the little window at the back—without having to be asked!

"That's brilliant," I tell him, though I wish I had less patronizing and/or dull things to say.

So it's something of a shock when he takes a big leap beyond silence or casual conversation or something boring.

He does it without warning, too, with his face turned away from mine.

"I'm used to keeping things neat, you know? My parents were pretty forgetful."

Something jumps inside me—a small electric shock. It's like being given an unexpected gift. It's like I've been digging in the dirt for weeks and weeks, and finally got to the treasure at the bottom.

Though the thought of what sort of treasure it's going to be makes me hesitate before digging further.

"Were you very close?"

Even with his back half to me like that, and his hands busy on a counter that's already perfectly neat, I can still make out the ex-pression on his face—an almost-grimace, as though he's just tasted something bad.

"We were...I took care of them. We weren't alike, though."

No sense in stopping now.

"In what way were you different?"

He shrugs, ever so slightly. A tight nudge of his shoulder.

"They weren't particularly sensible."

It's ridiculous, but my palms are sweating. I have broken into the Pentagon of him, and now I'm slinking down nuke-laced corridors. I am a Russian spy, interrogating him in a darkened room.

"So you were responsible for everything?"

"I...yes."

"For how long?"

I can feel him pulling away from me. He goes to the bookshelf adjacent to the counter, and tidies a mess that isn't there.

His back is fully to me, now.

"I don't know. Since I was a boy, I guess."

For some reason, Quentin Blake's drawings from *The Twits* comes to mind. Two scraggly, hairy weirdoes, living in a maze of filth. A small, slight Gabriel trying to keep on top of everything.

God, I should never have hired this one. He's making me feel obliged. I can sense it welling up inside me. It comes up my throat and spills out of my mouth:

"My father was very strict."

It's true. He was. But I don't know why I'm telling him so, when I've never told a soul. In fact, I can't remember the last time I told anyone anything about myself.

He turns, quite suddenly. There's a queerly eager look on his face that makes me both sick and something else. Something like excitement.

"I can tell," he says, which should make me even sicker. But somehow, it doesn't. Not when it's Gabriel. It would be different if it were Andy, sure of himself and rich with arrogance. But this isn't the same.

"How?"

His eyebrows lift, a little shrug of the face.

"Just something about you. Something so...in control."

How odd that he should say so, right when I haven't felt less in control in my entire life. I'm surprised my knees aren't knocking together. I need to get a hold on myself. I need to—

"Maybe that's just what you want to see. Maybe you like that about me."

"Why would I like that you're in control?" he asks, and even tilts his head to the side—for all the world like a curious little boy.

But I think he secretly knows. I think I know too—of course I know. I've been playing this game ever since I hired him.

"So is it all right if I go?" he says, quite abruptly. It sounds as though he's waiting for something—or looks like it, at least. But he's so closed and tightly wound, how can I know for certain what it is?

"Of course."

He flashes me that smile, the one with the pointed incisors and the curling tongue. The one that makes him boyish and not so weighed down by whatever he's weighed down by. And then all at once I know what he was waiting for.

Permission.

—◊—

I flick through *Sins of the Flesh*, looking for all the things he will have seen. He strummed her clit with thick fingers, that sort of thing. I want to get inside his brain and swim around in it, understand all the things he thought and felt when reading words like that.

It's not like with Andy. Andy's brain runs on one track; it's obvious he reads those words and gets an erection. It's a simple reflex.

But I remember what it was like to know nothing about words like that, to uncover a whole secret world one page at a time and be both baffled and awed. Is that the way Gabe thinks? Or has this always been his little furtive habit, while dodging around his crazy parents? If he reads this sort of stuff all the time, likely he knows more about fucking than Andy does.

That thought pulls me up short.

As does the scene in *Sins of the Flesh* where the heroine tells the hero to get on his knees. Though it's not the fact that the scene is hot that pulls at me. I think of Gabe liking it, instead, and feel my sex grow warm and plump. I'm supposed to be catching up on a little bookkeeping, but somehow the room has grown dark and my receipts have gone untouched and I've got this book in my hand while thoughts of Gabriel, downstairs in the shop, fill me up.

It's not the book, it's Gabriel. It's not that someone was watching; it's not the idea of being watched. It's the fact that it was someone so dark and strange and potentially pliable watching.

The realization makes me cover my face with the book.

I like it. I like teasing him and tormenting him, peeling away all his layers and giving him permission. I could have chosen the girl, if I wanted. I could have chosen Andy to be my assistant. But I didn't. I chose Gabriel Kauffman.

Probably because of my strict father, thanks so much, Dr. Gabriel Freud.

Fuck knows what I'm going to do from here. K-I-S-S-I-N-G, my brain sings, and I hate myself. Why can't I just be satisfied with Andy?

Because I've been satisfied with Andy all my life, maybe.

I throw the book aside and stand, straighten my shirt, smooth my trousers. I look neat and professional, which should help with the firing of my almost perfect assistant. I can tell him that we're just not busy enough—which is a lie—or that the economy is biting too hard, or some such nonsense. And then I can go back to the way things were and the way I was.

Straight, simple, professional.

Unfortunately, even before I get to the shop I know something's going on. I know the way I knew when I saw that little flash of hot pink and he stood up too hurriedly. The kitchen door opens out almost on top of the counter, and he's not there. He's not anywhere in the main space of the shop—though I suppose that isn't too unusual, considering that it's closing time. It could be that he's just tidying the second tier, the little alcove at the back of the store that made me buy the place.

And yet I know he's not tidying. I don't do anything as clichéd as keeping the filthiest books back there, but it's where I catch the most embarrassed-looking men in macs. I don't get all that many, however—I think because I sell so much romance, too. It's hard to lick the pornography amidst the hearts and flowers.

I like Gabe, a lot, for not seeming to mind how many hearts and flowers flutter around his smut. In fact, I think he prefers it that way. He's standing right in the corner, in front of the bookcase beside the window, reading *Passion's Flame*. I can tell it's *Passion's Flame*, because it's one of my all-time favorites.

I can also make out his teeth, biting deep into his lower lip. That furrow he sometimes gets between his heavy black brows, as though he's uncertain how to proceed. But then his head turns slightly—I think so he can look at the right-hand page—and I can no longer see the lovely slant of his face. His back is almost completely to me—though that's not exactly an unpleasant sight.

He isn't big, like Andy. But that curve, to his back. The narrowness of his hips—so clear in those tidy gray trousers he always wears—contrasting giddily with the broadness of his shoulders…

I don't want to alert him to my presence, just so that I can keep looking at his back. I don't want to alert him to my presence because then he would stop reading, and biting his lip, and acting like a nineteenth-century maid who's doing something she shouldn't.

I think I know when he becomes aware of me. His back stiffens ever so slightly. He doesn't turn the page when it comes time to.

My heart thuds, low and long. I'm not going to fire him. Oh my God, I'm not going to fire him. He's wrong, he's wrong—I'm not in control at all. I'm taking the step up. I'm strolling across the lovely plush carpet toward him.

When I get up close—so close that I can smell that old-fashioned pine-y aftershave he wears—the full pleasure of his height strikes me, as it did before, when I asked him if there was something he wanted. He must be six foot three, and yet so often he doesn't seem it. He hunches.

He's hunching right now. I can see him doing his best not to let me know he's looking at me out of the corner of his eye. He's keeping very still, juddery breathing aside.

I have to put my hand on his back. It's practically a necessity. I need to feel those unsteady breaths, vibrating through his sinewy body. I want to see him jerk when I touch him—and he does. But he keeps still, then, for the slide of my hand—all the way down that glorious curve to the hollow at the small of his back.

He won't look at me. So I just do my business while his back is turned. I slide my hands over his narrow hips and feel him tremble, then go further yet and pass them over the firm cheeks of his arse.

He makes a little startled sound when I touch him so intimately. His body vibrates with it, but he doesn't try to escape. So I rub harder, caress him more firmly. I slide my palms over the crease between his buttocks, pressing that tweedy material as deep as it will go.

He's taking tight shaky breaths, now. When I squeeze one arse cheek, the breathing gets even tighter, and shakier. He even lets out something that's almost a wavering moan—though not quite.

It definitely becomes a moan when I slide my hand around his hip, and go for the parts between his legs.

My hand immediately encounters the thing that's making him moan. A rigid erection, thick and pressing out the material of his trousers. It's so heavy and ready that just a brush of my fingertips makes it clear to me what's there, and he gasps, for extra clarification. He drops the book he's still holding, just so I'm sure.

I think he goes to say something then—something like stop. I can't. Don't. But when I finger the stiff shape of him through his trousers, the words trail away. He wants this. He's too eager for it to let propriety or repression or whatever else it might be stop him. I think about all the nights he must have spent with just his own hand for company, urging himself to lonely orgasms while flowery pages flutter through his head. I think about why he wanted this job, why he *must* have wanted it.

Because he's horny, so horny, even if other things inside him conspire to keep him alone. Just his little breathy sighs and his thick erection tell me how horny he is. Still, I want to hear him say it.

"Do you want me to give you a handjob?" I ask. Perhaps it's the wrong thing to do. He glances to the side, briefly—almost looking at me, but not quite. His teeth are worrying into his bottom lip, again, and there's a high glorious flush on the one pale cheek I can see.

Finally, he turns his face back to the bookshelf. Puts his hand over mine, suddenly, shockingly. He moans at the extra pressure.

"Yes," he forces out. "Yes."

I think about that point of mindlessness, when suddenly you just have to. When all possibilities open up. I think of him being there, of the book pushing him, of me pushing him, as I slide his zipper down.

Just the feel of his fingers pressing against my wrist, urging me on, is intensely arousing. My clit aches to be touched and wetness eases between my slippery pussy lips, sensation tight in the pit of my belly and ebbing and flowing with every new move I make. But it's building, and I want to build it higher. It'll be sweeter if I do. I want to come with the sounds of him going first in my ears.

The cotton of whatever underwear he's wearing is damp. More than damp. So much so that I wonder if he's already come, until I get my hands beneath the elastic and feel the slick bursting tip of his cock.

When I finally tug him free of his underwear and his trousers, I'm desperate to look. I need to look around his body and see what

I'm holding, because good Christ it feels big. He's swollen and taut with arousal—of course he is—but I don't think it's just him being turned on that's making his cock a challenge for my circling grip.

I think of his broad shoulders and his large hands. Of course he's got a big one. It would be weird if he were small. But this is something, even by those standards. It's something by any standards—heavy against my palm and straining against my grasp.

I map him out as much as I can while he judders and gasps, forming a picture in my mind of his length. No wonder he sometimes walks funny, with something in front of him. It's probably why he hunches. You couldn't hide an erection like this.

I wonder how many quick, tight orgasms he's jerked himself to, out of necessity. In the little toilet off the kitchen, perhaps, while I shop or bookkeep. Muffling his cries of pleasure in the sleeve of his jumper or against the back of his hand.

I thumb the slit at the head of his prick, and feel him buck against me.

"Please," he groans. "Please—"

I understand. I need it too. I'm rubbing my swollen nipples into his back, by the time I get around to tugging at his cock in rough little jerks.

Of course, I don't think it will take long. I squeeze and oil the way with all the slippery pre-come he seems to be producing. I twist my palm over all the good spots and work him nice and quickly. It shouldn't take long at all.

And yet it does. He grunts and rocks his hips into my hand, eventually giving in to leaning against the bookshelf. He rests his forehead on the arm he plants over the other copies of *Passion's Flame*, and his body trembles and trembles like a live wire, but he doesn't come.

He only comes when his own hand snaps down over mine, whips quick, and guides me desperately in a different sort of motion.

His gasps have turned frustrated and he's practically whining, but as soon as his own strong hand squeezes mine almost painfully tight around his shaft, it's clear that he's getting what he needs.

"Ah, that's it," he blurts out, body tensing suddenly and his hand speeding up on his swelling cock. My hand speeding up on his swelling cock.

It feels as though I *am* him. Bristling, shameful pleasure rocking through me, jerking at myself like a dirty little slut. More than likely about to spurt all over the books, and with thoughts of such only making the whole thing seedier, better, more.

My legs are shaking, in almost exactly the same way as his. I can't catch my breath, and I have to press myself right up against him to keep myself steady. Delicious urges thrill through me, and I give in to at least one of them—I turn my face against the bobbly wool of the little olive green tank top he's wearing, and bite, hard. I bite material, and the jut of his shoulder blade, and flesh.

My eyes open wide when he cries out in a way that suggests he doesn't hate a move like that. Not at all. In fact, he squeezes my hand tighter, around his cock. He jerks forward, as though pulled. And then his heavy prick leaps and spurts, thickly.

I know it does, because he cups his free hand around himself in this strange little jerky move, and everything spatters into the hollow he's made.

My immediate urge, however, is not what it was when Andy came all over my face—to get a tissue. Instead I want to turn him around, and lick my fingers clean right in front of him. I want to make him watch, and then I want to make him clean himself up, too.

Not that I get the opportunity to do either. Instead, he keeps his hand over mine—so that I have to sag forward when he does. He presses his forehead into the wood of one of the shelves, this time, but the impression I'm left with is the same. Frustration, and a mild sort of despair.

I don't think this has made him happy. I might have realized something about myself, but I don't think he's quite there yet. In fact, I'm not sure he's even in the vicinity.

I try to straighten and detach myself from him, but that's a mistake. The moment I do, he lets me go and jerks around, as flustered and blustery as ever I've seen him. He goes to pick up the dropped book, but then seems to realize that he's still exposed and covered in something that shouldn't be on books—which only makes him more agitated.

His hair is delightfully mussed. Or at least, it would be delightful if he weren't so clearly mortified.

"I'm so sorry," he says. His eyes flash ten types of panic at me, and all ten make my stomach twist in sickly knots.

However, before I can calm him down and reassure him that *I'm* actually the wicked pervert, he barges past me and out the door. He doesn't even remember to take his coat.

Lord, I hope he remembered to fasten his trousers.

Chapter Four

I LEAVE A SERIES of messages on his voice mail, but hold out no hope that they'll reach him. For some reason, I imagine his answering machine as a hand-cranked gramophone-type device, in a house full of similar items.

He probably has a mangle.

Either way, he doesn't call me back. Instead I get three hundred messages on *my* voice mail, from Andy. Some of them are dirty. None of them are as dirty as giving Gabe a handjob in the back of my shop. Though the "I want to come in your ass" one skirts extremely close.

I wonder if Gabe would dare to say words like that. I bet he's never even thought of such an idea, though I'm guessing his erotic romance education is getting him close. I bet it's making him want to pick up the phone and call me.

All I have to do is wait. Be patient. Don't force him. Why do I want to force him so badly?

Because I can still smell him on my skin—that sweet clean scent, like pine so strong and fine it's almost mint. Because when I think of his lean body strung out so taut and trembling against me, I go weak.

Because he needs a push, and maybe some tender loving care. And though I'm not that sort of person—or at least, I don't think I am—I can at least bake him a lasagna. If there are ulterior motives beneath the lasagna, like dirty fucking and not getting sued, well. At least he's getting a delicious pasta meal in the bargain.

I still feel foolish, however, when standing outside his over-varnished door, clutching food like some desperate-for-attention old lady. And, somehow, I'm sure he isn't going to open up. I can practically feel him peering at me through the peephole.

So it's a shock when the door practically lunges open. I almost take a step back, and then again when I see what sort of state he's in.

He has the tense harried look of a man who's about to be punched in the face. Or of a man who's been forced onto a ride he couldn't handle, and now he's about to throw up. His tie is slightly askew. A lick of hair dangles over his broad pale brow.

In his book, I'm pretty sure that's enough to indicate extreme stress. It makes me glad I brought the lasagna. It also makes me greedy to smooth that hair back into place, which is one of the strangest impulses I've ever encountered. I don't think I've ever smoothed a man's hair back into place before. Like I'm his mother or something!

Why doesn't it feel like a mother-y sort of thing?

"How did you find me?" he asks, like some gasping maiden, talking to her awful stalker. Though to his credit he seems to realize he sounds like a gasping maiden, and finishes with this: "I mean— what are you here for?"

I come very close to saying *to fuck you*, but luckily he gets in there before me.

"It's just that…my apartment is a mess and I…I don't usually have visitors."

It comes as no surprise to me at all that his apartment, far from being a mess, is almost unbearably clean and tidy. Reluctance skitters all over him, but he lets me by into the laboratory beyond. The one which he then tidies some more.

Despite the aroma of coffee wafting in from the undoubtedly sterile kitchen, the place smells like him: of that pine-y, soapy thing. And then there's the tang of furniture polish—of course there is. He's spraying some right now. On his books. Which are lined on shelves in so rigorous and orderly a fashion, it looks as though they've been covered in plastic.

Maybe they have been covered in plastic. The furniture certainly has been, after all. No word of a lie—the furniture is covered in plastic. The couch and chairs are what looks like a lovely and tasteful white and blue striped silk, but they're still covered in giant condoms.

There's not a speck of dust to be seen. Everything is at perfect right angles to everything else. Instead of a TV, he has a giant graph, plotting the space used by each item in his living room.

OK—perhaps not that last one. But it's a close thing.

"What a lovely apartment," I say, and I think he flinches—as though expecting sarcasm.

"Oh, well, I…" he begins, then gestures halfheartedly at nothing. "I know most men don't keep things this neat."

I get the impression that other people have not approved of his lifestyle choices.

"Who cares what most men do?" I say. He looks startled. Clearly the idea of not giving a shit has failed to occur to him.

I try to communicate my not-giving-a-shit-ness to him with just my gaze. Unfortunately, I think I send him extreme horniness, instead. He flushes from collar to eyeballs and looks down quickly, but there's no respite there. We're reflected back up at him in his over-polished floors.

I'm afraid to walk on it, this mirror floor. He's now looking at my shoes and it's reasonably obvious that he wants to ask me to take them off—but of course he can't. It makes me wonder how many people he's had in here, and been too terrified to ask them to remove their footwear.

When he meets my eyes again the flush that had died down returns, and he looks away. It's like a shove, to the small of my back.

"Was there something you wanted to ask me?" I say, but he goes in a completely unexpected direction. He blurts out, in a rush:

"Did you bring that for me?

Instead of anything about shoes. I don't know—I give him an inch, and he takes a mile!

Unfortunately, I love his mile. I want to run it, right now. I want to shout at him: of course I brought this for you!

But I just give him the barest flicker of a smile, instead, and hold the dish out to him.

"Why don't you go put it in the oven?"

His shoulders drop a little, but not in disappointment, I'm sure. It looks like relief, and the smile trying to curl the corners of his mouth suggests the same. When he reaches forward—from the waist, rather than actually taking a step closer to me—to take the lasagna, his tongue touches his upper teeth in that sweet and unintentionally lascivious way he has.

Or at least, I'm assuming it's unintentional. It certainly holds on to unintentional, when he stops halfway to the kitchen and turns—all big chocolate eyes and open mouth and oh my word, does he have little pointed incisors on the bottom row of teeth, too? Like a vampire, in reverse? How lovely he is. How lovely, and unsure of everything.

"Are you…were you going to stay and have some, too?"

He sounds so hopeful that my heart suddenly expands and devours my entire body. I think part of me had intended to punish him in some way for not answering my messages, but oh, that's not going to happen now. No no no.

I think he's going to get a treat, instead.

"Sure," I say. "Why not?"

He smiles properly, then, and when he comes back from the kitchen he even gets real close, to take my coat from me—like a gentleman.

His hands skim my shoulders once I've turned for him. They do slightly more than skim, however, when his fingers curl under the collar—I can feel him getting a sneaky stroke of my skin, at the nape of my neck beneath the dark fall of my hair. And then he slides the coat down my arms as slow as humanly possible, knuckles brushing me through my crisp shirt, all the way to the wrists.

Even sweeter and more sensuous than this strange repressed sort of touching: he leans forward and breathes in the scent of my hair. I know he does. I can feel and hear him doing it—just this side of obvious. Just enough so I'll know, without him having to say. That's Gabriel.

I turn back around on embarrassingly shaky legs. By this point I'm fairly certain that the barrier he puts up between himself and his desires is making a haze of tension drift between us, and I'm swimming in it. I'm drowning in it.

I think he's drowning, too. His gaze is foggy and his hair looks mussed, again—he must have straightened his tie in the kitchen, but the echo of that disarray still remains. I watch him fold my coat over his arm and an image floats up behind my eyes—him, putting my coat wherever he's going to put it. But pressing it to his face before he does so.

"The lasagna will be a while," he says, voice hoarse and oddly regretful. Though maybe it's not really so odd, when you consider that my mind has already progressed to him putting my wet knickers to his face, too.

He has to regret all the time we've got, all that while, when things like that are probably going to happen. Hell, maybe I'm going to make them happen, and then he can go ahead and not answer my messages for another hundred years.

"I'm sorry I didn't get back to you—before."

I think he's reading my mind.

"I just…I mean, my behavior…"

He rolls his eyes, as though his "behavior" was just that mind-boggling.

"I don't know what came over me. I'm not usually like that."

I raise one eyebrow, but don't contradict him. I don't really have time to—he darts back into the kitchen before I can say another embarrassing word.

Not that I mind. It gives me the opportunity to look around his tart little apartment without his nervous eyes holding me back. The books, in particular, need scrutinizing. I suspect that he doesn't put his money where his mouth is, and of course I'm proven right:

There isn't a single smutty book to be seen, on any of his many shelves. There are dry tomes on World War II and tasteful works of contemporary literature—you know, the sort that everybody likes— and the occasional manual on toy-making. But nothing that even feathers against the boundaries of naughtiness.

No one would ever guess that there's porn in his toilet cistern.

Even if there isn't, in reality. And I know this, because I check once I've invited myself into his immaculate bathroom. The one that's so immaculate that I bet myself he'll change the towels after I've gone, before washing the entire place down while wearing a biohazard suit.

And no, I've not a single clue as to why such an idea thrills me so. Even as I'm laughing to myself, I'm crackling with this strange sort of energy. The compulsion to do him wrong. I mist up the bathroom and write suck my cunt on his pristine mirror, then watch the words dissolve away into a little secret message, just for him.

For when he next has a shower, with all of his clothes on.

Unfortunately for Gabe, I don't feel like stopping at dirty words. The bathroom is en suite, with one door that leads to his living room, and another that I'm almost deathly certain lets a person through into the Fort Knox of his bedroom. The bedroom that's almost begging me not to stop at dirty words. The bedroom with the hotel-neat bed, and the weirdly drawn curtains, and the picture of Jesus over the headboard.

OK—not that last one. But even so.

The room smells of expensive air freshener, as though he's been doing bad things in here and needed something to cover them. However, finding what he's needing to cover proves almost impossible. The wardrobe is imposing and masculine, but there aren't any dead bodies inside—I know because I open it and find only rows and rows of identical shirts and trousers, with glossy shoes standing beneath.

The drawer at the base yields piles and piles of tank tops—his uniform of choice—while further bedside units are only filled with underwear, most monochrome and dull. I'm not even sure why I would expect anything else, and yet the more I search through his boring things, the sweatier my palms get. The more I anticipate his secret hiding places, his stash of the good stuff; after all, it can't just be a vice he indulges in while working at my shop.

I stand up, hands on hips. Frustrated and sure he's going to come in any minute, to make me feel guilty for rummaging through his stuff—though it's not as though he doesn't have a right to. This is a terrible invasion of his privacy and I *should* get guilt-stomped for it, I should feel bad, I'm an awful awful person, to do a thing like—

There's a drawer beneath his bed. There is a drawer beneath his bed, pretending to hide. I know there is because I had one just like it, and it makes those fat lines in the otherwise smooth underside of the frame. He's got a valance covering it, but really—he didn't think such a thing was secret, did he? Like a safe, for his valuables!

I crouch down and drag it out—so sure of myself that when there's nothing there, my disappointment is total. It's just more tank tops, more endlessly gray tank tops and so much monochrome that I wonder if the movie of my life has switched from color to black and white.

But oh my lad, you didn't think you were going to get away with it that easily, did you? Everyone knows that you have to check *under* the disguising items of clothing, too—like checking the layer of real notes to find the Monopoly money beneath!

And he has more than Monopoly money in his secret safe drawer of naughtiness, I tell you what. He has books, lovely books, of course he does—all the books I had under my own bed, back when I was far too innocent for this sort of stuff. Crimson Silk books, books by authors who disappeared into the wilds of "legitimate" fiction and never returned, books with bad girls on their covers.

He has my favorites: *Threesome, The Loner, All Business, World without End*. Spines laced with cracks, pages almost falling out. Exotically named authors like Felusia De La Ray. And all the scenes I still remember whenever I close my eyes and my body hums: the yellow scarf and the river and the tennis-playing girls.

I wonder if he remembers the tennis-playing girls. The ones who live on in infamy in my mind, apparently. Though I'm guessing it's more about the strong female protagonists in all of these books, doing things like writing the word cunt on bathroom mirrors.

Despite the fact that none of those amazing heroines ever do anything like that—mainly because they're strong and brave and cool. Whereas I'm just wicked and awful, and turned to water by desires I didn't even know I had five minutes ago.

Plus I jump and my legs don't want to help me stand, when Gabe finally discovers me and my many, many transgressions. If I was like them I'm sure I wouldn't feel conflicted about doing this, or nervous about hurting his feelings, and this would definitely be the moment where we continued what I shouldn't have started back at the shop.

The memory of which makes me stand up, book in hand. He looks angry at first, I think. That line appears between his thick brows; his dark eyes flash even darker. How dare you, that look says, as his hands ball into fists at his sides. Strangely, however, I feel no compulsion to apologize. I feel nothing besides the pulse between my legs, and the insistent buzz of a thousand heroines rattling their way through my mind.

"What are you doing in here?" he says, and the buzz grows louder, stronger.

"Looking through your things, dirty boy," I reply.

His face drops, the crease-frown and the balled fists forgotten. He blurts out, rather embarrassingly:

"They're not mine."

I love him for trying to deny it—it just makes the whole thing so much less awful, somehow. So much more like a game. Now I get to force him to confess.

"Really? Old girlfriend's, then?"

I can practically see him trying to work out the mathematical probability of such a thing being true. The odds do not look good.

"I'm keeping them here. For a friend."

"Did you read the books in my store for a friend, too?"

Even in the one-lamp-lit dimness of his bedroom, I can see that blush creeping up his throat. He fidgets, glancing from the book in my hand, to the open drawer, to me, and then back to the book again.

"No…"

"Then what?"

"I haven't read any of them."

"Really? Not even this one: 'Layla enjoys anonymous sex with hot young studs'? Or how about this one?"

I reach down and pick up another—a seedy-looking thing called *Breathless*.

"This looks fantastic. 'Before Cathy split up with her husband, she didn't understand the joy of a hard, healthy cock.' As opposed to a soft, sickly one I suppose."

I toss it back into the drawer and have to bite back a laugh when he winces. He's wincing for his injured, insulted books! As though I really mean it—as though I'm really mocking his taste when I love and sell books like this for a living.

"And what about this one?" I start, but he stops me, this time.

He lunges forward and snatches it out of my hand, clutching it to him like it's his dying love child.

"Don't," he says. "Don't say any more about them. There's nothing wrong with it, all right? I just like them."

He doesn't sound so sure, however. About the *nothing wrong* part, I mean.

"Tell me what you like about them, then," I say, and his expression confirms my assessment of what he really thinks is right and wrong.

"The psychological depth," he tries, but he doesn't seem convinced. I think he needs some convincing. I think he needs some help, from me.

"All right. Then why don't you read out some psychological depth to me."

His eyes freeze in place, wide and staring.

"I'm sure that Gemma Golightly you've got in your hand has plenty of choice moments."

Words are definitely trying to push against his pouty lips, but they're not making it out. Instead he shakes his head in this slow, almost resigned sort of way.

"Go ahead," I say. "Open it up and read something out to me."

At first I'm sure he's going to outright refuse. But he surprises me—he bends his head to read with barely another word or look.

I notice that he opens the book carefully, which makes the cracks on all of the spines something of a mystery. Until I consider what he must look like, clutching a book in one hand with the other on his cock. You don't typically think about spine cracks when busy masturbating to some psychological depth.

"'Kelly Matheson liked nothing better than a…she…when she went to work the next day…'"

He frantically rifles through pages, searching for the cracks in between what I know is steamy, steamy sex.

"'She told him without hesitation: it was him who had done this to her. He made her want to stop being prim and proper, and claw at him like a wild animal. Her puss—her...she...'"

More rifling. His face looks so hot, I'm sure it would burn me if I reached out and touched it.

"Why don't you just skip to the part where she has a threesome with those two hot gay guys?"

His gaze flicks up to me, bright and feverish already.

"I can't read that part aloud."

"So you know what I'm talking about, right? The bit where she gets fucked while the other guy fucks the guy on top of her. Right?"

His voice comes out wavery and oddly robotic.

"I'm not sure what you're referring to."

"Or how about the part where she makes him lick her pussy on that dirty staircase that leads up to her apartment? Oh, I like that bit. She's so good at describing all the juicy details—the way his tongue thrums back and forth over her clit, the way he begs her to let him come, the way she gets so hot all over—are you hot all over, right now?"

"I feel lukewarm, actually. Almost cold, in truth."

"Such a *liar*. You know what I said about lying to your boss. I think I'm going to have to punish you, now."

God, those heroines would be so proud of me! He swallows, again—looks to the book for inspiration. I really doubt he's going to find anything lukewarm there, though, I've got to say.

"Aren't I already being punished?" he asks, bless his heart.

I crouch, to find something even worse for him to read.

That seedy one by Barry Haydon, perhaps.

But while there, I find something much, much better. I can hear him protesting from somewhere above me, but he doesn't try to snatch anything away from my greedy grasp. He just waits, probably paralyzed with mortification, as I stand back up with something absolutely astonishing in my hands.

I could almost believe that he really did have a girlfriend who left all of this here. Because for the life of me, I can't imagine Gabriel going into Ann Summers to buy a sex toy.

He groans and his eyes flutter closed, briefly. But despite this humiliation—or maybe because of it—something is pushing at the front of his trousers.

"Don't be embarrassed," I tell him. "I have one just like it."

It's true. I do. A little pink toy—a real back to basics sort of thing. The kind of gift you get when you buy five books from certain online stores, maybe. I can just see him hunched over a computer, eagerly picking smut so that he can get something that buzzes neatly against the head of his cock or just behind his balls or something more, something else—good God, who knows?

"I've never used it. I don't use it—for anything."

"Are you sure? Because I wouldn't want to discover that you're lying to me, again."

Panic wrestles with his features.

"No—I'm not. I would never use that thing to—I don't. I don't."

"To what?"

"What?"

"You said *to*. You would never use that thing to. To what?"

He runs an addled hand through his hair, then smooths it back down again.

"To...you know."

"To bring yourself off?"

"Yes, exactly. Exactly."

He sounds relieved to have been given the answer. I've no idea why. Someone else is at the helm, now, and apparently she is a *hardass*.

"By...what? Rubbing it over your nipples? Pressing it to your stiff dick?"

"No! No, I don't use it to...do what you said."

"So if I put this in my mouth, I won't taste you all over it?"

He rolls his eyes skyward.

"Don't put it in your mouth."

"It smells like you. It smells like come," I tell him, though it doesn't really at all—it smells like antiseptic and soap and plastic. But he blunders into the trap, anyway.

"Oh God, does it?"

My sex shivers and pulses. The image of him wanking all over this pink plastic, hot streaks of come covering its surface—it's too much.

"What a liar you are," I say, and he moans helplessly.

"You know what liars have to do, don't you? Spread their legs."

He's sweating. I can see it gleaming on his upper lip. His cock has created all sorts of right angles in his trousers and he's practically squirming on the spot, but I don't blame him—only this new me is holding the real me up. The real me wants to faint beneath the pressure of this almighty arousal.

The arousal that's made me so wet I can feel it trickling into the crack of my arse.

"What are you waiting for? Spread them."

He glances at the bed and I understand immediately why—he thinks I mean get on the bed and spread your legs, like an eager slut. It makes me wish I had meant that, briefly, before I turn back to the matter at hand.

"No—just stand with your feet apart. Really, Gabriel—you're usually so good at taking direction."

He shuffles and makes this adorable little clucking noise at himself, the way people do when they've just fumbled something really easy and obvious. Then he just stands there and waits, and waits, for me to make my next move.

For some reason I'm certain that when I turn the base of this little ridiculous pink thing, it won't buzz to life. There'll be no batteries in it, he's never used it, it was a free toy for girls who buy books that are only meant for them.

But I'm wrong. It hums away merrily the moment I turn it on, and I feel his mortification press against my skin, sticky and delicious. It presses again when I step forward and whisper as close as I can get to his ear: *show me where you touch yourself with it.*

Of course he won't, I know he won't, but I also know that he doesn't have to say it at all. The little shuttered gasp he lets out when I pass the thrumming tip over his shoulder and down the inside of his arm gives me all the information I need.

He likes it everywhere.

I let it slide down his suddenly very thin tank top, clinging briefly to the poly-blend before finding that little hard nub—the one that's pressing eagerly against the material. So easily worked up, so sensitive—he gasps again when I let the vibrator trail over the jumping muscles of his stomach and ever down, down, down.

He knows where this is going to end up, I'm sure he does—he's vibrating too, with tension. And when I get to the twisted heavy shape of his cock, pressed tight against the material of his trousers, he lets out a low groan that makes my clit ache in sympathy.

I don't even have to get the vibrator that close. Just a light slide around his upper thigh, a twist beneath the buckle of his belt, and he sucks his lower lip into his mouth. He *mmmpfs* for me.

"Does that feel good?" I ask, but only to be cruel.

Before taking pity on him and inching that maddening buzz over the thick shape of his prick, through his trousers.

His eyes close. I don't think he knows he's rocking his hips toward me and my devilish little sex toy, but either way he's doing it, and he doesn't stop—not even when I pull back.

"Is this what you do when you're alone?" I ask, and this time he surprises me. He answers in a broken gasp, "Yes."

I don't think such a simple word has ever had this profound an effect on me. The urge to push my hand inside my knickers threatens to overwhelm me and I suddenly need that buzz all over *my* body, right now.

"What about here? Do you touch yourself here?"

I press the vibrator to his balls, firmly. Almost like an admonishment, I think, though he doesn't take it as such. He widens his stance, instead—almost unconsciously.

"Maybe," he says. "Maybe a little."

"I bet it feels so good buzzing you all over when you've got your hand on your cock, am I right?"

Before he can reply, I push said buzzing thing right between his spread legs.

He moans helplessly before I've even got it pressed tight to his flesh—his trousers are pulled taut and I have to work to get it in there, to get it flush against his perineum. But when I do finally get it, when I rub the thing nice and firm in the place he clearly likes it, he grunts and shivers.

His face is a picture of lust, hanging and absent, no longer looking away but looming over me. I missed out, the last time, on seeing him all body-shocked like this, but I revel in it now. His slick lips, parting. Those low lids lying heavy over his deep chocolate eyes. The way I can almost see his sighs wavering out of him.

And then beneath it all that steady buzz, prickling through my fingers as though it's already on my clit. Already sinking into my slick cunt.

"Is this what you do?" I ask, as I trail it back over the hump of his balls again.

"I don't remember," he replies, but he still jerks forward, when I suddenly remove that nagging pleasure.

"If you tell me, maybe I'll keep doing it," I say. "Maybe I'll unzip your trousers and run this thing all over the slippery tip of your cock. What do you say?"

He says *unnnhhh*, apparently.

"Or maybe I'll just stop it altogether."

I take a step back, and his expression snaps to attention

automatically. He even reaches a hand out, as though he's going to dare to pull me back.

"Please," he says.

I lick the tip of the vibrator, and he groans. That lust-blank look comes back to his face.

"Please what?"

"Please just…"

He searches the room for inspiration.

"Do you want to come?" I ask, even though it's blatantly obvious that he's gagging for it. It's obvious because I am too, and he's just me, mirrored.

"Yes, of course—"

"Then show me how you like it."

His face scrunches up in frustration. His shoulders bunch up.

"I can't do that."

"Why not? I bet you get enough practice. How many hours have you spent in here, doing yourself?"

"That's none of your business."

"What about if I tell you my business first? Think that'll make it easier?" I ask. I take a teasing step closer to him. "I masturbated yesterday, thinking about you. I fucked myself with something thick and fat, while rubbing my clit. I imagined it was your hands, and your cock. I came twice, thinking about how I'd probably have to instruct you. Boss you around. Then torment you until you gave it up to me, like you're going to give it up now."

He's breathing hard by the time I'm done. His hand is at his zipper, just hovering there.

"I do it…I sometimes do it three or four times a day.

"I've done it in the shop, too. I did it while you were on the phone with Barrett and Bates. I came so hard that my knees buckled when I thought about you telling them that they simply weren't satisfactory."

His words come out in a breathless rush, as though it's not really him talking at all. At the end, he swallows thickly—like everything just vomited out.

Me, on the other hand—I'm holding my breath. I've been electrocuted by his words about coming and masturbating and three or four times a day, and it seems incredible that I even manage to talk again at all. Never mind actually getting the following words to burst out of me:

"Now get on the bed, and show me how you do it."

He does so immediately. No protestations, no hesitation. He's even unzipping and shoving his trousers down his thighs as he goes, hands jerky and fumbling, legs tangling together. When he sprawls back on that pristine bed, it takes everything in me not to simply fall on him.

My entire body feels possessed by my cunt, and there's no longer just a trickle between the cheeks of my arse—there's a waterfall. My thighs are wet. My clit seems immense and it aches, solidly, relentlessly. But I stay standing, and I watch, I watch. I watch him stop watching me so that he can stare at the ceiling and maybe pretend I'm not here. I watch him shove his neat gray jockeys down and take his eager cock in his frantic hand.

His thighs stay caged by his trousers and underwear, but somehow that just adds to the overall effect: the one that fills me with bursting, slippery desire. It gets worse when in between rough tugs at his cock, he brings his hand up to his mouth, to lick a wet stripe over the palm before returning to stroke, all over and around his thick shaft.

He arches almost clean off the bed to feel it, body twisting and awkward but never losing that tight jerking grip on his thick shaft. The less he seems aware of me, the quicker and meaner he goes at it, rutting up into his hand like a filthy animal, stifling his groans against the press of his lips.

However, he has to look at me when I hand him the vibrator.

His expression makes me want to take off all my clothes and spread my legs—you know, for the view. But it seems I'm just fine fully clothed, because he bucks harder into his fist as his eyes travel down my body, and he presses that sweet buzz between his legs, no problem at all.

I watch him rub it over his perineum, his tight sac, the slick tip of his cock, all the time squirming and eventually moaning with abandon. And then finally—and strangely, most arousing of all—he discards his little toy and ruffles his shirt and tank top up, so that he can come all over his own belly.

He grunts once, gutturally, his eyes now on his own surging prick, and then thick ribbons of come spatter over the surprisingly hairy and pretty taut expanse of his stomach.

Though describing it so doesn't really cover how long it goes on for—long enough for his grunt to dissolve into whimpered moans. He makes a mess of his tank top despite his best efforts, too—he comes with such a force.

And then he's just quiet, and still, and probably very embarrassed.

Chapter Five

THE TIMER'S GOING OFF, somewhere in the kitchen. Of course I'm amazed I can hear anything what with this clanging alarm bell of arousal clamoring away inside me, but there it is.

I'm torn. On the one hand: extreme horniness. On the other: I don't want him to burn to death with his trousers around his ankles and spunk splattered all over him.

It just skirts way too close to dying of horniness.

While he's still immersed in bliss and not thinking too hard about what he's just done, I snap to a decision—quick to the kitchen, all heating appliances off, then back to appease the nagging harpy between my legs.

It takes longer than I had anticipated, however—mainly due to the fact that his cooker is three hundred years old. Immaculate, but still—most likely hand-cranked. The lasagna's probably being reheated by a lightbulb.

Plus there's the fact that I get distracted, by the photos that aren't on the front of his fridge, and the post-it notes that aren't stuck to his neat little cork notice board. He has a cat calendar, and the only thing on it for this month is *begin work*, in his tense handwriting.

I wonder if he ever wears the vaguely flowery apron hung on the back of the door. I wonder if I'm *ever* going to get satisfaction from a man who owns scented notepaper.

I'm guessing not, judging by his appearance when I make it back to the bedroom. If I hadn't seen it with my own eyes, I wouldn't have believed he jerked off not moments before. Would not have believed it. It looks like he's just finished chapter seven of Uninteresting Books for Boring People. He looks *tidied, cleaned, put back together again*. His trousers are zipped and his hair is smoothed, and he goes to say something that won't be explanatory—something light and irrelevant, I imagine, like *shall we eat*?

I'll tell him what he can eat, all right.

I can feel tension creeping up my back. My lips, pinching themselves together. I want to kick his legs out from under him, but instead words force their way up before he can talk about lasagna.

"Gabe—you weren't going to leave me like this, were you? How rude."

On the word *rude*, his lips part. He looks startled, uncomfortable.

"Of course not!" he blurts out.

"Then why are you dressed again?"

He searches the room for inspiration, and I'm pretty sure I can actually *see* his mind working. Figuring out the ratio of immorality to sex. If he puts a hand on my tit, is hell just around the corner, or down the next street?

But it's me who's too immersed in hell thoughts, it seems, because when he *does* step to me, it's so sudden that I start. He reaches out—almost wary, I think—and then strokes one hand down my arm. Just that. Nothing more.

Though it's still entirely possible that I gasp. I feel as though I haven't been touched in a decade, and if that wasn't bad enough, it's *Gabe* who's doing the touching. Gabe, who often seems too terrified to make eye contact.

Even if he's not too terrified to do this. He rubs his hand up and down, up and down—almost like a friendly reassurance, if it were not for my trembling response. I shudder as I watch him watching himself touching me, his too-dark and too-intense eyes following his own hand over the shivering sensitive inside of my arm. He follows it all the way up to my shoulder, where his fingers pinch and rub the material of my shirt in the most weirdly lewd way.

And then the lewdness flickers over to something else, as quickly as it had arrived. Something else worse, because I think he might actually be about to kiss me. He's very tall, so it's not hard to miss. He has to lean down, and come so close to me, and I think of all those cheesy movies with the hero going in finally, finally for a kiss. The heroine swooning, hardly able to believe it.

This wasn't what I had in mind when I started this. And yet I find myself tilting my face up to his, as his parted lips get closer and closer, and all I can think of is the utter hilarity of an odd backwards movie kiss.

That doesn't make me want to laugh. By God, I think I might actually be swooning—at the very least, I don't think I've ever closed my eyes before on feeling someone's mouth pressed to mine. And he's so tender and so gentle that it makes me ache, in a hundred odd and completely unused places. Unfortunate, really, that I don't have all day.

I want to touch his body and I want him to touch mine, and I want to be naked and writhing with him, immediately. So I worm one sly hand beneath the prison of his olive green tank top. And maybe I also curl my tongue around his earlobe.

He goes stiff against me, and stiffer yet when I poke said tongue right into his ear. Though really I think it's the combined effect of me gripping his jaw hard and holding his face down where I can reach, on top of my exploratory probings.

He makes a sound like this: *unf.* And when I lean in to kiss him, his mouth is soft and yielding. He sags against me, lips no longer quite so mean, fingers finding the slick mess I've made of his right ear.

Clearly, he's still sensitive from that earlier orgasm—he can't seem to take it when he touches the wetness, and his reaction gets even more pronounced when I stroke over one still hard nipple.

There is whining, and wriggling, and when I move to pinching that firm little bud, he lurches forward as though doing so will get more contact on his cock.

It doesn't, however. I shy my lower body away from him in perfect tandem, and then tug and twist at the nipple I'm still playing with until he gives even more over to me. Even more cries of pleasure, even more squirming and whining—it opens him up to such an extent that when I push for it, he lets me slide my tongue into his mouth.

And of course I know that, ordinarily, such a thing wouldn't be world-shaking. I can't remember the last time I had a kiss without some tongue. But with Gabe, everything seems to have a new level of lewd—my hand up his tank top is like a hand on someone's cock. Pinching his nipples through his clothes seems akin to something far dirtier, like, say, forcing someone to masturbate with a vibrator.

And sticking my tongue in his mouth is like fucking it.

He makes a little startled sound before moaning blissfully— exactly the way I imagine he'd respond if I did just fuck him. His mouth moves against mine tentatively, at first, but then with a little more boldness as my hand slips beneath the confines of his shirt.

It takes some tugging and wrestling, but I manage it. And then my hand is on his bare stomach, his bare chest, while he presses his lips to mine, wetly.

It's a shock to discover that he's as hairy everywhere as that glimpse had suggested. Somehow I'd imagined him largely smooth and soft, but there's nothing to apply those two adjectives to. His torso is uniformly hard and lean, thick with hair and utterly masculine.

He goes to say something, when I twist a few strands around my fingers. Something embarrassed or awkward that I muffle with my mouth forced against his. This time when I kiss him, his tongue flickers against mine. Just a little. Almost as though it isn't doing such a thing at all.

And when I move back, he moves forward, eating at my mouth hungrily, slippery tongue getting bolder and bolder until I'm trembling again, and more aware than ever of just how wet I am.

It comes in fits and starts, however. He'll kiss and kiss me and explore my mouth until our jaws ache, but then he'll stop and pull back, and every muscle in his body will suddenly tense against mine. Only when I grasp a handful of the thick hair at the nape of his neck does he push forward again, seek me out again, moan thickly into my mouth.

But I can see that this is all building to him pushing me away. He feels hot and too feverish, shivery-sensitive everywhere and eager to get away from my prying hands. And sure enough, after what seems like a desperate age of frantic making out, he tugs away from me, turns his face to one side.

Even in the low light of his bedroom, I can see the flush devouring his cheeks and throat. His lips are kiss bruised and pouty-slick, and I just want to go for another round, just one more round of this juvenile sticky fumbling—like I'm back in college again, wrestling with my boyfriend in the backseat of his Ford Fiesta. Tongue-y kissing seeming like the height of filth, my sex so wet and filled with ache that I could die from it.

I am going to die if it isn't my turn, soon.

"Don't—" he starts, but he doesn't get any further. Or at least, not with words. Instead he tries to shove my hands down and out of his shirt, struggling to straighten himself before he's even free of me.

Even stranger, as soon as my hands are away from his bare body, he actually *reaches* for me, again. His left hand—much bigger and broader than his lean frame suggests—cups the back of my neck, my jaw. He reels me in as though forgetting how nervous and hesitant he appears in every other way, and when he kisses me this time, it's hotter. Bolder.

While his right hand…his right hand moves forward, to cup my breast.

I go rigid. I think I come. Either way my defenses are down and all rational thought flees—I don't care what he does next, or what I do next, or what he wants. Just please have him carry on doing what I think he's doing: unbuttoning my shirt.

Whatever it is, he does it quickly and with fumbling fingers, as though at any moment I might stop him. His kisses grow sloppy and erratic, each one punctuated by a desperate groan or hum of pleasure.

It's clear: he didn't want me to undress him. But he sure wants me to be undressed.

I let him push me back onto the bed, body thrilling at this brief new side to him. So eager and hungry for something, for me—indeed, once my shirt is unbuttoned he moves back, almost crouching on the edge of the bed with my body sprawled out before him, and the look he gives me as he does it…

His dark eyes gleam, assessing me, and he chews on that plump bottom lip as his hands wander over the skin he has exposed: the almost-flat plain of my stomach, the steep hills of my breasts still encased in black silk. My nipples are standing out stiff and proud through the material, I know, but I don't *know* it until his lips part on seeing them. On seeing my tits, my throat, my collarbone. The little dip of my belly button that he touches first.

I feel him press just one finger there, tentative and curious, before laying his big hand over my stomach. Then he spreads his fingers wide, taking in as much skin as possible, before sliding his hand up, up, to the valley between my breasts.

He doesn't quite let himself touch them, however. I think he might be waiting for permission, but his soft shaking breaths and marveling eyes tell a different story. I think he knows he's allowed—more than allowed. This is his chance to explore.

I don't have any choice. I have to ask, "You want me to take off the rest?"

His patiently wandering gaze flicks up to meet mine, suddenly agitated again but no less arousing for it. I like his agitation, his nervousness—both rub against my tingling hot spots like calloused fingertips, though I couldn't say why.

"Is that what you want?"

He doesn't answer again, but his jaw tightens when I shimmy back on the bed and away from him. I lean against the headboard, smoothing my skirt and almost closing my shirt as I go. Prim, again. Neat.

"Tell me you want me bare, and I'll give it to you."

His eyes flash wide for the barest second, before he composes himself again. Though in all honesty, his composure is not what it should be. His hair has slanted sideways and his mouth can't seem to close, and I can see the tension in his thighs and his shoulders. The tremble through every inch of him.

And of course, he's hard again—I can see the thick jut of his cock through his tweedy trousers. When he passes one hand over this obscene bulge, unconsciously, my sex swells against its cotton confines. I feel as though I've been straitjacketed, down there. I feel too full and uncomfortable, just aching all over to remove my clothes in ways my words belie.

"You're teasing me," he says after a second—but he doesn't sound upset. "Are you going to refuse if I ask?"

I suppose he would seem very practical and ordered, like usual, if it were not for the tremor running through his voice. That cut of hoarseness, right at the back.

"Is that what other girls did, on this prim little bed?"

His face doesn't darken, the way I expect it to. The question bounces right off him, not hitting the mark of offense that someone who'd been snubbed would certainly have.

He just shakes his head. As though there haven't been any girls *to* snub him.

"If you want it, you have to ask," I say.

His thick brows gather together, but not really in anger or frustration. Again, I can practically see him considering and struggling, attempting to plot out his next move.

"Shouldn't you just be telling me what to do?" he asks, and though it's true that a thick gush of pleasure goes through me when he says such a thing, I wonder what ideas about sex are floating around in that complicated brain of his.

"No—I think I'd like this, instead. I think I'd like you to ask me. I think I'd like for you to come and get it."

His brow smooths out, but he looks no less disconcerted.

"Take—" he begins. And then again: "Take…"

I think about him looking at my shoes. My dirty, sharp little shoes on his beautiful polished floors.

"What do you want, Gabe? Would you like to see my tits?"

His eyes close briefly on the word *tits*.

"Yes."

"Then ask."

"Why do I have to—"

He stops himself, before his words become a frustrated shout.

"Because I say so. Go on, be dirty. Say 'I want to see your tits, Madison.'"

He shakes his head, almost amused.

"I can't say that."

"Then say Ms. Morris. 'Ms. Morris, I'd like to see your tits.' You can make an appointment, if you like: Mr. Kauffman to view the breasts of Ms. Morris five seconds hence."

Of course he knows I'm mocking him—just a little, not enough to singe, I hope—but he goes for it anyway. All in a jumbled rush, as though the words are sharp and scour his insides as they go.

"Take off your bra for me," he says.

It's close enough. Who am I to deny him, after an internal battle like that? And when he adds the word *please* on the end, well.

I just want to shove my hand into my knickers and get myself off, immediately.

"Shirt first?" I prompt, and his mouth almost makes a smile.

"Yes," he replies, breathy and bashful.

I kneel up on his uncomfortable bed, stockings almost making me lose my way, and then I take my time. I unbutton the cuffs of my shirt; I fold it neatly once it's off. And all the while his impatience vibrates against me, a living, arousing thing, made worse by his inability to push through it. He doesn't demand or ask anything further of me, though he shakes with the need to.

When I unclip the bra and slide it down my arms, finally exposing my breasts to his heavy gaze, he passes one hand over the bulge in his trousers, again. This time, it lingers there. It really rubs, and his tongue flickers out to lick his firm lips.

The cool air feels wonderful on my tense nipples, but I bet that tongue would feel even better. Not that I think he's going to do anything like that, of course. No, instead he says in this blank, strange voice, "Turn around."

At first I'm sure I've misheard. Not only because it's Gabe actually telling me to do something off his own bat, but because the request itself is so…odd. I thought he wanted to see my tits. The back view's not half so interesting.

And yet he's waiting, he's just waiting for me to obey.

So I do. I turn slowly, on my knees. Consider putting my hands on the headboard—even though that seems much more like an Andy sort of request. It seems like an Andy thing to do, too, when he puts one firm hand on my back and bends me forward.

Somehow I end up on my hands and knees, facing the giant cross that isn't over his bed. And though I adore many deliciously naive and awkward things about Gabe, I won't lie. The newness and unexpectedness of this act prickles delightfully along the length of my spine.

For a moment, I'm sure he's going to fuck me. His hands even go to my thighs, and he pushes my skirt up until I know most of me is exposed to him. Just a strip of white knickers between his gaze and my cunt, and that's got to be see-through by now. I can feel the sodden material trying to merge with my flesh, in some sort of awful, shameful fashion.

Even though it's Gabe who should be ashamed. He's the one with all that baggage on him. And yet when I imagine his precise eyes assessing me, his carefully measured repression doling out his slight, sighing reactions—my cheeks heat. I clench his perfect bedspread into white-knuckled fists, expecting maybe disapproving words: *You little slut. Look at that soaking wet pussy. You know what you need? You need a big fat dick in that whore's cunt.*

Of course, no such words come. Instead I hear and feel him move off the bed, and I bark it out before I can stop myself:

"Don't you fucking go anywhere, boy."

He hiccups around his response, but that's OK. I hiccupped inside, while saying those words.

"I won't—don't worry, I'm not." A pause, full with heat and tension. "Come closer to the end of the bed."

I do, without looking—looking would spoil the surprise. Maybe he's going to fuck me, long and hard. Maybe he's going to tease and torment me. Maybe he's going to play the sudden authoritarian and spank me. How dare I toy with him like this!

And it could be that's what I want. Or what I deserve, at the very least.

However, I know what he's actually doing, when I hear it—and it makes me thrill more deeply than any shame-based fantasy. He's kneeling on the ground.

"Gabe," I say, but he just tells me, in this breathless sort of voice, "It's OK. It's fine—I know what I'm doing. I know how to work this out."

And then he just presses that gorgeous mouth to the tense strip of material between my legs, without having to be asked.

I have to hold in the sob of relief and pleasure because there's no way I want him to hear it. It seems that I don't want to do anything, apart from focus on the sudden slow drag of what must be his tongue over that wet material.

His hands skate over the backs of my thighs and then up, beneath the folds of my skirt—and I think I know what he's going for, even if the way he lets himself squeeze and fondle my arse—even daring to explore the cleft between—makes me doubt his intentions. I get a sense of being uncovered, or being detailed and mapped out like a science experiment…

And then his hands slide further up, and find the elastic of my knickers.

Most of which would be just as excruciatingly pleasurable even if he weren't feverishly tonguing my slit through clinging material, at the same time. But as it happens he's doing both, and so it seems that I'm getting close to coming without anything like serious contact on my clit.

I think of Greg, saying *oh, do I have to*? I think of Kevin, getting bored after five minutes. I think of Andy's cock in my mouth.

And I judder, from head to toe.

I don't think I can stand him inching my knickers down. Of course I knew he was going to do it, but it still makes me delirious when the thin straps dig and roll against my tensing flesh. Cool and blissful air hits the furnace between my legs—God, I wish he'd go on peeling these off me forever.

But all too soon they're at my knees, and dear Lord he's *lifting* my leg—just a little, just enough so that he can complete the operation. Knickers all the way off. Bare arse and pussy exposed. I bet it looks like sticky honey in this low light. I bet I look as lewd as fuck.

Though of course he doesn't say so. He doesn't say anything at all. Instead his breathing gets higher and tighter, and he sighs like the dying wind just before touching me right. *There.*

Nothing more. More's enough.

I immediately push back against his delicately probing fingers, but only because I can't help myself. It's my intention to be patient—I want this pleasure to go on coiling itself forever in the pit of my belly, but I'm desperate. I'm so wet that the barest touch slicks and slides his fingers the entire length of my slit, whether he wanted to go there or not.

It makes me sure that the first time he sinks something into me is not because he intended to. He just presses and fondles and runs unsteady fingers over and around each fold until suddenly he's inside me, and I'm spread right open for him.

He moans, then—a real moan, tremulous and deep. I think he goes to say actual words, too—maybe about how hot I am, how slick—but like me he's probably too engrossed in the slippery sounds I'm making. That click when he pushes a second finger into my greedy hole, then separates them. Tests me out, until whatever he's feeling makes him shudder far more than it should.

It's only when he starts fucking into me, though, that I know for certain he's masturbating while doing so. He's now groaning, quietly, almost constantly, and there's another rhythm to his movements alongside this jerky fingering.

I think it's all just having a cascade sort of effect. He pumps his fingers into me faster, twisting and searching in my slick heat, and then just as he finds what I think he's actively looking for—that little bump inside me, that small collection of nerves—his mouth presses messily to my sex once more, over and around the slow steady push of his hand.

The first flicker of his tongue against my pussy is electric and impossible. I doubt it's actually happened—he feels too greedy, too open-mouthed, suddenly feverish and hungry for my slippery cunt.

And that's definitely my G-spot he's found. I don't know how, but he's curling his fingers and rubbing and all I can think is *science experiment science experiment hey Professor, Gabriel found her G-spot first! Look, she's going to come!*

It makes me long to see him. I think I know why he didn't want me to face him—so bad, such a dirty boy!—but I need to. I need to see and know and I need a lot of other things, too, until he slithers his tongue over every inch of me, before coming to rest right on my clit.

Then I don't need anything at all. I find my voice at that point, all right. I shout. I boil with obscenities. *Yes, lick my clit*, I tell him. *Lick it, you dirty little slut. Fuck my cunt.*

Words come out of me that I'm sure would make him melt through the floor, if we were fully clothed and face to face. And all the while I rock against his teasing mouth and tear at the sheets and pant as though I'm possessed, each kiss of my clit he manages to land promising to be *that* one, the one that pushes me into orgasm.

I'm so close I can taste my climax on the soaring edge of each fumbling, greedy lick. *Harder*, I tell him, *harder*, and though he obliges, I've been too excited for far too long. I'm jammed up, locked down tight. I have to put my face to the bed because I definitely can't hold myself up.

"Just your fingers," I say, finally. "Just your fingers, and then tell me, tell me exactly what you're doing."

I think it makes it better that he obeys me immediately, without restraint. His voice jangles through me, thick with desire, as his thumb slides down to rub the tense underside of my clit.

"I'm—" he begins, but maybe he doesn't finish with what he thought he was going to. Instead, he rushes out:

"Oh Jesus—I'm gonna come."

Just before my entire body clenches and gush after gush of pleasure goes through me, so intense I trap his hand and shout into his bedspread. I can feel my cunt spasming around his still working fingers, my clit jumping against his pressing thumb, everything inside me pushing toward one thing for what seems like forever. It goes on so long, I can't remember when it began, and when I'm done, through a haze of utter dissolution and shivering aftershocks, he asks, "Would you like another?"

Chapter Six

HE LOOKS FLUSHED AND pleased with himself when he comes into work the next day. Like he has a secret that no one else knows—the secret of my pussy, obviously.

I puzzle about it all day as we dance around each other—him coy, me so eager to slap his gorgeous arse it's like a sickness—serving customers, straightening and tidying and making idle chitchat about the weather. *God, it's icy*, he says. *Yes it is*, I say, as thoughts of the body I still haven't properly seen and of his furtive, dirty knowledge eat away at my insides.

I want to run *my* finger down the cleft of his bare arse—maybe while his rigid cock is deep in my mouth or my pussy. I want *him* to kneel on a bed and spread for me. I want him to tell me everything, everything about how he knew to do me so good.

I'm guessing it's the books. He knew what he was doing because on page thirty-six of *Hearts Aflame*, the hero sticks his tongue into the hot wet mess of the heroine's cunt.

But I've got to ask, anyway. I ask after I've run a couple of errands, and come back to find him making me a coffee in the kitchen.

It's become a sort of tradition, now. I come back or come down from my luxurious moments of time to myself, and he has a closing-time cup of coffee ready for both of us—the only one he has all day. I've tried to get him to take more breaks, but he just won't. In truth, I don't think he even drinks coffee.

But he does it when we can drink it together, and I always want to sacrifice my me-time for the exact same thing. If I spent the afternoons with him, instead, why—think of the things we could get up to! Think of the things we could get up to if I didn't open the shop at all. Think of the things we could get up to if I did nothing but roll around with him naked, in my bed or his bed or maybe not even a bed—

"Hey," he says. His face lights up when he sees me—it really does. He had seemed flustered and withdrawn once everything was done with the night before.

But I think he's ready to talk, now.

Even if he does go very still all over when I put my hand on his arse. Not sweetly, either—not a pat or something you could mistake for another thing. I spread my greedy fingers over the entirety of one cheek, and let them wander into the cleft between. It's a hard task, pushing tweed into someone's butt crack. But I persevere.

The coffees in front of him are briefly forgotten—and they're forgotten even more when I stroke. When I squeeze he doesn't look at me, but I can almost feel his awareness of my hand and my body, now pressing ever so lightly against his side.

I get my mouth very close to his ear, calves straining as I go up on tiptoe, and whisper,

"Where did you learn how to be such a filthy little pussy eater?"

He looks at me, then, big-eyed, but with that same pleased-with-himself-ness playing around his mouth. It doesn't stop him glancing toward the kitchen door, however.

"Someone could come in," he says. I guess he knows the drill, by now. It's not as though I'm going to leave things at an arse grab and a dirty question. "The door isn't locked."

"No one ever comes in past five," I reply, and then squeeze, nice and tight, until *he* goes up on tiptoe. "So come on. Where did you get it from?"

"I *read*," he blurts out. I think he's already half-cut with arousal and jangling nerves and other things delicious. "You know I do."

"You've read about fucking a woman with your fingers while licking her clit?"

He meets my eyes straight on, then. His pupils are fat and I think he might be almost smiling, but his expression still says—don't play silly beggars.

"You know what's in those books, Madison."

I think my nipples peak when he says my name. He's got quite a deep voice, really, and it curls around *Madison* as though savoring its flavor.

"I do. But it could be you got the idea from somewhere else. Maybe some older woman, when you were too young to know any better. Shoving your hand between her legs after you'd mowed her lawn."

He actually chuckles. Ducks his head.

"I didn't mow lawns. And there was no older woman. I just... I've always been good at putting theory into practice." His eyes dart all over my face. "I'm good with diagrams and working things out. I always have been."

"Are you going to work me out?" I say, and that little faintly exasperated, tremulous smile becomes something more solid.

"Is that what you want?"

"I want you to show me all the theory you know, in great and varied detail," I say, and then I take his hand and put it between my legs.

He lets out a little puffing breath and glances at the door again, but as he does so, he finds the time to run the pads of his fingers over my cotton-clad slit. Just a little test-out, to see what it's like.

I'll tell him what it's like: wet and full and ready.

When he turns back I go to remove his glasses, but he shrugs me off. His gaze is fixed, concentrated on the hand between my legs, and he murmurs after a moment that he *needs to see what he's doing*.

Right before pushing busy fingers into my knickers. And then he presses, lightly, on the first thing he finds.

"Mons," he says, in such a sweet explanatory tone that I would laugh, if I wasn't fizzing and popping with anticipation. Is this what he's going to do? Tell me all the theory, before we get to the practice?

I think it might well be.

He slides two v-ed fingers downward, the way eased by lubrication I'm already producing in excess. I think he says something about my near smoothness, my lack of fuzz, but it's hard to tell when I'm breathing so hard and anything but strict anatomy comes out of him pushy and tense.

"Labia," he says, clear as a bell, while his fingers skid stickily over my heated flesh. A little dart of feeling arrows through my chest and belly, but I can't tell if it's due to the simple, straightforward descriptions or the purposeful fondling.

"Well—actually, this is your labia majora. *This* is your labia minora. It's meant to be more sensitive here, does it feel more—"

"Oh, yes."

His eyes spark with delight, before he looks back down at his careful, meticulous work. He's so good, so clever, my Gabe.

Oh God. *My* Gabe?

"And then here…here's your clitoris." He frowns, ever so slightly. "I thought it would be less obvious—people talk about not being able to find it. But I can feel it really easily. I can feel it—though maybe that's because you're aroused."

He looks up again, eyes big and searching.

"Are you? You must be—you're all slippery. And your clit's all firm and swollen." He pauses. His eyes flick down.

"Is it all for me?"

I guess what comes out of my mouth could be described as words, but they feel more like gargles of disbelief. Is he actually saying this stuff? What is it—OK if it's an anatomy lesson? He got it all out so calmly, the bit about my slipperiness and my smoothness aside.

Yeah, that made him stutter, all right.

"Who are you thinking about? That guy I saw you with?" He doesn't sound angry. His tone is almost…resigned.

"You looked like you were enjoying what he was doing to you. I don't know if I could ever be…I don't know if…"

"Kiss me. Kiss me while you touch me," I gasp, and he presses a chaste one to my lips as his fingers circle round and round my bursting clit. His caress is in no way hard enough, but it's maddening and glorious all the same.

I have to grasp the nape of his neck and hold his mouth on mine, as I rut into that teasing touch. But he doesn't pick up the pace or pressure—far from it. Instead his fingers slide down, down, to my greedy, grasping hole.

He makes a sound into my mouth, as he sinks into me. I guess it feels good—I know it feels good to me. His fingers are so strong and thick, and he lets them glide and ease in and out, rather than pushing or forcing.

Before I might have said I liked it hard, but this is somehow just as good. It's all so ripe and raw, his fingers stirring my slickness and his hot eager mouth on mine. His kisses are much wetter and more open, now, and he lets me fuck his mouth with my tongue. And when he pulls away, it's only to tell me what he's touching, and how. Not because he doesn't enjoy the shameful thrill of being pushed and used by a woman.

He curls his fingers sharply, and rubs, and tells me he thought *that* would be hard to find too. But I guess he knows it isn't, now— especially as I'm up on tiptoe, holding onto his shoulder, babbling at him to *let me sit down, let me sit down, I'm going to come* as though he's the one in charge.

Though he doesn't look it. He looks intense and fascinated, as his fingers twist in my pussy, thumb rubbing fitfully over my clit. He looks pleased that he's got it all worked out, all the world forgotten— including his obvious erection—apart from my slick cunt.

"Yes, yes—right there," I say, and then my thighs lock and my clit pulses and I moan my way through a shivering orgasm. I press his hand tight, between my legs—which is when he moans, too. Just a slight sound, but we're suddenly so close that I can feel it, vibrating against me.

When I put my head on his shoulder, and relax all over—that's when I notice Andy, in the doorway. Just standing there, leaning against the frame, arms folded over his chest.

He looks amused, I think—though it's hard to tell when another man's hand is still in my knickers, and I'm still buzzed and lax from a huge orgasm. I just want to lean against Gabe forever, and not have to think about anything.

Especially not about whatever is probably coming, now. Somehow, I don't think Andy is the type of guy to run away from a situation like this.

"This your new boyfriend?" he says. I can't recall Andy being my old one, but I refrain from saying such a thing.

Gabe, on the other hand, snaps his full attention to Andy immediately. Though he does so without removing his fingers from the insides of my knickers.

"He looks like a real sweetheart."

I wince, inwardly. Yeah, I don't think this is going to go well, at all. What had he called Gabe last time? A pansy?

"Got him in the back of your shop, working real hard for you—I'm impressed."

There are many possible things I could say here: You shouldn't be back here, Andy. You're a pervert, Andy. Piss off, Andy. But I don't say any of them. I just watch, and wait, as Gabe goes tense against me.

He doesn't remove his hand from my knickers, however. I guess it's a better mark of ownership, if it remains where it is. A badge of his good work and dedication—what a good boy he is!

Not like Andy. Nasty, spying, gorgeous Andy. Who's getting closer by the second to get a better look at what we're doing.

"Do you think she enjoyed that, mate?" he asks, and I have to yank back my protective instincts—protective instincts I didn't even know I had—on a leash.

But Gabe answers anyway, before I have to say anything.

"Yes," he says simply. It makes me want to pump my fist in the air for him.

Lord, this is all going horribly, horribly wrong.

"I bet she did. I bet she did. You're her little puppy dog, I'll bet, jumping for a treat when she says jump."

I hate Andy. I don't know why I'm not telling him to get out.

"No," Gabe says, but he doesn't sound sure. There's only so much effort you can pack into monosyllables, after all.

Andy raises an eyebrow. I think—*fuck*—I think he's got an erection, and it looks almost as good as Gabe's does in those tight jeans. I guess tweed or otherwise—it doesn't really matter. It's still a fat thick cock, making perfect triangular shapes in material.

"Really?" he says, and then he's close enough to touch my face. It seems incestuous, somehow, while Gabe and I are still attached like this.

"She's such a sexy bitch, though. I'd obey her."

You liar, I think, but I *still* don't say. It could be that I want to see how this all plays out. Just a suspicion. And maybe more than a suspicion when Gabe says, sudden and through gritted teeth, "That's not what I saw."

And oh my heart goes pitty-pat, pitty-pat.

"Yeah? What did you see, mate? Did you see me getting a little rough? Getting her to do what I wanted?" He shrugs.

"Maybe she needs a little of that, sometimes. After all—looks like she's left you kind of high and dry."

That is an *outrageous* accusation. If true.

"But then I guess you're not the sort of bloke who likes to order someone around. Am I right?"

Gabe doesn't answer him. I don't think the obvious intense arousal he's laboring under is really helping him articulate. He seems trapped between confusion and suspicious anger.

"But it's real easy, I promise. Look, you just get her all worked up—and hey, you've already done that! Then you rub your groin, like there's something pretty hot in there."

I almost laugh. Is he serious? He's got exactly *zero* chance of getting Gabriel to consciously do something so lascivious. He might as well ask Uwe Boll to make a good movie.

And I'm right, because he comes close to throwing an amused smile Andy's way. I like his smile. It says: *You're a Neanderthal*—which I suppose is true. But it's also true that when Gabe starts to shake his head, Andy says, "No? OK—I'll do it for you, mate. No worries."

And then he *puts* his *hand* over Gabe's *erection*.

I'm so stunned, I almost stop to check we haven't flipped into an alternate dimension. I almost stop Andy myself, and I *definitely* expect Gabe to push him away. As passive as he sometimes appears to be, he doesn't seem the type to accept a man's hand on his groin—seriously, his sexuality is confused and shame-filled enough as it is. Another brick on top of the sandcastle and he's going to end up underground.

Only he *does* take it. His cheeks burn a brilliant red and he shuts his eyes, briefly, but he doesn't move an inch. He neither pushes away, nor pushes toward. He doesn't even flinch when Andy whispers in his ear, "So now she's seen what you've got, you tell her you're going to give it to her. Right? Tell her you want her on her knees, your cock in her mouth."

I've no idea what to think of Andy, at this point. I mean, he doesn't seem gay. Or bisexual, even. And what's even weirder—none of this seems either gay, or bisexual. Andy is just a cocky fuck and Gabe… well. Apparently Gabe will be into anything you order him to be into.

I think. I'm not sure. Someone explain it to me.

"Go on. What are you waiting for? She's primed. She's just waiting to swallow your cock…unless you want her to have a go at me, first?"

Whatever this is, *Andy is very good* at it. Gabe blurts out a *no* before he's even got to the word *first*. Not only that, but I think he's been reading my secret Big Book of Horny Fantasies, because I'm sure I've imagined something very like this before.

At the very least, I guessed right. I knew Andy would be like this, do things like this, and I was one hundred percent correct.

"No! No—I'll ask—I'll *tell* her. I'll tell her to…do that."

"Do what?"

"S-suck my cock."

I lick my lips for him, for getting those words out.

"Come on and do it," he says to me. "Come on and do it to me."

He's shaking and flushed. His hands are clenched into fists at his sides. It's clear that this is all bothering him in probably weird ways, and yet he *still* sighs disappointedly when Andy moves his hand away.

Andy just grins—his expression saying *dance, puppets, dance*, very clearly. I've no idea how he took the reins so quickly, but I understand this much for sure: my own efforts seem weak and third-rate by comparison.

"Undo your pants," he says to Gabe. And Gabe obeys, in flustered fumbles. He's looking right at me, but I don't think he'd hear me if I spoke.

"Get it out, get it ready. You don't want to make her wait, do you? She's so horny for it, mate, seriously."

It's obvious why his filthy arrogant words have an effect on Gabe, but I'm amazed at the effect they have on me. It feels as though I haven't come for a week, though in reality it was about five minutes ago. My body's agitated, restless—Andy's right. I'm horny for cock. I can hardly wait to taste him.

When Gabe finally, *finally* wrestles himself from his trousers, Andy laughs. Not meanly—just a short bark—before he leans back against my table, arms crossed.

"No wonder she likes you, hey?"

He glances at Andy, then—more directly than he's dared to since this whole weird force-Madison-to-give-you-a-blowjob thing started. He looks confused, I think, though alarmingly not because of the scenario.

It's clear—he just doesn't know what Andy means by *no wonder she likes you*. He just doesn't get it. Though to his credit, he's probably not used to guys complimenting his dick.

"You're hung like a donkey, mate," Andy helpfully fills in, because he apparently picked up on the same clues I did. Gabe wouldn't know how big his dick was if you put a block of wood in front of him and told him to chop. He even looks to me for something like confirmation.

I guess most of his favorite books weren't really specific on how big "totally hung" was. Though I know some of them go with "he filled her with his full ginormous eight inches," so perhaps I'm wrong. Perhaps Gabe just thinks he's some sort of mutant.

I'm up close to him again, now, so I press kiss-reassurances against his mouth, his cheek, and for a moment it's just us, and I think he understands me real well. There's nothing wrong with you. Nothing wrong at all. And I won't let anything happen to you, because apparently you're turning my insides to goo.

From somewhere off to the side, Andy says, "Now put your hand in her hair."

His voice sounds flatter, more commanding. Not quite as mischievous as before.

"That's it—tighten your grip. Like you're going to pull." He glances at Andy, then.

"I don't want to do anything that will hurt her."

Such a sweetheart. Seriously—why aren't my insides gooier?

"You won't hurt her—here, like this."

I can hear my breath coming high and fast, while my heart pounds in my brain, my clit, the ends of my fingers and toes. This can't be really happening, and yet I'm sure it is. I can feel Gabe's heavy erection pressing into my skirt, as Andy stands and gets too close to me. Gabe's hand has dropped away, and Andy replaces it with his—so that he can get a fistful of my hair, and pull it just pleasantly tight.

I guess he's had practice. Lots and lots of practice, with other horny sluts.

"Then you whisper in her ear: go on, baby. Go down on me."

But Gabe doesn't have to say the words. I'm on my knees before he's even processed them. I'm on my knees and my hands are on his thighs and I feel his juddering, desperate moan pass all the way through his body.

"Tell her you're gagging for it. You can't wait for her hot, wet mouth around your dick. I bet you're primed, too, right? You're gonna shoot in about ten seconds."

Far from making him cringe, as I expect, the words seem to spur him on. He bucks his hips, and the slick tip of his cock slides wetly along my cheek.

"But don't worry, mate. After you've had your slippery go, I'll finish her off."

Jesus, where does he get this stuff? Has he spent the hours in between all those messages he left, plotting what to do with us once he had us cornered? He's like a fantasy sex villain.

Gabe just makes a sound—a little guttural ah right in the back of his throat that should probably suggest mortification—but it doesn't quite get there, not entirely. It lingers around aroused, trapped, and I can't help thinking:

He really *does* enjoy it. He likes being humiliated and ordered around, even in this fantasy sex villain sort of scenario. His balls are drawn tight to his body, and a little strand of liquid has worked its way down the stem of his prick, and whenever Andy touches him he jerks, as though a hand on his arm is going to be the thing that pushes him over the edge. *That's* what's going to make him spurt helplessly into the air between us, without anything tugging or sucking him along.

I want it in my mouth, however, and Andy doesn't have to push or force me—I just stick out my tongue and lick loud and wet from root to tip, catching that thin streamer of pre-come as I go. He tastes like soap, and salt—of course he does—and I lap at him, wanting more. Wanting more of the tensely smooth feel of him against my tongue—the one that I know will be so much sweeter, when he's filling my mouth.

So I let it happen quite suddenly, sinking down as far as I can go—which isn't very far at all. He presses at the back of my throat barely halfway in, and then he grunts, and his hips buck forward minutely, and Andy forces me to do what Gabe wants but won't ask for.

Take more.

I gag and Gabe flinches back, but I think Andy's hand is pressing against him, somewhere, so it's not as though he can go far. *No, no*, he moans, until I reach up, and dig my nails into his clenching backside.

Then he surges forward again, whether Andy's there to force him or not. He fills my mouth, hot and thick, sometimes just a hint too rough and groaning when Andy tells him *yes, go on, fuck her face.*

Just like I knew he would.

I feel what could well be a reassuring hand of Gabe's, fluttering over my cheek, but it's sweaty and obviously as wound tight as the rest of him. When I circle all the parts of his dick I can't quite reach with my fingers, and jerk him off as I suck, I feel his entire body stiffen as though this is going to be it.

But he doesn't come. And Andy's kind enough to acknowledge that fact.

"I'm impressed, mate. You're really not doing all that bad." And then, even worse, "Wanna have a go in her pussy?"

Gabe makes this terrific whining sound that somehow sends little jolts of pleasure straight to said place. He's trying to hold off, I can feel it, and unlike Andy I know that Gabe holding off is akin to concrete holding off a squirt of silly string. But even so, this is a lot to take—and he tells us just that in lovely wavering words.

"Oh my *God*," he says, and there's a note of delicious contempt in there—as though Andy is just the most disgusting beast to ever walk the earth.

And maybe I am, too. Is that what you're thinking, Gabe?

"Come on, babe," Andy says. "Stand up. Let him get a look at your snatch."

Apparently I *am* a disgusting beast, because I stand up when Andy tells me to. I clamber up Gabe's body on wobbly legs, one hand clasped in Andy's—so thoughtful. And then he leads me back until I'm right up against the table, and watches Gabe watch him as he pushes my skirt up my thighs.

And pulls my knickers down my legs.

I think it's the part of me that wants to resist Andy that climbs up onto the table and spreads my legs. It's definitely that part that makes me tell Gabe, "Fuck me, fuck me now."

Even though that's technically obeying Andy's directive. But then, I don't look at Andy when I say it, and it's not him who Gabe's obeying in that moment, and although I seem to like being a dirty whore, ordered around like I'm nothing, I think I liked having the final word, too.

I like it when Gabe steps toward me, and looks down on my bare, glistening cunt. I think about how lewd I must look, and heat strips me down to nothing. *Go on*, I think, *go on*, but he only stands over me, cock pointing at my body, eyes all over me at once.

"Give it to her," Andy says, but I'm not sure Gabe's really hearing him any longer. He puts a hand on my body without having to be told or asked or anything, and strokes downward from collarbone to stomach, skimming my breasts as he goes.

I have to put my head back—the swell of pleasure is too intense.

"Fuck me, please fuck me," I say, but he doesn't. He shoves my skirt right up with one hand, and jerks himself roughly with the other.

And when he comes, with a startled gasp that thrills me to the core, he spurts all over my sweet little wet pussy, in thick, heavy ribbons.

Chapter Seven

HE DOESN'T SAY A word about what went on between us and him and what-have-you when he walks in the next day. His lips are sealed. His face and body and everything else are sealed, too. He couldn't look more uncomfortable if he donned rubber underwear and did seven hundred lunges.

But I press on. *I* make *him* a cup of coffee. I stay with him in the shop, and make pleasing small talk until he starts to unwind and forget that we did a weird threesome the day before. That Andy jerked off all over the place *he* had jerked off all over, like a dog marking me.

Then said *see you again*, as though we'd all had a nice tea party with cake and crumpets, and wouldn't it be wonderful if we repeated the experience sometime soon? I don't think Gabe thinks it would be wonderful if we repeated the experience sometime soon. I'm only glad Andy didn't try to fuck me, because I don't know where that would have ended up.

I'm not sure how jealous Gabe is. I'm not sure if it's just the sex that disturbed him, or the humiliation, or some sort of unholy association of all three.

So I go with small talk, and not thinking about how his face looks when he comes. Works like a charm, every time. Works even better if you start talking to him about his favorite books—though of course by favorite, I don't mean his *real* favorites.

He's a big fan of Charles Dickens, apparently. He tells me

he used to imagine himself living in those times—well of course! Everything so repressed and straight-laced! But then he says, quite unexpectedly, "I don't think I'd have lasted five minutes."

I turn from the window—the trinket shop across the way is still selling those stupid red penis-looking lampshades—and look right at him, for the first time this morning. He's sitting at the desk, meticulously putting together something that's probably far below his skill-set—this little bookstand we got from a supplier. Such long, careful fingers. I want to suck them into my mouth, right now.

Though I refrain, of course. I probably wouldn't, if Andy were here. He could just tell me what to do and I'd obey and humiliate Gabe into oblivion.

God, have I pushed him to oblivion? He seems…OK. I don't want him to be anything less than OK, even if he had seemed to really, really enjoy a lot of it. Maybe there's another way he can really, really enjoy it, without seeming much less pleased than he had when we first screwed around.

"What makes you say that?" I ask.

He sort of half-glances up from his work, then, as though realizing he might have said too much. Though about what, I can't say.

"Times were hard," he says, finally. "I'm not exactly made of stern stuff."

He turns back to his bookstand, too quickly.

"I'm not even stern enough for right now."

I sip my coffee, as though my insides aren't churning. So *that's* the issue.

"Why do you have to be stern?" I ask, as he slots tab A into opening B. I think he's considering, but it's hard to tell.

"Women generally prefer assertive men."

"You don't think you're assertive?"

"No. No—of course I'm not." A pause. God, I wish a customer would come in. "I can't even ask for what I want."

"There are other ways to go about getting something."

"Well yes, maybe. But I don't think that you…I don't want to be some sort of game."

I can't believe how quickly this conversation has turned into sex alley. I'm amazed he's still talking.

"You seemed to like it."

"No—I…yes. I…enjoy being with you. In that way. But the first time I make love to you, I don't want it to be something ridiculous."

That last comes out all in a rush, and he seems embarrassed as he says it. I'm embarrassed, too. I'm so embarrassed that I think I need to lie down for a little while. Did he just use the words make and love? Was the word love there already?

I don't love Gabe. We're just a…thing.

"I mean, that is, if you want me to make love to you. Or have sex with you or whatever it is that you want to do." He pauses. He's no longer putting together the bookstand, but I can see him piecing together and ordering something in his head, anyway. "I realize you might not want those things from me. Like that, you know? Because I'm not assertive. And I can't ask. Apart from that last bit, I did ask that. About the sex, I mean."

I think that's the longest bit of speech I've ever heard him say, all in one go. He talked a lot about *Oliver Twist* when we got onto that, but discussing literature and Nancy's boobs in the musical really doesn't count. Even if he had laughed when I had pointed out how magnificent they were.

The boobs, I mean. Not the long bits of literature.

I mull this over for a moment. In all honesty, I can't think what to say in response. There are a number of things that he needs to be told: I don't care that you're not assertive, I want to…I want to have sex with you. Have sex, not other ways of describing it that make me feel a little bit weird. I don't want things to make you feel ridiculous or humiliated.

I need to know how much humiliation you want in order to get you to that place of shuddery, red-faced excitement, without the uncomfortable self-doubt and awkwardness afterward.

But I'm just not practiced enough, at any of this. This all seems very dom/sub or something like it, and although I've read a great deal of material on the subject, I've no idea how to carry myself like Andy.

Though the words that finally come out of me seem very (a) Andy-like and (b) as though I do actually know what I'm doing, and want this all to continue, immediately.

"If you find it hard to ask for what you want, then we need to find another way for you to go about that. Don't we?"

There's something that definitely clicks into place in his expression when I talk a certain way or say a certain thing. His lips part and his eyes meet mine, without a hint of trying to squirm away. I think there's even something of a smile playing at the corners of his mouth.

That secret smile—the one that I do think of as ours. Somehow I doubt he's offered it to too many people.

"Whatever you think's best," he says, and I like that. I like that a lot.

I park myself on the edge of the desk, one leg crossed over the other. His eyes go immediately to the expanse of thigh I've exposed.

"So, for example. You could try reading to me, again. I did enjoy you reading to me."

"Chapter eleven of *Great Expectations*?"

He has such a hidden sense of humor! It's *fabulous*.

"How about chapter five of some dirty book you enjoy that tells me exactly what you really like and how to go about it."

A crease appears, between his brows.

"Or we could make a much more fun game of it. I mean—make a game of it that you would appreciate. You circle all your favorite bits in all your *real* favorite books, and I can go out and find them, and surprise you. How about that?"

His shoulders drop a little, and he glances around the shop. Could be that I've hit on the wrong sort of thing. But then he says, "It would ruin the stock."

And I have to laugh. *That's* the first place his mind goes to—ha!

"I'll pay for the books you use, personally," I say, and maybe it's the dirty connotations of the word *use* that make him color. Maybe it's something else. He's fidgeting, now—all the focus on the book-stand drained away. Even as I think he might resist, I can see his eyes darting busily over all my lovely books, searching.

It's a hungry sort of search. He bites his bottom lip.

"Go ahead," I tell him. "I won't look."

I slide off the desk and make as though to turn back to the window—though I wait long enough to watch him stand and wipe his sweaty palms on his trousers. He's in gray, today—gray pants, gray tank top, checked shirt underneath. Tie so firmly knotted it looks as though it's about to strangle him.

"You're still looking," he says, mouth curled up at the corner—and I could eat him up, I really could.

This. This is it. This is what he needs and what I need, immediately.

I turn and look out of the window, but this time I don't see the little crooked street beyond.

"Should I just…" he begins, but I tell him not to say anything at all. Just do.

And then I can hear him, somewhere behind me, running his fingers over the books. I know that's what he's doing—it's a slick, almost fluttering sound. And I'm so tuned to it that I can hear him taking one off the shelf, too.

It doesn't take long for him to apply pencil to paper. I recognize that sound, as much as I recognize any of the others—if not more so. A kind of scratching swoop, like music to my ears.

I'm not Andy, I think. *Show me who you are, really. Show me the limits.*

When someone comes into the shop, I almost jump right out of this brand new skin I've found myself in. And the way he looks at me suggests I seem as though that's just happened. Like I'm examining him as though he's an alien from Mars.

"Hello," the customer says, and I remember to reply in English. Not Martian.

"How are you today?" I say, which sounds reasonably human to my ears.

The customer—we'll call him guy-in-cardigan—nods, and then starts pretending he's not really looking for what he's bound to be looking for. Which I suppose wouldn't be so bad—it's very unthreatening, after all. Only Jeanette comes in then, too, right after Cardigan, and Gabe is visibly a little more disturbed by that.

Lovely chipper Jeanette, whom he knows works next door.

I glance back at him, and he's just stood, open book and pencil in hand, eyes wide. As though we were caught having sex, rather than caught reading. But I guess I'm a little bit of the harsh taskmaster, because as I'm saying hello to Jeanette and oh yes isn't it *bitter* out and so on, I raise my eyebrows at him.

He understands me perfectly, and shakes his head minutely.

Bad boy.

"Oh, hello there, Gabriel," Jeanette says, as she shakes out her umbrella and puts it in the helpful little stand I provide for customers. Mainly so they don't get a ton of York rain on all of my books.

That I want Gabe to deface with his dirty pencil.

"Hi," he replies, because he's a genial sort. It's not his fault that his *hi* sounds like a balloon deflating.

"You look a little stressed. Is she working you hard?"

I grin, and he tries not to.

"Oh, very hard," I say, and take a step toward him. "You can keep doing what you're doing, by the way…unless you have any objections?"

His tongue peeps out—just briefly—to wet his lips. He glances down at the book, still open in his hands. God knows what page it's open at. Or what I'm expecting him to circle while Jeanette and I chitchat inanely and Cardigan shops for porn.

"She made him figure out what he wanted, sexually, while people stared at him," probably.

"No," he says. "No, that's fine."

He turns his back to us, though. I think he even makes to walk into the little alcove, until he realizes Cardigan is there. Ha! *Trapped*. And he must look it, too, because Jeanette's face is a picture. I guess we're not being as sly as I think we're being. Some of the undertones are definitely leaking out to become overtures. Our text is not sub. Maybe it was the up and down wavering of his voice, or *dammit*—I didn't check. Did he have a hard-on?

Fabulous.

"What are you having him do?" she whispers, leaning right in as though that's going to stop Gabe hearing. I don't think there's anything sexual in her implication, however. She probably *imagines* sexual, but she's not the sort to come out and say it.

Unless I'm hearing it through our bedroom walls. Then she says all sorts.

"Ah…" I say, while I try to imagine what pencil-circling tasks there are for bookstore assistants to complete. "Some errors in some of the stock we got in. He's finding them for me."

She doesn't look convinced—though she still takes a seat when I offer it. And pulls it right up to the desk when I sit down behind it.

"I just thought I'd pop in," she says. "I haven't spoken to you in a while."

I think it's been about a day, but I don't say anything. She keeps just popping in to see how Gabriel is doing, and by this point I'm fairly certain that either (a) she has taken a shine to him, (b) she's desperate for the filthy gossip I'm not sharing, or (c) both.

After all, he is attractive. He might not think so, but he's really not a reliable witness. He seems surprised when people comment on his huge cock, for God's sake.

"The shop seems busy," she says, just as another customer walks in. Unfortunately, Gabe has pressed himself into a corner with his back to everybody in the world, so I can't see how mortified he is.

He's definitely still circling, however.

"Yes—it's been a good week. Hasn't it, Gabe?"

He doesn't hear me. He's engrossed in *Demon Seed*.

Jeanette leans in, again.

"He's very odd, isn't he," she says, but she's making pointed eyebrows and licking her lips as she does so. She has this very expressive, chipmunk-y face, with all this bubbly red hair, so when she's trying to squeeze information out of you, it's really obvious she's doing so. Like a cartoon character trying to do said same thing.

I think about Gabe, getting to that bit in chapter twenty-two—or is it chapter twenty-three?—where the two guys fuck both the girl's holes. Is he hard yet? Is he making himself read it, until he stiffens in his gray trousers and wonders how he's going to hide it?

"You think so?" I reply, but I leave a gap. So that perhaps she might think I'm suspicious, too, of odd Gabriel Kauffman.

"I think he fancies you."

She's as subtle as a brick through the window.

"Do you? No—I don't think so. I think he likes men, anyway."

Her eyes get even wider at that little fake-revelation. Though in relation to the so-called fake part of that revelation, my mind *does* go to Andy's hand over his groin.

"No! *Really?*" she gasps—not quietly at all. Clearly she *did* think something was going on between us. "But I thought…well. I don't know what I thought."

That I was sacrificing him to the God of lust? It wouldn't be that far from the truth.

"Yes. And you wouldn't believe what he's into."

She snaps words out immediately, as though I was asking her to guess. I don't think Derek is doing it for her, anymore, I really don't.

"Cottoning!" she says, and I almost burst out laughing.

I think she means *cottaging*. In fact, I'm deathly certain of it. I glance up at Gabe, wondering if this conversation is being heard and whether or not he's hurt/confused/disturbed by my revelations, and find him looking over his shoulder, a frown so cartoonishly incredulous all over his face that it belongs on Jeanette.

I almost giggle seeing it there. Even more so when quite stupendously he mouths *cottoning*? at me.

Sometimes I forget about Gabe's wealth of knowledge.

"Glory-holing," I say, and now his expression is just pure *don't tell her that, are you talking about me, don't tell her that!*

But of course, he can't come over here and tell us that he's neither gay nor into sticking his dick through holes so that someone can suck it. Mainly because I'm fairly certain that he has an erection, by now.

The look over his shoulder says it all, really—he can't turn his body, because then she'd see.

"I don't even know what that *is*."

She's still whispering. So am I—I don't want to unduly disturb the female customer who's currently looking at a copy of *Despairing Love*. You don't want to destroy your business just because you're trying to gently humiliate your little love slave, who's standing squirming in the corner.

Woman-in-raincoat buys five books—four tame, one dirty, naturally. Cardigan is far bolder—three works of absolute filth. It's usually the case. Men are much more furtive during the coming in and browsing portion of the book shop experience, but they tend to buy the naughtier stuff.

Jeanette raises her eyebrows at me when she sees the covers. I wonder if they'd make a loop all the way around her head if she knew

I'd ordered Gabe to circle passages in a book almost identical to one of the ones Cardigan has chosen.

When Cardigan's gone, she leans in and asks me if Gabriel behaves himself while he's working.

"Oh God yes," I reply. "He does everything to my complete satisfaction."

—◦◦◦—

I bet he's aching by the time Jeanette and the last customer of the day leaves. He was offered no respite. It's been busy, and Jeanette wanted to talk during all the times we weren't busy, and though he went and hid in the alcove, I know he's been sorely tested.

Still, when I lock the door and make my way slowly to the corner he's standing in, the first thing he says to me is: "Should I carry on?"

He doesn't keep his back to me. I can see the long line of his cock through all that gray.

"No. I think you've done enough for today."

"I don't think I've really earned my wage," he says. I think he has, but saying so would probably just make us seem much more like a prostitute and his perverted client.

I'll save that for later, when he's needing just that little extra twist of humiliation.

"Well, I suppose you'll have to work twice as hard for me tomorrow, then, won't you?"

He looks satisfied by that—or as satisfied as someone can be, when he's breathless and lust-glazed. His hand—the one that's not still holding a book and pencil—hovers restlessly close to his groin, as though it can't wait to get at what's there.

"Do you want to masturbate?" I ask, and he replies with a little muffled groan. "Don't be ashamed. I do—I want to. I've been sitting on my little hard chair, grinding my wet pussy against it whenever I thought about the dirty things you've been reading."

"Really?"

Why does he always sound so surprised?

"Of course." I take a step toward him. "Now—are you going to show me what you've been reading? Or do I have to guess?"

He moves quickly, then. To a stack of books behind him on the little white windowsill. I hadn't even noticed, but I thrill when I do. He didn't just put them back on the shelf—he made a pile, for everyone to see!

"I was going to let you guess," he says, still breathless—but now there's an almost giddy quality to it. "But I thought it would be much more efficient to put them all together and give them to you. In order of preference."

He's a wonder, he really is. What would I do without him?

"How thoughtful," I say, as he hands them to me. There are eight books in total, and none of them look like the sorts of things a sweet, middle-aged, female customer would comfortably buy without a romance bolster.

When he leans in close, briefly, I can see the perspiration on his upper lip.

"You can go, now."

It kills me to say it. It really does. I've never wanted someone's face between my legs so badly in all my life. But his expression tells me I've made the right decision—caught somewhere between frustration and a kind of odd delight.

He doesn't say a word in protest. He just nods, and as he goes to pass me, he does the strangest, most tender thing.

He leans in and kisses my cheek, softly. Just a sweet little kiss that makes a sound of sudden and intense arousal escape my lips.

I turn in time to see him fold his coat over his arm to hide what walking funny will probably give away, regardless.

"Good night, Madison," he says.

I can't think of anything to say in reply.

Chapter Eight

I TAKE MY TIME getting to the books. It's like I'm getting ready for a lover, only he's made out of paper and pencil markings and I'm insane.

I shower and wear something silky and black, and arrange them in front of me on the bed, in order of Gabe's preference. Apparently he likes *Sin in Red* the most, and *Outdoor Pursuits* the least. Though I don't think the word *least* really comes into it.

He's not really judging them, after all. He's just picking what he wants most, and I'm now going to get to find that out.

I open book one, and there it is, circled on page thirty-eight.

"He could feel the silk chafing against the head of his cock, a maddening reminder of what she had made him do. The panties felt too tight, restricting, as though her hand was constantly clasped there, around his aching shaft."

How utterly, utterly delicious. And also how open to interpretation. What is it that he likes about this? That a woman forced a man to wear her underwear? Is it just the idea of something silky against his cock? Does he want to be restricted in some way, confined; is it the tightness?

I wonder—would I have found a pair of lacy knickers if I'd have searched more thoroughly through his drawers? Dirty boy, filthy boy, fuck I love it.

And then there's book two:

"His cock leaped in his hand, climax surging up from his tightly drawn balls. He couldn't keep the strangled gasp in, as surge after surge of pleasure went through his already over-taxed body.

"And it was at that moment, as thick spurts of come splashed against her pristine porcelain basin, that Delaney Marcus burst into the bathroom."

God bless Delaney Marcus for pretending she didn't know he was in there.

I remember Gabe saying how he'd jerked off after hearing me on the phone, but I had no idea he did it while thinking about me bursting in on him. I mean—that's what he's saying here, right? I might not be as cool and daring as Delaney Marcus, but I'm sure I could fill in, quite convincingly.

I want to burst on him, just as he's coming. That would be absolutely excellent, I have to say.

And this is before I get to some of the other stuff—God, the things he's into! He's twice circled the scene in *Going Down* where the group of girls makes the arrogant hero strip for them. And then there's the bit where Marnie Sheriden slides a slick finger into Gregory Tate's arse, and the bit in *Desperate Measures* when the reluctant heroine spanks the conflicted hero.

I'm amazed he's even managed to find this much submissive guy/dominant heroine stuff, but he's got laser guidance when it comes to it, it seems. He got the bit in *All Business*, when Bree makes Dirk wait, and wait, and wait. He got the bit in *The Hard Way*, when the two girls tease some little office schmuck until he cries for mercy.

It doesn't escape my notice that a lot of them are my favorite parts of these various books. It makes me wet just reading them, never mind the layer of Gabe's tortured desires over the top of all of it.

I can't stop myself from putting my hand between my legs, while thinking about him doing the same. He'll probably still be wearing something—pajamas or sweatpants, maybe. Hand burrowed inside, to get at his straining cock. Me—I just flip this little black thing all the way up to my stomach, legs spread, uncaring.

It's not as though anyone's going to walk in and see. I wonder if Gabe imagines that's what's going to happen, and so is forced to keep his clothes on, just in case. Or perhaps he simply doesn't like his clothes off—maybe it's the furtiveness of it that gets him going. It's certainly something, because he didn't circle that forced-to-be-naked scene for nothing. Maybe it's that he simply doesn't like his own body, which makes me want to stop touching myself and start thinking about him in annoying, frustrating ways.

But I persevere. I picture him, again, with his hand pumping inside the material of something or other, hips rocking ever so slightly. Head pressed back into the pillow, mouth open—probably being noisy, too.

Or maybe he's got his fist stuffed into his mouth, for fear that the neighbors will hear him. He hadn't seemed to mind making a little bit of noise in the shop, but I remember him pressing sounds against his squeezed-together lips when we were in his apartment.

I guess it's all about who's around to hear—the old lady from next door, listening to him be a dirty masturbator...that just wouldn't do. And especially if he does it three or four times a day.

What on earth would everybody think of him if they knew?

I come downstairs the next morning to find him already waiting outside. As though perhaps he has something to talk about with me, and just can't wait to get to it. An hour later simply wouldn't be good enough.

But when I open the door and let him in, he still can't seem to find the words. He looks happy, and when he takes off his coat he does so in the oddest way—like he wants me to see him do it, like he wants me to think of stripteases and other things he clearly finds terrifying.

I think I might be able to persuade him to take his clothes off sometime soon.

"Did you have a nice time last night?" I ask, and the grin he breaks into is delightful.

"I don't know what you mean," he says, and then there's this weird pause, this sort of tense moment in which we just stare at each other.

Before I step to him, he leans down, and we kiss, long and wet and stuffed full of this strange languid sort of sensuality. His hands slip around my waist and he caresses me, suddenly soft and sure, the slippery push of his tongue like a reminder of all the things he didn't dare do before.

I take a step back, smoothing my hair and catching my breath as I go. He seems reluctant to let me do so.

"Describe what you did last night," I say after a moment, and I see him wipe his palms on his trousers. Could be they're as sweaty as mine are.

"I made myself paella."

"And before that?"

I expect him to evade, again, but he doesn't. He keeps his face turned to one side, but he sticks to it.

"I masturbated."

"Where?"

"Standing up. With my back to the door."

"You couldn't even wait, you dirty little mess."

His eyelids flutter and almost shut.

"No. I can't wait, now. I did it once and then I promised myself I wouldn't do it again, not until later, but I couldn't concentrate on the television."

"Why not?"

"I kept thinking about you, reading all those…things."

"Like how you want me to make you wear women's underwear?"

His gaze clicks with mine, but it doesn't look as terrified as I'm sure it would have not so long ago. Instead he looks furtive—he licks his lips. His eyes are big and round and his chest seems to be almost heaving.

"Would you…you wouldn't really do that, would you?" I'm glad I put a pair into my trouser pocket.

"I thought hot pink might be your color," I say, as I pull them out for him to get a look at.

He immediately shakes his head—but I think it's just a reflex, really. I've hit him on the knee with a hammer of sex, and he has to voice some sort of protest. Otherwise he's just easy as well as kink-riddled.

"No," he says, faintly disbelieving.

"I bet you'll look fabulous in them. All that lovely pale skin against shimmering pink. Very nice."

He screws up his nose, but then goes with something I don't expect, "They won't fit, Madison."

"What are you talking about? You're skinnier around the hips than I am."

"I doubt that—but the hips aren't my problem. You know they won't fit." And then he leans forward, and whispers in this fabulous and hilarious co-conspiratorial way, "Because…you know. Because of my—I have trouble with underwear as it is."

I giggle. I can't help it. He rolls his eyes.

"Well, I guess you'll like it all the more then, right? Nice and tight on your big dick."

He groans—I think partly with embarrassment.

"Go on. Go to the bathroom and put them on. Or would you rather I make you do it here?"

He snatches the dangling slip of pink silk from my hand at that. Almost angry, but not quite. And then he makes his way into the back, material bunched in his fist.

I wait until I hear the door lock before I follow him back there. It's no fun if I don't get to hear him mutter and curse, after all, as he slides those little knickers up his thighs. Everything comes through muffled and jumbled up, but one thing gets to me loud and clear: the way he moans, when that silk clasps around his cock.

"Feel good?" I ask, and he makes a little startled sound. I guess he hadn't known I was there.

"It's...can I take them off?"

"Is it hurting you?"

He takes a moment with that one.

"I—no."

"Is it pressing nice and snug against your dick?"

Even more reluctant, this time.

"Yes."

"Does it feel good?"

"It feels like women's underwear."

I like it when he's funny.

"Good. Now put your trousers back on and come out here. You do remember how you said you'd work extra hard for me today, don't you?"

"I—wait. Wait, I can't. Madison, I can't."

"You mean you're not going to keep your word?"

"I can't walk around with these on. You know I can't."

"Then maybe you gave me the wrong passage to read."

He makes a little exasperated sound.

"No. No. It's not that—I do want—God. OK." I hear him take a deep breath. "I can't walk around with these on because they... they're rubbing against me. It'll just be too much."

He sounds wretched. But in some really, really awesome sort of way.

"You know what I mean, don't you?"

"You mean you might come in your brand new underwear. God, how disgusting." I pause. Just for effect, you know. "Now get out here."

It takes a minute, but eventually the lock snaps. The door opens. He's sweating and smoothing down hair that doesn't need smoothing.

"Show me," I say, and he makes a sound like the wind, dying. "Just lift your jumper and pull down the waistband of your trousers, so I can see."

The flash of pink is a sight to behold. As is him, showing it off. I love how he twists his body and rudely reveals it, like a dirty bitch showing off her obscene tattoo.

"Very nice," I tell him, and he groans. Not in a despairing way, either. In an excited sort of way.

It turns out to be a very amusing day. At one point I see him crouch to get at a lower shelf, and when he does so his entire face changes, as though someone twanged a little string inside him. He has to stay like that, on his hands and knees, before whatever is going on inside him dies down.

But it's OK, because luckily, a customer stoops to ask him if he's all right. I guess she heard the faint noise of protest he made—that sigh of pleasure and frustration and fear, all the sounds so sweet and fumblingly sexual.

When it gets to lunchtime, I turn the open sign to closed and wait for him to go to the bathroom. Of course, I know what he's going to do. He knows that I know. I can see him watching me out of the corner of his eye. I can see him trying to hide the stiffness in his trousers by holding a box in front of his groin.

He's done the same all day. Such an assortment of things to keep prying eyes off his erection. A cardboard sign, a plastic bag. Though really, it's not as bad as it would usually be. The knickers seem to be holding him in nicely.

And by nice I mean in all senses of the word.

"Where are you going?" I say, but he doesn't answer. He's grim-faced and determined, likely not thinking about the scene he circled, where the heroine catches the hero masturbating frantically.

Or maybe he is thinking of that. He probably is. What else would he be thinking about?

When I go to the door I can hear him breathing through it. At first a little hectic, but then with more rhythm. And every now and then, he'll cut a sound or a high breath short, and it's so real and strong that I can picture exactly what he's doing:

Pressing his hand to his mouth, to stifle his moans of pleasure.

"Gabe, are you all right in there?" I say, and it's so much like a game I could cry with happiness. I can feel it filling my chest as much as it's filling other places, even when I try to hold it down.

Don't, I think, *don't*, but then he answers, "I'm fine. Really. Don't come in here."

And I'm not sure I can stop it. He's playing with me. It's obvious. I think he means it, but at the same time…

The door won't be locked. I know it before I even get close to trying it. And I just reach out and turn the handle and push it open, not quite bursting in because I'll never be Delaney, but close enough.

He has his trousers shoved down—not around his ankles in a pathetic puddle. Taut between his legs, and no further than mid-thigh. He hasn't taken the underwear off, and it flashes pink and gleaming against his delightfully hairy and finely muscled thighs.

I can't see his balls, because the elastic is cutting over them—likely too tight for comfort. Though I suppose that's the point. It doesn't seem to be putting him off to have a pair of little knickers digging into him.

Quite the contrary. His cock's in his fist, the ruddy tip peeping between his tense, squeezing fingers, everything so clearly ready to go off that I freeze in delicious anticipation. I run my gaze all over this frankly startling tableau—one that's so sexy and dirty and fabulous that I'm sure he must have planned it just so, oh God, you little whore—just waiting for it to happen.

But I guess he's in no rush.

He squirms, first, and stutters some sort of apology that I think is at least half-faked. Though the flush that spreads over his cheeks and down his neck is real enough. He swallows, audibly, and that seems real, too. We might be playing dress-up, but clearly he can press the actual feelings down on himself hard enough.

"Ms. Morris," he says, and I can feel myself slipping into the role as easily as I would glide into a warm bath. "I can explain."

"Really?" I ask. I notice that although he's straightening up and trying to act presentable, he can't resist pumping his shaft just once. I think he does it when I raise one stern eyebrow.

I raise the other, in the hopes that he'll do it again.

"I'm sorry—I won't do it again. I swear I won't do it again." His eyes dart to one side, but not in shameful penitence. I think he's actually considering—probably mentally flicking through every dirty book he's ever read for just the right thing. "Can I pull my trousers back up?"

Ah, asking permission. Always a bad thing to do when you've just been caught doing something naughty and you're starring in an erotic novel.

"I don't think so, Gabriel."

Again, he surreptitiously strokes himself. Or not so surreptitiously, really. More like he wanks right in front of my face and waits for me to punish him for it.

"I think you need to finish the job. Don't you think so, too? I mean, how can you come back out onto my shop floor with that thing waving between your legs? You'd frighten all the customers."

He groans. He shuts his eyes tight. His cock jumps in his twisting grasp.

"No. I think what you need to do is jerk off until you come, right here, in front of me."

"Oh," he says—so lustily despairing. I didn't even know there was such a thing. How can despair be lust-filled? And yet somehow, he manages it.

"On my tits, I think. Wouldn't that be nice? You do want to come all over my tits, don't you?"

He bites his lip. I'll take that as a yes.

Though I don't have to. I don't have to make do with subtle, because when I get up close to him he actually reaches forward and starts fumbling with the buttons on my shirt. And he kisses me—he really kisses me, while I just stand there, frozen.

It feels good, though. I won't deny that. His cock pokes into my skirt, coming close to the V between my thighs. His mouth is warm and soft and patient, not frantic as I had expected. And then he pushes his hand inside my shirt, and fondles my half-clad breasts, and I forget every single thought in my head.

I wonder if he's going to try and make love to me on the bathroom floor.

"Gabe, wait—"

He's somehow got my bra undone. The shirt is off my shoulders.

"Don't you want me to do this, anymore?" he asks, but he rubs his erection against my skirt as he does so.

"No—I do—"

"It'll be messy. I'm really close."

God. God. Fuck.

"Do you want me to climb up, or are you going to…to kneel down. Like before, when you…"

"When I sucked you?"

"Yes, yes exactly."

He's stroking himself, again. Short, restrained tugs, squeezing when he hits the base.

"When Andy forced you to put your cock in my mouth?"

"Oh my God, oh…oh Maddie, I'm gonna come." Did he just call me Maddie? He did. I'm sure he did.

"I can't hold off—please," he says, so I get on my knees in front of him for the second time. Not that I care about little details like that, when he just called me *Maddie*. When I keep flashing on us on the bathroom floor, holding each other.

His hot come spurting over my breasts is a nice clean slap to the face. Something to wake me up and get me focused on the matter at hand: him groaning above me as his cock jerks in his fist, streamer after streamer of spunk coating my nipples and my chest and even all the way up to my throat.

Feels good. Silky and dirty and cooling on my heated flesh. And then I get to say this as he breathes unsteadily and tries to sit down where no seat is, "Now clean me up, you filthy little mess."

I don't look at him as I say it, but I hear him simultaneously trying to tidy himself up, while obtaining some tissue for me. He should really know me better, by now.

"No," I tell him. "No tissue. I want you to lick me clean."

I hear him pause. I can see tweed out of the corner of my eye. At first I think he's going to balk, and he makes a little sound that could be turning into a protest. But then he just gets to his knees in front of me, as determined as he had looked earlier on his way to the bathroom to start this game off.

"Quickly," I say. "I don't have all day."

And then he puts his tongue to the drop of sticky fluid that landed right on my left nipple, and laps, and laps, and laps. I can't help the little cry that escapes from between my supposedly pressed-together lips.

When he hears it, he suckles instead of licking. I clasp a hand to the back of his head—I can't stop that, either. Just the sight of him, hungrily licking and sucking at my covered tits, groaning softly as he does so. His pink tongue against my pale skin, against the near translucent liquid…

"Oh baby," I say, even though I hate myself for doing it.

He gets to my throat, and my knees would buckle if they had anywhere to go. I just want to kiss and lick and suck him back, plunge my hands deeper into his silky black hair—but if I do, what then?

I don't mind admitting that it's a relief when someone bangs on the outside door.

—⁓—

He tastes like come when I kiss him. The streets are rain-slicked and gray and we stand briefly under a shop awning, when it rushes down heavily, suddenly. He looks out onto the street as it thunders down, oblivious to my eyes on him. He's talking about nothing in particular, and ends by saying that we're not going to make it to the cinema in time.

I think he might be beautiful. Not classically so, but just—he looks so lovely in the low light. He's worrying about some little thing, and yet he seems so much less concerned than he once did, as though the weight on his back has gradually lifted.

There's more stubble than there used to be on his face. It looks good—especially at the firm curve of his jaw. His hair isn't as tightly smoothed to his head, and there's no tie today. It's just little things, really. Little things that become big, on him.

So I kiss him when he's busy not looking. And he kisses me back, because that's what we do, now.

We also apparently go to the cinema to see a double bill of probably inadvisable steamy French movies. I wonder if he's going to want me to hold his hand in the dark. Or put my hand over his eyes. Or put my hand down his pants.

He's still wearing the pink knickers.

"What was that for?" he asks when I pull away. And I have to consider: Is it really that unusual for me to just kiss him? Or is it that we're outside, in the open, like a proper couple?

I hope he doesn't want to hold my hand in the dark.

"I want to taste what you've been doing lately," I say.

But I'm lying. The real answer was: because you looked so gorgeous, I just couldn't resist. And he's blushing, now, too, which always makes him look even hotter, somehow. Though nothing on him even comes close to this, in the hotness stakes. "I've been licking your tits."

God, I wish a customer hadn't interrupted us. Maybe I could just let my business go to hell and spend my days playing kinky games with Gabe until I turn myself inside out.

"Really?" I say, and he touches a cheeky tongue to his upper teeth. "And what else did you do while you were there?"

He leans in, then, too close for comfort. Whispers in my ear as an old lady hurries past.

"I tasted myself on you."

My world narrows down to just his words. Not an anatomy lesson, not something he read out for me—his words, freely given. I kiss his cheek, as a reward, but somehow that's even worse than the one I've just planted on his lips. So intimate and sweet—I can't resist at all when his hand slides down my arm and closes around mine.

It seems as though we're supposed to do that, now. I guess it was only a matter of time.

We walk in silence to the cinema, getting a little wet around the edges. By the time we get there, I'm certain *The Hairdresser's Husband* is a terrible idea. It's all romance and tragedy and sex, people foofing around in French until you just want to drink coffee and have tortured affairs with the entire world.

Through the darkness, he whispers to me, "I'm not even a fan of French films. I prefer spaceships and aliens."

And I want to cry, because that's almost exactly what I wanted to tell him. But I don't say anything at all, and then a little later he asks me if I think he's uncultured for saying so.

"Why would I ever think that? You're intelligent and well-read and…"

Stop. Stop.

"...let's just watch the movie."

But of course we don't just watch the movie. How can we, when I can't keep my hands off him and apparently he can't keep his hands off me? Even when he's just got his fingers wrapped around mine, I can feel him stroking over my knuckles, methodically, one at a time. Pushing between each finger, in a way that seems lewd and is probably now intended as such.

And everything is only exacerbated by the orgasm I didn't get a few hours ago. I had almost retired to the bathroom myself, when the ache through my swollen sex got just a little too much. And by too much I mean: please come into the bathroom and catch me masturbating, so I can lick my come off your chest.

I still haven't seen him without any clothes on.

"Madison?" he whispers. There are only two other people in the entire cinema, but as we all know by now he's the considerate type. "Are you all right?"

I guess I must be visibly squirming in my seat. He's not helping by continuing to rub between my fingers. His thumb makes it to my wrist, and I have to lean over and kiss him. It's just a necessity.

On the screen, they're sprawled on the floor. Doing stuff. If I can just hold off, I'm pretty sure she tops herself, soon. That'll kill the mood of warm sensuous love-things, crawling all over me.

Though probably not the mood that his hand inside my coat is creating. I think he really, really likes my breasts, because he seems to have no qualms about fondling them, anymore. Once the top three buttons are undone, it could be that he traces all the places he marked earlier on.

"Madison," he whispers, but it's not a question this time. And I can hear words stirring against my ear before they're even out, his hand now at my throat and my coat almost off.

So I push him back into his seat and grab a handful of what he's got between his legs.

His hands immediately go up and off me, hovering just above the armrests as though they're on fire. As though he's being held at gunpoint.

"Wait…wait…" he says, but he was only too eager a second ago, when his hands were full of my tits.

I'm sure he intends to sit straighter and away from my grip, but he only winds up sinking in further, deeper. The chair ruffles his hair at the back, and the sandy jacket he's wearing swallows him whole.

"For what?" I say, and I do so loudly. The person sitting three rows down and to the left turns his head, just ever so slightly. And of course, Gabe notices.

But he doesn't say what I expect.

"Shouldn't it be your turn, now?"

I kiss his mouth, before he can say anything worse. I don't know what sort of person he's becoming, but it's just different enough from the person he was to be both disturbing and as electric as ever.

He still does what I tell him to do. He still obeys me. But he pushes the armrest up between us, too. His hands go around my waist, right inside my coat.

I think we might be making out in a movie theater. I stir the silk over his erect cock, but it doesn't change the fact that we're kissing like teenagers, in a way I never did when actually that age. When my father died, that's when I went on my first date.

I seem to remember being nineteen, but it's hard to recall. Mostly I can just picture the backseat of his car, the slippery weight of his cock in my hand. Him asking me if I was ready, me laughing in response.

I rub harder, with the heel of my palm. He gusts a warm excited breath into my open mouth, before sliding his hand from my waist to cup my arse. Only I don't think he's just cupping my arse—I think he's trying to slide my skirt up my thigh.

"Madison," he moans, though I wish he'd stop saying my name. "Oh, that feels so good."

I bet it does—all that smooth material slithering the length of his prick. The pressure of my hand, rubbing and rubbing.

"You like that?" I ask, and the person in front definitely turns around, now. I don't blame him. We're doing this to the credits.

"I always like it. I like it so much—God." His head goes back against the sticky seat. "You do all the things I've ever wanted, always."

"Really?" I say. I want to pull away, but I can't. "Aren't I cruel to you, Gabe? Am I not a bitch?"

He laughs. He actually laughs—though not unkindly. And when he looks at me, his eyes are bright and disbelieving.

My hand falls away, but he doesn't seem to mind.

"Yes. But it's good. It's so good. Everything you do, the way you look and act and speak—I never thought…I never thought I'd be so lucky." He touches the side of my face, just to cement the crashing impact. "You're what I've always wanted. Everything about you is what I want."

And then even worse, "You do know that, don't you?"

When we get back to the shop, I tell him he should go. I don't want to tell him that—I need to fuck so badly it's making my insides weak. It's making me want to shoot myself in the head. But, unfortunately, I don't have a gun and instead there's just Gabe's concerned expression, as though he's sensible of some wrong thing he's done.

But it's OK, Gabe, really. At least you didn't tell me you loved me while I gave you a handjob in the back of a cinema.

"I just…need to be on my own for a little while," I say, but he's much smarter than I've given him credit for.

"I don't think we're boyfriend and girlfriend, you know," he says, while I try to stay calm. I think we are boyfriend and girlfriend. More so than I ever was with Greg or Kevin or what-the-fuck.

"I know."

"We don't have to be anything."

"Of course."

"You seem afraid of me. I kind of thought it was supposed to be the other way around."

I almost laugh at that. Despite the fact that I seem to have some sort of almighty intimacy issue that relates directly to him—one that he is, apparently, aware of—he almost laughs, too.

Why am I spazzing out? I don't understand. I didn't spazz out with Greg or Kevin or all of the other utterly meaningless throwaway men that I absolutely despised.

"I'll be here tomorrow morning," he says, and he sounds a little sad, this time. So I squeeze his arm, and then wish I hadn't.

"Bye, Madison."

I want to say don't go. Don't go. Instead, let's go upstairs and make love, because good Lord I desperately want to. I want to feel you inside me and have you over me and tell you while you're doing both that I think you might be everything I've ever wanted, or similar.

So why is it that once he's gone, I pick up the phone and dial Andy's number?

Chapter Nine

HE DOESN'T RUB IT in, like I thought he would. No "knew you'd come running to me, eventually" or "I guess that simpering nancy just wasn't doing it for you, huh?" It's good that he doesn't go with either, because then I'd have to tell him that Gabe is doing it for me so much that I'm all confused inside.

Though I don't mind so much when he orders me to take my clothes off. Or when he shoves a rough hand between my legs and tells me how soaking wet I am. Just dripping, he says, so messy.

And then he surprises me with, "Did he get you like this?"

Now they've both asked if the other one turns me on more. Maybe I should call it a draw.

"You like it, don't you? When he does what you ask him to."

He's probably bugged the shop. Or maybe he's that guy with an eye patch who came into the store the other day. He had a terrible Australian accent—I knew he was a faker.

"Maybe you even like it a little bit more than what I've got to offer."

Or it could be that he's just a mind reader. He knew about my Big Book of Horny Fantasies, after all.

"And what do you have to offer?" I ask, but he's way ahead of me.

"Turn around and bend over," he says.

It's very cold in the kitchen, without all my clothes on. I was going to take him upstairs, to my apartment, but why break with tradition? And then, of course, there's the fact that I didn't want to. Why should he get to come up when Gabe hasn't?

"So has he fucked you?" he asks, as I obey him. Over the table, just like before. He spreads my legs wider, with rough but not unkind hands.

"I don't want to talk."

"You mean, you don't want to talk about Gabriel. That's his name, right? Is it that he wouldn't fuck you? He didn't seem to want to back when we had that bit of fun."

"Please just fuck me, Andy," I say, but he isn't listening. My sex gapes wide and wet, desperate to be filled—but he ignores it.

"God, I bet he'd feel good in your cunt. Don't you think? Could you not bring yourself to order him to fuck you?" He pauses, his big hands on my arse cheeks. Squeezing, just ever so slightly. "Shame. I'd love to see that one—you on top of him, ordering him to fuck up into your sweet wet pussy. Making him stop just as he's about to come. I could rub you off as you're doing it, make you go around his prick until he's begging for mercy."

"Sadist."

He laughs and slaps my arse just once, lightly. It makes me shiver. And then he damns me with something that feels even better than the smack, "I'm only saying what you want to hear, babe."

A finger trails down, between the cheeks of my arse. It doesn't take much for him to glide into my cunt, as easy as you please. I gasp and twist, and he chuckles.

"I don't mind saying all the dirty things you'd like to do to someone else if it turns you on this bad."

He has two fingers in me, now. They feel *fabulous*.

"Oh, that's it, babe. Buck back into my hand. You like that, huh? Are you thinking about him while I do it?"

"No."

"Liar," he says, and then he slaps my arse. Hard. "Have you done this to him? Spanked him? Man, I bet you look hot doing something like that. Him bent over, crying, while you—"

I turn my head and spit at him, "I think I know *someone* who wants to spank Gabriel Kauffman."

But he just looks as laid-back and unfazed as ever. As though I suggested he likes bicycles or teapots.

"There's nothing like a good submissive, Maddie," he says, finally—as though gender isn't even in the equation. *And* he called me Maddie. What the fuck is going on?

"Now spread your legs wider, so I can fuck you. I've been dying for that gorgeous cunt for weeks, while you dicked around with your sweetheart."

I do as I'm told. There's the snap and twang of rubber, and then he's easing into me, good and slow. I moan, with something like relief.

"Feel good? Just need things straightforward sometimes, huh?"

I wish he'd stop talking.

"You feel good to me, babe. So hot and tight—it's like you haven't been fucked in a month."

He puts his hand into the hollow of my lower back, and shoves into me, hard. Then again. And again. Soon he's got a good strong rhythm going, and it's hitting all the right places, and he's grunting roughly, which I don't mind at all.

But I don't think it's going to be enough.

"Want me to rub your clit?" he asks, and in answer I squeeze my eyes tight shut, so that I can think of nothing but his cock drilling into me. And the thumb he's now slid between my cheeks, so that he can press it hard and dirty to my arsehole.

The table is shaking. It feels good, it does.

Though not good enough.

"Oh baby," he says. "Oh Madison, God—I'm gonna come soon, sweetheart. I'm gonna—"

Which is where I cut him off, in a rushed and ill-thought out blurt, "Would you fuck him?"

The pounding I'm getting slows, then stills. After a moment he laughs.

"You want me to talk a little man-on-man until you get off, is that it?"

I press my face into the table. He hasn't quite got the point, but that's OK. He doesn't need to know that just picturing Gabe's face sends a bolt of pleasure all the way through me.

"No."

"I wouldn't mind seeing the look on his face. Or yours."

"So you would. You'd fuck a man."

Gabe, facedown, over this table. And maybe it's a man. Maybe it's not. Who cares?

"Are you asking me if I'm bisexual, Maddie?"

"No—yes. I don't know."

"Make up your mind, hon. I'm going to come pretty soon and then you'll kick my arse out of here."

He's right. How did he get to be so right? Why does it now feel so much better when he rocks slow and steady in and out of me? Gabe—Jesus. What have I done?

"Are you?"

"I don't think so. I don't want to fuck him. But man, I do love watching people do what they're told."

Me too, I think, and I see Gabe spread out before me, hands tied above his head. Gabe bent over me, fucking me the way Andy is while I tell him—I don't beg him—to do it harder. Do it harder, babe, yes. Give it to me, God give it to me I want you. I want you. Just you.

"Oh that's it, babe, that's it—come for me!" Andy says, as his cock swells in my pussy. He calls out my name, but I don't call his in response. Of course I don't.

I call out Gabe's, and then want to die.

I pretend to be ill. It's tough doing it, but my dignity makes me. I just don't think it could stand him seeing my puffy eyes and all the tears that keep leaking out of me. Especially when they're tears of evil, evil guilt and other things I've never felt before.

I don't want to feel guilt over fucking Andy. Me and Gabe— we're not boyfriend and girlfriend.

So why do I feel like shit? Thanks a lot, latent conscience.

I leave a key over the door for him, and then wait in the kitchen like a cowardly fucking coward for the sound of it in the lock. When I'm sure it's him—that's when I run back upstairs and make a burrow in my bedcovers and try to fool myself into thinking that I'm actually sick. I'm so sick I might have to stay in bed forever. I'm so sick that I might have to leave the country for special medical treatment.

Hopefully from Dr. Freud. Yeah, Madison, apparently you have ze intimacy issues. Probably 'cause you want to doink your Father, yez.

I have absolutely no idea why fake Freud ends the word yes with a Z.

At lunchtime, I think he comes up to my apartment door. I stand in the living room, duvet wrapped around me, certain I can hear him breathing through the wood. He has very intense breathing—it's easily recognizable.

Also he says my name, so that's a bit of a clue.

"I brought you some soup," he says, and I hate him, I *hate* him. What in God's name would Freud with a Z have to say about Gabe? He's nothing like my father. I know for a fact that he doesn't want to slipper my arse for reading dirty books.

Though maybe *his arse* got slippered for reading dirty books.

My God, are we ever fucked up. He doesn't even give in after the dinnertime silence! He comes back at five, and tells me that he's really worried. He's so worried about me. He wants to come in and make me dinner. He thinks I should eat—but Gabe, I really don't think I can. It's so hard to eat when you're shaking all over like some pathetic idiot.

"Madison," he says, after so long a silence I'm sure he's gone. "I know you're there. And probably not really sick, either."

Sometimes I think Gabe is the naive one in this…thing. Then I realize I'm an idiot.

"Whatever you're thinking—whatever's wrong…you don't have to worry. I mean—I'm hardly likely to push you into anything you don't want to be pushed into."

Or maybe he *is* the idiot. Doesn't he get it? That's the entire fucking problem! He doesn't push, but I'm goddamned going, anyway. I'm going worse than if he'd shoved me with a fucking steamroller.

"Or maybe you really are sick and I'm just reading too much into things. In which case, I have something for that, too. Chicken soup, and…" I hear him rummaging. "…some plain noodles, orange juice, cough drops, throat lozenges—I've covered all my bases."

I have to open the door for throat lozenges. I can just picture him wandering around Sainsbury's, ticking off a list of potentially helpful things for sick people.

"Whoa. So sick that you need a duvet force field."

"When did you get such a smart mouth?"

"When I realized you didn't mind," he replies, and somehow that's even worse than all the other stuff.

"Just…come in."

He peers around the corner, into the room beyond.

"Are you sure? I don't have to—"

"Just come in, Gabe, come in now, quickly, before I go insane."

He does so, but barely gets beyond the doorway.

"Your apartment's really nice," he says, even though it isn't. It's a mess.

"You're not really thinking that, Gabe, OK. I know you're not, because apparently I now know you well enough to make that assessment."

His little curl of a smile almost hits rueful, and he shakes his head.

"I don't know you at all. This is an absolute disaster." He marvels at my piles of paperwork and the three plates on the coffee table that I haven't washed. "You keep the shop so *immaculate*."

"That's work. This is…I don't have to do anything here."

"You know, I could just…run the hoover around in here, maybe—"

"Sit down, Gabe. Sit down on my filthy couch."

He eyes said couch with something like trepidation. It's really not that dirty, however. It just has an old cardigan and maybe a pair of pants strewn over it. He asks me how I have any clothes left with none of this laundry done, but somehow I just end up blurting out, "When I was a girl, all my clothes had to be ordered in my wardrobe from light to dark."

Which doesn't seem like a good idea. Especially not when he then says, "You don't think I want to make you order your clothes from light to dark, do you?"

In all earnestness. He glances around with those assessing eyes.

"I mean—if you *wanted* it doing, I could do it for you…"

I sit down opposite him, on my dirty coffee table, when he takes a seat on my couch.

"Like you did for your parents?"

He flicks his gaze back to me, expression somewhere close to bemused.

"Why? Are you going to forget to take your tablets and then lock me in the attic?"

This talk is not going the way I wanted it to. My palms are sweating.

"How Virginia Andrews of you."

"Have you ever seen that documentary—*Gray Gardens*?" Lord have mercy. I wish I hadn't.

"They had a toy museum once—my parents, I mean. It was an

amazing thing…just so meticulous and beautiful. But then they—"
He pauses, and his gaze sinks down, down into some bizarre past. "I
guess they never really wanted me. I always felt as though I was some
alien who had landed in their life."

When he looks back up at me, he doesn't seem sad, however. I
don't know why, because he really did when he first started working
for me. He seemed like the saddest man alive.

"But I'm not saying this so you'll feel sorry for me, Maddie. I
know what you're probably going to say—and that's OK. At least
you seem pretty torn up over it."

For some reason, him giving me this speech—probably the only
one of its kind that I've ever felt was threaded with sincerity so sweet
it hurts—makes me crumble like year-old cake. Maybe it's the fact
that I know without a shadow of a doubt that he's not trying to twist
my arm that makes me blub like a girl.

I also realize something pretty profound: I wasn't even *going* to
break up with him. Though he's probably going to break up with
me, after I tell him this. We had something to break, too!

"Are you—are you *crying*?" He sounds so incredulous that I have
to check my face to see if I really am. "I thought you had been, but
God, it's so weird to see. Why are you upset, Maddie—please don't
cry. It really wasn't all that *Flowers in the Attic* and even if it was I'm
so much better, now. Really—I feel so much stronger and happier
and I can't tell you how much you—"

"Please don't say anything else. Just don't say anything else."

"Has it freaked you out? It usually freaks people out. Though I
promise, I never slept with my sister."

Now I'm a crying, *laughing* snotball. He hands me an immaculately clean and folded handkerchief.

"I don't even have a sister—though not that I would have com-
mitted incest had I had one. I mean, I had this cousin who said some
pretty dirty things to me, but that doesn't seem quite as perverted."

I laugh again, only this time, right in the middle of drying myself and giggling, he leans forward and rubs my arm. And then the side of my face—I have a strand of hair stuck wetly to my cheek, and he brushes it away. Though his hand doesn't leave my cheek once he's finished the job. And I think it's obvious that I don't want it to go anywhere, too.

I seem to be breathing hard. He's breathing hard. It's fair to say that I launch myself at him, fiercely enough to knock him back against the couch. I straddle him the way I imagine maniacs straddle, with one knee almost up to his armpit and my crotch pressed to his…belly somewhere. It's not hard to imagine that I look like a giant spider.

And I kiss him hard enough to force this noise out of him: *mmph*.

He kisses me back. Of course he does. Prior to me he only ever kissed his sister-cousin. Though I'll admit, it doesn't seem that way. Sometimes his mouth starts off clumsy, but then he'll get into this rhythm and his tongue will flicker in this tentative-but-hot way in and out of my mouth, like he's fucking me even though he's not all that sure he should be doing it.

It's difficult to pull away. He's hypnotizing me with his lips.

"Maddie," he says, between kisses. I think it's the first time I've ever liked anyone calling me that. "Maddie, wait."

But I don't want to wait. If I wait, I'll have to tell him what I did and then he'll probably never kiss me again. I don't deserve kisses, cheating whore that I am.

"Maddie, come on!" he says through laughter. I'm glad he can laugh. I'm also glad that he can get an erection—I can feel it pressing against my thigh and God it makes me want to rub myself over it.

I pull away when he pushes. He asks if he can make love to me, and then I pull away even further.

"You don't have to…want to," he starts. He's half-frowning and flushed—as usual—clearly confused but Lord I don't want to take away that confusion. Let it stay all over him forever, for all I care.

I do care. I do.

"I mean, maybe you don't ever want to do that with—"

"I fucked Andy. Yesterday. I fucked him."

I blurt it out, just like that! Right in the middle of whatever nice thing he was going to say. Or awful thing, depending on your point of view. Because I do want to do it with him. I do, so badly. I can almost *taste* what it would be like.

I don't want to meet his eyes. If I meet them, then I'll have to go back to the way things were before I knew him—

I won't have an assistant, suddenly, or a man I almost want to call my boyfriend. My lover. My whatever you're supposed to call it when you're too old for teenage things like going steady.

I can just see his hands, each one curled on their respective thighs. They don't start fidgeting, and they don't clench into fists—though granted, he might not be showing his emotions through the medium of fingers. Perhaps it's all in his chest or his shoulders—though when I creep my gaze up a little, they don't look tense/angry/upset, either.

But I can only bring myself to look at his face when he says:

"And then what?"

Mainly because it seems like an odd thing to say, at best. I need to see what expression goes with *and then what.*

Apparently it's *expectant.*

"I…what?"

"Then what did you do after you fucked him? Did you…are you in love with him?"

He swallows, directly after the word *love.*

"Because if you are, that's OK—I mean, he's strong and handsome and…other things. I wouldn't expect you to…I don't know. Why are you telling me this, again?"

I honestly have no idea. I look back on those cheating whore thoughts and find them faintly ridiculous, now. What claim did Gabe really have on me, after all—beyond the one I made for myself?

"I don't love Andy," I say, because that's the most explainable part of all of this. Why does he look so…bemused?

And somewhat relieved, after the whole *don't love* part.

"Good," he says. "Good." And though he says it fiercely—for a moment, his eyes flash bright and dark, all at the same time—he doesn't linger on that feeling for long. Instead, quite suddenly—and sort of breathlessly, I have to say—he spits out:

"What was it like?" Oh Lord. Not this.

"It was…it was nothing! Just nothing. I did it because I—because I think I have feelings—"

"Tell me what he did. Did he do it hard?"

"Gabe—" I try, but he ploughs on. Eyes suddenly distant and to one side, chest rising and falling rapidly.

"Where did he do it to you? Downstairs, in the kitchen? I know you did things in the shop once, because I could see the print you left on the desk…God, that print. I had to polish it away, but even after I did I kept thinking about it and thinking about it. I still do, sometimes."

At which point, understanding begins to dawn. What an idiot I am!

"It was in the kitchen."

"Did he…from behind? Or were you sat on the table?" he asks, and actually licks his lips. He's leaning forward, now, and I lean forward right back at him. I should have known, I should have known. What does he like better than anything else?

Humiliation.

I think about Connie, in *Behind the Bedroom Door*, telling Peter all about the escapades she'd just been on. Gabe had circled the scene where she tells him about the two guys, filling both her holes, I remember. Though I don't have anything as good as that to tell him.

I only have this, "He was so good. He pounded me so hard, I thought I'd die."

Though it seems to have the desired effect. He's leaning over, but I can see his hand sliding between his legs. I can see the back of it, as it flexes—as though he's squeezing something, hard.

"Like when I saw you? Like when I saw you with him?"

"Yes—exactly like that. He got hold of my hips, and yanked me back on his thick cock."

And then he does the most extraordinary thing—or at least, extraordinary for him. He leans right back into the couch, and starts unbuttoning and unzipping his trousers, with fumbling, unsteady hands.

The thought: *he's going to masturbate right in front of me, while I talk about this* rolls up behind my eyes, sudden and so thrilling that my entire sex contracts and swells. I feel my nipples stiffen underneath layers of shirt and duvet.

"Keep talking," he pants, and I have to stop and gather myself. I'm just not sure what I expected, but it absolutely wasn't this. I'm a fool, and apparently a weirdly conservative one.

"Gabe—wait," I say, and he immediately stops with his zipper halfway down and one hand already inside his trousers. It makes me wish I had a camera to take a picture of him being a loose little slut.

"What do you want me to do?" he asks. He definitely, definitely knows what presses my buttons. And all along I thought I was the one doing the leading, setting the rules, laying the groundwork.

Now I'm not so sure.

When I speak, my voice comes out hoarse.

"I want you to…follow me into my bedroom. OK? I want to go to my bedroom."

A smile pulls at his mouth, but it's a nervous sort of thing. And when I get up and turn around, I can hear him behind me, blundering into the coffee table. Knocking things over. I wonder if he knows that my heart's pounding, too.

Chapter Ten

I KEEP THE LIGHTS off and get him to close the door. My bedroom curtains are always closed, so it's very dim and quiet once we're inside. He trails his eyes over everything—the bed, covered only in a crisp white sheet. The books I have haphazardly stacked on the bedside chest of drawers, the small desk in the corner, the top of the wardrobe, the floor. It's a jungle of books in here, I know.

Not much else by way of decoration.

"It's lovely in here," he says, because he's clearly mad. "I can smell your perfume."

"Take your clothes off," I say in reply.

His eyes flick back to me, suddenly stormy. I can see what the words do to him, even through the faint darkness. It's been clear all along that he doesn't like to be naked, but this is intense. I actually think he might refuse.

But in the end, he just goes with, "Will you take yours off, too?" before he starts peeling off his tank top.

I watch it go over his head, glasses still on—of course! It almost makes me laugh, but I catch myself just in time. I don't want him to feel any more awkward than he already clearly does.

I start unbuttoning my shirt, in sync with him. However, unlike me, he hesitates halfway down. His words come out ever so slightly unsteady.

"Do I have to?"

"Yes," I tell him and he grimaces, but continues unbuttoning his shirt. When he starts tugging it off his shoulders, the urge to ask him what, exactly, the hang-up is rings out strongly inside me.

There's nothing wrong with him at all. His skin is gorgeous—I can tell, even in the low light. That same liquid paleness, everywhere, and then the sharp contrast of the dark hair all over him. It's thick over his chest—much thicker than you'd suspect, when thinking about his passive demeanor—before trailing down in a thin line over his taut belly—so much like an arrow that I want to lick it immediately.

But it's clear that he doesn't appreciate it as much as I do. He murmurs something about Andy's relative smoothness, though I've no idea how he knows that. Was he checking him out, when Andy lifted his shirt? Specifically measuring the ratio of his hairiness to another man's?

It makes me restless and agitated to think that he doesn't understand his own attractiveness. So I step forward and touch him. He should be touched—it's a crime that he hasn't been. Or at least, I think he hasn't been. He certainly shivers when I run my hands over the rough fur all over his chest, and then up to the strong shape of his shoulders.

When I get close to that curve of his lower back, he *almost* flinches away. But I insist, and smooth my hand over and around and down to that sweet hollow just above his arse.

"Madison," he moans, though I can't tell if it's a request for me to stop, or a need for more, or anything at all, really.

But he does start unbuckling his belt with fumbling fingers without me having to ask. And when I find his stiff little nipples and pinch, he fumbles faster. Draws it from its loops, slow, slow, while behind my eyes I see that leather looped around my fist.

I think he sees the same thing, too, because when I step back a little and watch it come free, he pulls slower yet.

Almost like a nervous striptease, begging me to think about certain slutty things.

And I do, I do.

"Touch yourself," I say, so close to him suddenly that he must be able to feel my breath against his lips. So close that he finds it a struggle to slip his hand between our bodies, and stroke all over the places I tell him to.

He toes off his shoes and socks, first—and I let him, because that's a nice easy start. Before I progress into making him unbutton and unzip his trousers, and shove down the too-tight underpants he seems to be wearing. They're not quite as bad as the ones I requested he wear, but they're not far off, either. As clingy and bright as men's underwear probably gets, and he seems to know it too. He tries to kick them away before I've seen, and as a punishment I make him run his hands over his own arse.

That seems to get him into stuttering, red-faced mode. Though shortly after fondling himself like a little trollop, he licks his top lip in this greedy sort of fashion, and the hand that's trying to pretend it doesn't want to run through his chest hair finds a nipple, and pinches it in much the same way I did.

Harder, in fact. He pinches it really hard, and then makes a sound halfway between a groan and gasp.

"That good?" I say, at which point he notices that I'm still in the room. His eyes flick back to mine, too dark and greedy-looking. He licks his upper lip, again, but this time I catch it coming. I swipe my own over his, just as he's reaching that firm bow in the middle—in a teasing way, I suppose.

He certainly seems teased after I've done it. He jerks as though startled, then presses himself against me, quite suddenly, pushing for a kiss before I'm sure I've had my fill of him discovering himself for my pleasure.

Or his pleasure, depending on how you want to look at it. He certainly seems steeped in eager excitement when he kisses me— it's far from closed and tight-lipped. His tongue flickers quick and urgent over mine, and when he can't get close enough he actually pulls back and takes off his glasses.

So that he can really get at me, you know.

I try to tell him to slow down, but I've got my hand pressed to the nape of his neck at the same time—so what sort of reliable narrator am I? All of this is heady and delicious, and even more so when I realize that he's rocking his hips. He's rutting his prick against my skirt, my belly, and when I go to pull away he actually grasps at my arse, so that he can press more firmly into me.

He's probably leaving sticky trails all over the material. He's probably going to come all over one of my nicest skirts. Certainly he's shaking enough—and he shakes even harder when my wandering hands find the cleft between his arse cheeks.

But of course he doesn't go over—not even when we tangle briefly on the bed, or when I curl down and find the slick, swollen head of his prick with my mouth.

That sharp pine scent fills me up, and I suck hard as he tries to push himself up or back or anywhere onto the bed. I feel his hand, briefly, in my hair, but it moves away almost as soon as it gets there, and then it's just his moans, his bucking hips, his wavering voice telling me I don't have to.

I think about Andy, "making" me. It makes him nervous, I think—that idea of forcing me. Though he doesn't seem to mind being forced to do anything at all. When I push him down—one hand spread over his chest—he goes easily enough. When I stroke a firm finger over his perineum, he squirms but doesn't stop me.

He doesn't stop me when I drag just the bluntest edge of my teeth the length of his cock, either. Instead he whispers *go on, go on*, and bucks up at me.

I don't start out wanting to make him come in my mouth, but it's hard to stop once I've begun. He tastes so good—salt-sweet and immaculately clean, naturally—and the little fluttery noises he makes, the way he jerks forward then holds back, and oh God, his thigh muscles jumping against my chest and stomach…it's all good. It's so good that I think I've soaked through my knickers before he's even had a chance to have a go at me.

I'm still almost fully dressed, though he seems to be trying to rectify that. My body's half across his, so it's not hard for him to get at my skirt—though it's definitely surprising when I feel him push his hand inside, rather than trying to remove it.

When he gets to my inner thighs—eagerly spread for him—he slides his fingers between, stroking the soft skin there first before progressing to the material that's pulled taut over my plump sex.

I think it's the feel of it—material probably sodden and my cunt so hot and ready—that makes him go rigid. His voice comes out panicky and breathless, and with his free hand he tries to pull me away from his cock.

"No, Maddie—stop. Stop. I don't want to come in your mouth."

The implication of which I find even more exciting than if he actually had—just sudden, a flood of hot liquid. God, I'm sure I get wetter under the pressure of such thoughts. I certainly get wetter thinking about what he means by *not in your mouth*.

It's pretty close to him asking me for a fuck, I reckon.

"Maddie, I'm almost there, come on. Please."

I pull away with largely feigned reluctance, and for a second I am startled by the look of him. He's almost weirdly different without his glasses—features suddenly too big for his face without something else there to offset them. But there's still that odd attractiveness there, something fierce and dark and matched by his sinewy, oh-so-masculine body.

His legs seem to go on forever—right off the end of my bed—which probably should seem girlish, but doesn't. He's just so *hairy*. And his prick juts up like a fist, between solid thighs and a belly you could actually bounce pennies off of, as I had suspected.

Suddenly I'm imagining frantic stomach-crunch sessions, while he tries to drill non-sex thoughts into his smut-addled brain.

He has a tight little line between his brows, when I finally work my way back up to his face. Then he swallows—both visibly and audibly—as though someone staring at his naked body is a hard thing to get down.

But he stays quite still for me, all the same.

"Good boy," I say, and quite delightfully the frown melts a little. His mouth quirks into that almost smile of his, and it grows wider when I start sliding my shirt off my shoulders.

"Do I get to examine you, now?" he says—jokingly, I think. Though he still circles his cock and squeezes, briefly, once the idea is out there. And he does it again when I peel off my bra, and unzip my skirt, until I'm almost naked and only watching his prick.

I'm watching it so much that I accidentally blurt out, "God, I love how big and slippery you get."

Which sounds so ridiculous and rude all at the same time that I think I flush. I know my cunt does. And that same bright spread of pleasure goes through me, when he sort of glances down at himself as though to check if I'm right before giving in to that bristling embarrassment he so often wears all over him.

"Oh…" he says. "Well…"

As though it's something to be ashamed of, to be so completely turned on. I wish I could explain to him how much I enjoy that—such a sweet guy, being a complete slave to his desires and his hormones.

But instead I just have to go with, "Get the condoms out of the drawer next to you."

That pulls his attention back. Enough to say the hottest words ever invented, at least.

"Don't you want me to lick you, first?"

Ah, Gabe.

"I want you to be really wet."

Lord, Gabe.

"I don't want to hurt you."

With your gigantic glorious cock, Gabe.

"I think I'm good to go," I say, though he still looks unsure, as he fumbles for the rubbers. And then less so when I wriggle my knickers down my legs. He watches me spread out beside him, while I watch him. Of course he knows what he's doing, but it's still a tense fight between rubber and dick. *I don't think these were made for me,* he says, but I think he seems just a little bit smug, too.

And then he turns, and leans down, and kisses me—obviously hungry, but strangely chaste, at the same time.

Oddly, I think of my first boyfriend. Lying like a starfish on his single bed, waiting for him to do it to me.

I don't know what it is about this that reminds me of that, but it seems to be a recurring theme in my head, just the same. Fumblings on narrow mattresses and in the backseats of cars. All of that excitement gone so quickly, and replaced with the dull grayness of reality.

I don't know what kind of reality this is. I'm breathing hard, and he's barely touching me. He asks me how I want it, and I can't say anything. I'm not sure. I think about telling him I want it with him lying facedown, but God knows what response that will get.

Instead I spread my legs and he slides over me, slick with perspiration and tense as anything. I think his teeth might be chattering just a little bit. And when his cock slides through my soaking wet folds—unintentionally, I think—his eyes widen and he jerks back.

"I should probably make myself come, first, and then…" he says, but it's OK because I think *I* almost come, hearing him say that. I definitely moan aloud when he follows it with a quick hand between my legs, and a moan of his own.

He sounds despairing—he *looks* despairing. His face goes slack and lust-glazed when his fingers get lost in my completely over-excited pussy.

"You're so wet," he murmurs. "You're so wet and burning hot, God."

I can't stop myself bucking up into his probing fingers.

Especially when he puts two fingers together and swipes down over my clit—just once, but once is almost enough. I nearly ask him not to stop, but then I think about his cock sliding back and forth in me, while those same fingers play right where they are now.

I just have to put a hand to the small of his back and urge him forward.

"Let me make you come, first," he says, so I kiss him to keep him quiet. I don't think I can stand to hear him say anything else. I just want his mouth on mine and his cock pressing into me and oh holy mother of…I don't think I'm going to survive this. Not on any level.

He slides just a little way in, and that's too much. I think he knows it is, too, because he stops being able to kiss me properly, and turns his face to one side. His damp cheek presses against mine, fitfully, and I'm sure I hear him tell me to *relax, please relax*.

But I don't need to, I really don't. He feels big, but not impossible. I guess it only seems impossible to him, because he gasps out, "You're too—"

Then can't seem to remember what other words he was going to say. Mainly because he sinks all the way in, sudden and lo-o-ong. I see his eyelids flutter and his lips part, and then he's rocking his hips, just a little. Just experimentally.

His hair has fallen over his forehead, but he doesn't stroke it back. Instead he drops down so that he's just propped up on his elbows, and brings his hands to my face. Strokes a thumb over an eyebrow, too soft and too much.

I slide myself back and forth, back and forth—nice and quick— before he can say anything. And after that, I'm pretty sure he forgets. He jerks forward in what seems like an instinctive sort of way when I rock into him, and then when my legs are hooked over his hips, he just has to test the waters further.

He gets this little jerky, shallow rhythm going—one that makes that flush on his cheeks spread down over his neck and chest. But it's not quite enough—not for me, or for him—and it's obvious he's holding back. The time comes for him to speed up and hit it hard, but instead he just shudders all over, and makes these bone-melting desperate sounds. Almost like *ohs*, but not quite.

"Don't worry, don't worry," I tell him, but I don't think my words come out right either, and his *ohs* definitely get louder when I add, "You won't hurt me, fuck me hard, OK? Fuck me, Gabe."

But he still holds himself back. I can feel his body, straining against the leash. His thrusts turn sloppy and uncoordinated, and the sound he makes when he presses his face into the crook of my neck—it's almost like a sob.

I just have to fuck myself on him. It's not difficult—I just grab a handful of his arse and rut up and down beneath him like a maniac, sobbing myself whenever that gorgeous cock rubs hard and solid against that sweet spot inside me.

His belly keeps grazing my clit, too—which is more maddening than anything else. But luckily he hasn't forgotten his manners, because he lifts himself up and gets a hand between our bodies.

Those two fingers, sliding down. And down. And down. Oh.

But I only come when he says, "Yes, yes. Fuck me harder."

Both because of the gasping, breathless, slutty tone to his voice, and the realization that his body is jolting and juddering like that because I'm ramming myself down on his cock.

I say his name. I don't care. I don't think my pussy has ever clamped down so hard on anything in all its days, and I know I've never gone so tense all over. When he goes to move his hand away, I mash mine down on top of it, because it's so good and so expansive that I don't mind it going on forever—long past the point where it's comfortable.

When I finally come out of it, he looks sweaty and startled and in absolute agony—though I don't think we've been having this weird push-me-pull-you sex for all that long.

"You seemed to…like that," he says, half trying to laugh, I think, but he doesn't laugh at all when I tell him it's his turn, now. He tries to say some desperate unsure thing like *I can't get there*, but that's OK because it's obvious why.

"Harder," I tell him, and when he tries to squirm out of it I *order* him. I think I maybe call him my fuck toy. I tell him I want him to do it to me so hard I won't be able to walk straight tomorrow, and in response he tries an experimental thrust.

It's pathetic, really.

"I can see I'm going to have to spank you, until you do it right," I say, and he moans, *No, Maddie, don't*, while pushing his arse into the sudden firm clasp of my hand.

It's an awkward twist to do it, but worth it for the way he bites his lip too hard and shivers once, like a wet dog. When I do smack him, it's more of a firm and sudden squeeze, a handful of arse that makes him surge forward.

I think I choke on his cock. But it's OK, it's good. He draws back and then seems to fumble his way to an almost hard enough rhythm—which improves when I slap and squeeze again. In fact, it improves so much that I feel my inner thighs go oddly weak at the firm and constant pressure right…there.

He's kind of still twisted to one side a little, and the way he rolls his hips…God. No snapping back and forth like a jackhammer—actual rolling, hard and steady. One of his hands goes to my hip and…I don't know. I think he just presses down, but it feels like a trigger. It sets off something tense and heated.

I definitely pant for him to keep doing that, and it's then that his body tightens. I see it happen, and know he's holding it off—breathing suddenly absent and lips pressed together in a thin line.

So I dig *my* nails in, and watch him jerk against me, all that pent up need coming out of him in a sound I never thought I'd hear him make. It's loud and frantic and he can't seem to stop once he's started; he squeezes hard enough to leave bruises at my hip.

I feel him swell inside me—impossible as that seems—and then his eyes snap open and he tells me *Maddie, Maddie*, as his body jerks through an orgasm that never ends.

When he's finally through, I think he's managed to lock himself in one position. His hand won't unclasp from my hip, and I notice his other hand has fisted the pillow into some impossible shape.

It takes some unwinding and unraveling. And when I finally manage it, he collapses all over me like an undercooked soufflé. Hugs me and hugs me and won't let me go.

But I don't mind. I don't. I really don't think I mind any of this at all.

Chapter Eleven

I THINK I DOZED. I'm sure there was a dream about some sort of Christopher-Pike-Gabe-turns-out-to-be-an-alien-thing. He probably is, come to think of it. *Cosmo* never talks about men like him.

But I come to rested and warm and still weak from the waist down, curled around his pillow. I can't remember the last time someone owned a pillow in my bed, but there it is. And he does.

He can have all my pillows, for being seated against the wall by the closed door, legs crooked up, with a book between them.

He's wearing one of my towels around his waist, but other than that he's naked. Just seated there, half-nude, uncaring! I want to ruffle his still wet hair. I want to kick him for not waking me up for shower time. It would have been a real treat to see him trying to scrub away naughty sex.

But then he looks up, face lineless and open, and I don't think he really believes that we're being naughty. Instead he focuses on the silliest, most innocuous thing:

"You don't mind, do you? That I had a shower? I didn't think you'd mind."

"Why would I mind?" I ask, and am shocked by how sleepy and satisfied it comes out. I'm practically drawling. And I think I can still feel the echo of his cock between my legs.

He shrugs one shoulder. He really has the most adorable bashful look—lips sort of turned inwards, eyebrows raised.

"Didn't think you'd mind the book, either. You seem to enjoy encouraging my education."

I laugh, at that—though it comes out warm and dozy. How did he manage to make me so comfortable in my own skin? Wish I knew.

"I do," I say. "I'm all for bettering oneself."

He glances at the cover—a classic: *Ultimate Threesomes Four*—and laughs right back at me. Though when he laughs, it's never really that. It's more of a sound struggling to fight past his lips. A little chuff, pulled right out of him.

"Is it good?"

Again, a one-shouldered shrug.

"*Ultimate Threesomes Two* was definitely the masterpiece of the quartet. This one's lacking." He tosses it aside. "I wasn't really reading it, anyway."

"Oh, that old excuse."

"I wasn't. I wouldn't lie. I don't have to lie with you."

He meets my gaze, steady as anything. Mine's not doing quite as good.

"Mainly I was just…looking at you. You went to sleep in the crook of my arm—never had anyone do that before."

I keep my eyes on him. I keep them there. I don't try and get away. Especially as I think he's just going to keep talking. He seems completely relaxed, and he's going to keep talking. I wonder how much of it I can take.

"But then I was just creepily staring at you, so I thought I'd better get up and distract myself. Shower. Books. The books didn't work very well."

"You weren't looking at me when I woke up."

"Lucky, I guess. Though I *have* just told you all of this, so…"

"Pointless, trying to hide your creepy staring."

"Exactly."

He breaks off the locked gaze thing, then. Maybe he couldn't stand it—I don't know. It doesn't seem like it, but what do I know? I'm some sort of insane emotional cripple.

"You know—I think there are some clothes that would fit you in the drawer over there," I say, and only when he gets up do I know why I directed him to them—because he won't be facing me anymore. He won't.

And I can say the words I want to say when his back is to me, with the sound turned down.

The next time I wake up, it's after a take-out dinner in bed, and more talk about random things that somehow lead to me wanting to declare undying love, and it's late. Around 3 a.m., I think, though the sudden war zone bed doesn't seem to know it.

Did he really think I wouldn't feel it shaking like that? He's not exactly gentle when he jerks off. He's vigorous, and hard on himself, and God it makes me wet just listening to him trying to be quiet.

Though I kind of suspect that he's not exactly trying to be as quiet as he can be. He hasn't got his hand pressed to his mouth, for a start. I can hear him breathing too hard and occasionally stifling a moan against the seam of his lips.

And when I say his name, he just moans louder.

"You could have woken me, you know," I say into the semi-darkness, and I can hear his hand speeding up on his cock. That slick, rapid sound—ah, delicious.

"I'm sorry, I'm sorry. I don't sleep very well. Especially when—especially with—oh, oh yes—Maddie!"

"Are you going to come?"

"Soon. It's really coming easy."

"I'll take that as a compliment."

"You should—ah!"

I listen to him going at it for a few blissful seconds more, then have to get him over here. I'm human—there's only so much I can take.

So I reach behind myself and fumble over whatever I can find, until his hand stills and his body stills and he does his little non-laugh.

"I don't know if I can ask you for sex," he says, through said amused sound. And I suppose it is amusing, really.

We're both stumbling around in the dark, unsure. Happy, somehow, to be unsure.

"You can ask me for anything. Come up against me, OK?"

He does as I ask far too slowly, settling around the curve of my body with an even more amused *are we spooning now*? To which I reply that I guess we are. He isn't touching himself anymore, but I can feel the hot press of his erection against my bare back. Against my arse, occasionally—not sliding in or between anything, but certainly eager.

And then his arm loops over and around me, and he pushes his face—his mouth—against the all too sensitive nape of my neck. When I shiver, he pulls away a little, startled. But I soon fix that with a hand behind me, on the nape of *his* neck.

I clamp down hard, and yank him back rough, and now it's his turn to shiver. *Do what you want*, I tell him, and his hand immediately comes up to cup and squeeze my right breast. Though it's not him suddenly tugging at my nipple—just once, light and good— that pushes me over the edge into do-anything-excitement. It's when I feel his tongue sliding cool and slick over the back of my neck.

That's when I buck and order him to put his hand between my legs. Of course, by this point I'm sure he'd get there eventually all on his own. He's got my tits and all the licking in hand, after all. But I won't lie—I don't want to wait.

And he doesn't make me. He slides his hand down my belly and squeezes between my closed thighs, wriggling his way in until he's cupping my sex in almost the same way as he'd cupped my breast. Insistently, firmly.

"What do you want me to do next?" he says, and my mind forgets everything, everything but him. I could eat those words every time he says or implies them.

Instead, I squirm back against the heated bar of his cock. He makes a little startled sound and backs off—though his hand remains exactly where it is. His shoulder clicks, somewhere close to my ear—probably trying hard to stay in its socket.

"Tell me what to do," he demands, again, and really—who am I to deny him?

"Rub my clit until I come," I say, then think to add, "And don't do anything to yourself while you do me. Not anything. Understood?"

There's a pause, and when he speaks it's hoarse and faint.

"I don't think I can wait much longer."

And it's the weirdest thing. I am almost certain that he's only saying that for my benefit. In fact, I think I know it. I do know it. He's now somehow aware enough of my likes and dislikes to understand that I enjoy the idea of him not being able to wait.

Like he's going to go off any second while he's touching me, and come all over my back and my arse. Like he's so excited that he's going to fail, and fall to frantic jerking off in the middle of making me come.

"You can finish after I've gone—any sooner and I'll be very disappointed. You don't want that, do you?"

"No, God—no. Help me, though—show me how you like it. You like it quick and light, don't you, Maddie? Just like this. In circles, like this."

I try to get words out. I try. But he's doing exactly what he's saying and by God he's right.

"Because I'll bet it feels good when you really press down hard on your clit, but teasing makes it better, in the end."

He really is good at putting theory into practice.

"Maybe that's why you hold off all the time and get me to put on a show for you. So it's better when you finally get it." He's half right, this time. "Sometimes I do the same thing. I wait, and wait, and then when I do it I stroke lightly, like this, because I know I need pressure to really get off. And it feels so good, so good, when I go a little faster, a little harder. It feels so good to talk to you like this, Maddie."

It's fabulous that he's really finding his voice. Because I seem to have lost mine. I press my face into the pillow, and squeeze my grip tight around his straining-to-work hand. I think he's got just his middle finger on my clit, and it feels like it's barely touching. It feels like it's setting me on fire, right there.

"I guess I'm talking dirty to you," he says, after a moment of this torture—but it's his little bemused and shocked at himself laugh that really catches some previously unknown triggers. I babble his name, and press against his hand.

"Do you like me doing that? I've never said any of this, or talked like this, to anyone." He presses down just once, hard and shocking. And I have to wonder if he read about doing this somewhere, because Jesus it feels amazing. Like little mini orgasms are going off in all the places he isn't touching. Or is. Or fuck, I don't know.

And he just keeps on talking! I've busted a dam. I've cracked a hole in the dyke.

"But then, I've never done *any* of this before, with anyone. I've never stroked anyone like this, or rubbed my stiff prick against their back, or fondled their breasts and wanted to be inside them again. God, I want to do that again, Maddie. I never thought it could feel like someone's fucking you while they're underneath you—that was amazing. It was amazing. Oh Maddie, I think I'm going to come—hurry. Don't make me wait any longer."

It's funny—I didn't think I was the one in control anymore,

until he said that last bit. But when he does, everything all boils over and mingles together and goes crazy inside me. I tell him harder, harder, and he presses just that one finger down on my insanely swollen clit.

And then such intense sensation pushes outward from that one point—I think I wet myself. I can't even make a sound of pleasure. My mouth just opens and my legs lock around his hand and I jerk and make a mess of him.

Before blissful bonelessness takes over I think I sag all the way through the mattress to the floor below. I'm pretty sure I'm never going to stop sagging—or regain the ability to speak. So good— Jesus. So good that I'm not going to say anything about the still slippery hand he clamps over my hip so that he can go at me.

He doesn't try to fuck me, however. No—I guess he can't wait for that. He just ruts against me—first over my back and the firm swell of my arse, and then…oh then. He fumbles and finds the cleft between, and suddenly increases the frantic, jerking pace.

I just lie there, and let him. Mainly because I can't believe that the slick feel of his prick between the cheeks of my arse, rubbing and rutting, filthily, actually manages to thrill arousal through me. After that huge orgasm. Still.

"Is this OK, is it OK?" he asks, but it's a minute after he's started and his voice is so up and down that I can't take it seriously. I'm right not to, too, because almost at the same time as those words, his body locks against mine. He grunts so gutturally, it sets my hair on end.

And then I feel the hot spurt of his come all over my arse and my lower back. Which feels so delicious and dirty, I bite my lip and try not to wonder when he'll be up for another round. I'm guessing it's not going to be soon, because a second after he's done it all over me, he apologizes. He apologizes for making a mess. For fucking… whatever it was he fucked.

At which I definitely want to do it all over again. Immediately. Continually. Forever.

Seriously—when can we do it again, forever?

———

Dawn's just coming in through the curtains when I next open my eyes. And find him already awake, staring at me through the rising light. I know he's slept, because I felt him press heavy and sudden against my back, soon after cleaning me up. Still spooning, him satisfied with my assurances that I had no complaints.

Though I didn't use the word complaint. It was much more like: my God, you're a sexual wizard. I honestly don't mind telling him that. He deserves it. He says sorry far too much, too.

Like now, when I catch him staring.

"Why?" I ask, and he tells me frankly that he knows it's weird. That he's weird.

So I reach out and touch his face. Overnight really gives him some serious stubble.

"It's not weird, Gabe. I like it. I…you know. I like you."

I can feel I'm blushing, but it's too dark for him to see. God knows what would happen if I ever managed to say the words I mouthed at his back last night. My face would explode, probably.

But he looks delighted with just *like*. I guess there haven't been many of those in his life—never mind the other one.

"You've really never done any of that stuff before, have you."

I don't know why I ask. Though I suppose I'm not really asking. It's a given. It's obvious. We've been doing sexual things for what must be months, and he's only just got around to being comfortable with talking dirty to me. To considering the idea of asking for sex.

Still, something inside me twangs when he says, "Are you asking me if I was a virgin?"

Somehow, him saying the word smashes it right into me: last night I popped someone's cherry. I don't even think my first boyfriend was a virgin when he banged me in the back of his dad's Ford Fiesta.

I've just fucked a thirty-year-old virgin. I'm like the less impressive sequel to a Steve Carrell movie.

"Did it seem like I was?"

I know what he's really asking: Was it awful? He's actually asking me that. Sometimes I honestly think he's bonkers. I mean, the virginity's a hell of a clue.

"It seems like you are on a daily basis, Gabe. But that doesn't mean you didn't fuck me into goo last night. I mean, you must know that you fucked me into goo. I know how smart you are—don't pretend."

He smiles, showing teeth. I watch it slowly light up his face.

"I told you. I know my theory."

"You know me, too."

He seems to sort of shrug with just a turn of his head.

"You're easy. I always thought it would be hard, but there are so many little signs and hints. The way you move your hips or sigh or sometimes you don't say anything, but I know the words are kind of trapped in your throat. Then it's good. It's really good."

The urge to call him a sexual wizard surfaces again.

"I knew you wanted me to do it harder before you asked. Before you did anything. But I didn't want to hurt you—you felt… really…small."

"No—you're just that immense. I swear—no one would ever guess you're packing what you're packing, babe."

He laughs at that, but then his eyes get that faraway look, again. The one he often gets when he starts talking about, say, how small my pussy felt. Though this time, it's something entirely unexpected that comes out.

"I always thought there was something wrong with me when I was a kid."

And I'm not sure how to respond, at first. It's always so much like he's peeling off raw skin when he shares something about his past. Though he seems relaxed, much more relaxed than usual. The words come easy, and untroubled.

It's simple to go with amusing.

"Because you had a gigantic monster dick?"

Sure enough, his smile spreads. He chuff-laughs at me, and kind of ducks his gaze.

"No. No. Well—maybe a little. I got a shock in the changing room showers, I'll say that much."

I picture it. Of course I do.

"But it wasn't just that. The other boys…they all…you know. I felt so different to them. And I guess they knew I was different, too. They weren't ever cruel, exactly, but they'd talk about doing stuff and how many times they did it, going into loads of detail—things I'd never heard of. How this girl or that made them get a stiffy, that sort of thing. And I just…"

"You didn't pop a boner 'til you hit your twenties."

He squirms onto his back and stares up at the ceiling. Though somehow I don't think it's a sign of discomfort. He still seems relaxed—no hair smoothing, no fidgeting. Just lost in time and slightly amused, probably by *pop a boner*.

"No—no. It was before then. But I clearly remember getting to seventeen without ever really…God, I was so worried about it. I used to lie awake at night, wondering if there was something wrong with me—you know, bodily? Like a tumor or something. I kind of knew I wasn't gay, because I liked the look and smell of girls. Sometimes I'd feel good, being close to them—though none really wanted to be close to me so maybe it was just that I hadn't had the opportunities other boys had. Sex was just a formless, physical education thing to me. No *Playboys*, no *Hustlers*. No secret porn movies."

I raise an eyebrow.

"No books?"

He glances at me, eyebrows raised right back.

"No—God no. My parents would never have allowed it in the house. Until I was permitted to go to high school, I'd never heard of any of this stuff. I didn't even know books like…like the ones I've got now existed."

"So when did you get your first…stiffy?"

The word almost makes me giggle, but he doesn't seem to notice. He's looking at the ceiling again, without really seeing it. However, it seems to take him no effort at all to answer. His voice is low, almost like a soothing hum.

"When my cousin came to stay."

I poke him and see his mouth slant into a half-smile. Everything is half with him. He's not allowed full measures because his mad parents aren't going to let him. I think of those words: *permitted* to go to high school. Like ordinary life is a privilege, not a right.

God knows what they taught him at home.

"Led you astray, did she?" I ask, and his smile widens. He knows all the old clichés, all right.

"No. Yes. Yeah, I guess she did. My parents liked her, so she got away with a lot while she was there. She was allowed to wear short skirts, and she brought books that weren't manuals or history things into the house."

He glances quickly at me and then back again, and waits—I think for my laughter. But he's not going to get any—I'm hooked, now.

"So she introduced you to—"

"No. They weren't erotic—I don't think even she would have got away with that." He pauses. I think it's actually intended as a dramatic one, too. "They were horror books. These boring looking things, with houses on the covers or else nothing at all."

My mind immediately goes to those old-school horror novels, with giant peeling lettering on the front. The author's name in ten-foot-high font. I'll confess I was hoping for secret *Playboys* passed to him under cover of darkness—but this is weird enough for me to want to find out what it has to do with erections. Or feeling different to everyone else.

And he's apparently comfortable enough to oblige. He's even—quite startlingly—trailing his fingers back and forth over the hair all over his bare chest. Just absentmindedly, though I can see his cock rising beneath the sheets.

"I didn't think anything to them. I wanted to read them, maybe, because I always wanted to read different stuff. But I didn't ask her. I didn't talk to her at all. I never had time, really—my parents were getting pretty bad by then. Forgetful. I think that's why she was sent, from some uncle I didn't know and never saw again. To 'help.'

"But she didn't help. God, she never helped. She used to torment me—all the time. I remember distinctly—feeling *forced* to read these really gory parts of her books. She would force me. I'm not sure how, exactly, but I always felt like I'd better do it, you know? Or else."

Is it weird that I understand why he's getting an erection? Because I completely do. Though granted, it's not exactly the riddle of the sphinx.

"You were only seventeen, for God's sake. And you'd had about a millisecond of experience dealing with other people. Of course you did what she wanted you to."

But that's not what I'm thinking, of course. I'm thinking: you were like this all along, weren't you. You were just waiting for someone to come along and show you.

"I was taller than her, too. Much taller. I was six foot two at *fourteen*, with hair all over my chest. But it didn't matter—I had to do what she asked. And it wasn't...it wasn't in the same way as having to do what my parents wanted."

I'm propped up on one elbow. It's pretty easy to trail the hand that's already close to him through his thick and completely unruly hair. I don't know what product he uses to create the rigid side-parting but there's none of it here, and without it his hair remains straight but heavy and all over the place.

When I rake my nails over his scalp, just lightly, he pushes into the touch.

"Your parents didn't ask, though, did they. Or even demand."

"No."

"I bet they just expected you to be the one on top of things all the time."

He pushes harder into my hand. I think he might actually be toying with one of his nipples, now, and when he answers he pinches it harder.

"Yeah. They did."

He's silent for a moment, then. Just still, and pliant under my touch. I run the backs of my fingers over all the stubble he's managed to produce overnight, and he lets me. Until some other thought occurs to him, and that almost-smile comes back to his lips, and he blusters out, "God, some of those things she made me read!"

I think of Kevin Collinson in the playground, trying to get everyone to look at pictures of Freddy Krueger. Couldn't even look at his face when I hit college.

"They were gross—they gave me nightmares. Heads being smashed open, zombies eating people…just awful stuff. I was terrified. And I told her, too—I said I couldn't stand it anymore. I know I was seventeen, but I just hadn't read anything like that before. I hadn't seen anything like it. So I told her to stop."

"Did she?"

He shifts on the bed, and his still hard cock bobs beneath the sheets. I'm sure he's going to progress to touching himself—any second now. Any second.

"Yes. For a time. Then one day she just came up to me and said, 'Here, Gabe. Try this bit.' And I did."

Of course I understand what he's getting at—or what she was getting at. It's clear, now. But I still want to ask, and hear him say.

"What bit was it?"

That flush is creeping up his face. He's moving more often, now—I think because it makes his cock brush against the material covering it.

"I don't remember the name of the book. Something was coming to get the main characters, I think, and they were…"

He clears his throat. One of his hands is now beneath the sheets—though not quite at its destination yet. It's just pretending it's on its way to Brazil, for the moment.

"…they were having sex, oblivious. I remember I had to hide the book and act like I hadn't read it after I saw the first words. I acted like that, and wouldn't talk to her."

I wait, with baited breath, for him to tell me what she did next. I can't imagine she let him off so easy, and I unfortunately know this because I wouldn't have done that. I *didn't*. He doesn't *want* to be let off easy.

"So she told me—she said—God. I'll never forget what she said as long as I live. She said *if you don't read your book assignment, Gabe, I'll have to punish you*. To this day I've no idea if she really meant it… the way I later found out people sometimes mean it. She never got to the punishment, whatever it was going to be. I was too terrified of her telling on me to let it go that far."

He swallows, thickly.

"But I wanted it to. That was what was worse about the whole thing. I knew inside that I wanted her to punish me. I wanted her to punish me *for* reading what she'd asked me to. Because I did—read it, I mean."

He glances at me, all over me, eyes bright and sort of…confused. It takes me a minute to realize why—it's because I'm rolling my hips. I'm rolling my hips and squeezing my thighs together, and it's as much for this story he's telling as it is for the way he looks.

"You like hearing this, don't you," he says, soft as anything.

"Do you mind me liking it?"

His expression fades into bemusement.

"Why would I mind? You know it's turning me on, too. It always does, I can't help it."

His flush deepens when he gets to that part. He looks off to the side at nothing.

"Finish telling it, then. What happened next?"

"I told you. I read it."

Now he's going to withdraw? Get awkward, close himself off? It's a bit late for that, my lad.

"And what was in it?"

"I don't remember."

I can't resist. It's so obvious, I have to wonder if he's pushing for it. He's tensed up a little, but he's not exactly pulling the covers up to his chin and smoothing down his hair. So I go with what I want to most, "Tell me, or I'll punish you."

His eyes flash to me, bright with an emotion I can't identify. It looks like a mixture of around seventeen feelings, all at the same time. His breathing roughens, almost immediately—like I cocked a trigger at the back of his head.

"Well? What's it to be?"

At first I'm sure he's going to refuse. A tight pulse of arousal blooms outwards from my sex, just thinking about it.

I've no idea what I'll dole out punishment-wise if he does refuse, but man alive does it excite me thinking about it.

Only the tension holding fast between us melts, and his eyes flick down, and he says in this breathless sort of voice:

"I recognized what they were doing—in the book, I mean. They were having sex, but it wasn't like in physical education. It wasn't like anything I'd heard other boys talking about."

He pauses, when I curl right down next to him, and kiss just below the curve of his jaw. Lower still, on the stretch of skin beneath his ear—at which he makes a contented sound before continuing.

"It was...schlocky and messy. I don't know, I—is this my reward? One way I get a punishment, the other way a reward?"

I like the sudden puzzling tone to his voice. Like his need to work things out breaks through all the memories and arousal and fuck knows what else.

"Why don't you carry on and find out?" I say, between wet kisses. He definitely enjoys it when I suck his earlobe into my mouth.

"Hm—oh. Maddie, if you're going to do that I'm going to stop making sense." He brings a hand up, then seems to consider whether he should put it on my bare shoulder or not. Desire wins. "And then I guess...I guess he kissed her, between her legs. I always remember that part the best. He—you know. He went down on her."

This story is turning out *really* good. And he's definitely getting back into it, now.

"But I'd never heard of anything like that before! I couldn't believe it. I had to keep re-reading it. And then—Jeez, the most terrible writing. It said something like 'he popped just the thick head of his cock into her slick love tunnel' and I—I don't know what happened to me. I guess it started with her, telling me...that. But it got really strong when I actually read what she'd told me to."

It's getting strong, now. He moans when I slide my hand under the sheets, over his already jumping belly.

But I don't touch his prick. I wait, until he carries on.

"I remember thinking: there's nothing wrong with me, there's nothing wrong with me—I'm just like the other boys—and being really happy about that. But it was shameful, too. She knew that I was reading this part, and probably getting stiff, and she'd made me do it.

"Which just made it worse. I know I thought: how am I ever going to be able to stand up and leave my bedroom? I knew that my body was doing the right thing, but it felt really wrong—massive. And like I couldn't think straight. Usually, everything in my head was calm, and right. This was just...I know I wanted to touch myself. I knew what to do—in school, they'd all talked about it.

"But then I thought about my parents catching me, and it sort of just died away."

He's *really* touching me by this point. Hand on my back, smoothing around and around. Other hand at my hip, tugging me toward him.

His dark eyes meet mine—rueful, I think. And he backs that assessment up with, "I think *this* might be my punishment."

"So when did you first masturbate?" I say in reply—and he grimaces and laughs, somehow at the same time.

"Later that night. In bed. I made dinner, I washed up, I took a bath. I did everything like normal, calmly—I didn't even think about anything, though Missy kept trying to nudge me, you know. And then when I got into bed, my mind just filled up with all these thoughts and all those words, and Missy saying...those words.

"Only in my head they became—if you don't *touch yourself,* I'll punish you.

"So I did."

Permission, I think. *Permission to be bad.*

"What was it like?"

He answers immediately, despite the thigh I now have hooked over his. And the way I'm rutting against him, slow and steady. Something on me grazes his cock, and he jumps, as though struck.

But he doesn't move to touch himself.

"Frustrating. I know that people usually do it really fast the first time. But it didn't come easy to me. I remember being really, really excited—really worked up. And it built up and up and I knew I was supposed to get somewhere and stuff was meant to come out of me but it just wouldn't happen.

"I think I sweated through my pajamas. I had the covers pulled right up so it was boiling, and I definitely thought more than once that I wished I'd had a book telling me how to do it."

I try not to laugh at that—but God. It's just so *him*.

"Then it finally occurred to me to actually think about the stuff in Missy's book *while* I did it. I know—usually I'm quick to figure things out. But not with myself. Never with myself. I thought about the man, licking her between her legs. And I rubbed hard—harder than I thought I should. I was sure I'd hurt myself—you know, not be able to pee the next day, or something like that.

"But it felt so good. It felt so good. I made a noise when I rubbed it nice and tight. I didn't mean to and afterward I was terrified, but I couldn't help it. And when I came, it went on forever. I bit right into my lip—the only part of me that was actually damaged the next day. And I had to wash the sheets, too, because I made a mess everywhere. I was pretty careful after that—taking tissues to bed, that sort of thing. Or I'd do it in the bathroom, or the shed—because no one ever went in there. I had to find places quickly, because by then I really...I...well."

I know. I understand. You've come twice tonight, and you're still so horny that you're rubbing against a leg that's barely touching your always eager cock.

"How did you stand it?" I say, against the open mouth I'm kissing. And kissing. "How did you stand it?"

He moans in reply, and asks me if he can stop talking now. If he can. If he's permitted to. And I kiss him and kiss him and kiss him for being strong enough to ask.

Chapter Twelve

"I'VE NEVER TOLD ANYONE any of that," he says, as he watches me get dressed. He's sitting on the end of the bed, starkers. Still hard, because we kissed, and rolled around on the bed, but no further orgasms took place.

Further orgasms would have just been insane, and eager to eat into proper adult work time.

"I like that you've never told anyone any of that," I say, as I zip my skirt. Pull it down taut, and neat. "I like that you've got it to tell."

The sudden lines of worry that have crept over his brow smooth out at that.

"Will you tell me about you?" He still isn't getting dressed yet—but that's OK. I have other plans for him. "Later, I mean."

"What do you want to know?" I ask from inside the confines of the sweater I'm pulling over my head. When I finally break free, I finish with, "That I first masturbated at an age much younger than yours, while reading Judy Blume and thinking about Corey Haim?"

He surprises me with a head duck and an eyebrow raise.

"The dirty Judy Blume," he says, and it's not a question. I give him a wry smile for that one. I guess all kids—even sexually stunted ones—know about the dirty Judy Blume.

"Yeah. That one. I didn't have any epic voyage of discovery, like you." He comes close to grinning. I think because I called it an epic voyage. "Though looking back, I've always been attracted to a certain sort of man. And I think that…maybe I haven't understood myself very well."

I eye him, as I say it. See him really clear. I wonder if in ten years' time I won't ever forget what he's given me over these past couple of months. It's been something, all right.

It still is something.

"No," I tell him. "Don't get up. Don't get dressed."

He's half-standing, when his face floods with surprise. I think he even starts to protest, though that soon disappears. I think it goes when he sees my expression, which feels flat and calm and right on me.

"I want you to stay up here. Naked—all the time," I say, and suddenly wish I'd made time for that last orgasm. He was right—you just know it, inside. You know.

"Maddie—" he starts, but I interrupt.

"You have to go the bathroom, naked, and make yourself breakfast, naked, and when you're done, I want you to read or watch television or whatever you want, also naked. Feel free to explore my apartment."

"People will see me. Through the window—the window in your living room is huge!"

"And?"

My hands are on my hips. I don't know how they got there.

"What about work? Don't you want me to—"

"I'm going to pay you to be up here, waiting for me, naked. Like my little whore."

He actually makes a noise when I use that last word. A real, guttural, excited sort of noise. His cock lurches, between his legs.

"And you can touch yourself, and play with any of the toys you find in my drawers, and smother your face in my underwear if you feel like it—" I pause, watching him squirm after each one of those options. Then the *pièce de resistance*. "—but you're not allowed to come."

His eyes snap to mine at that. Fierce, like before—when I said

I'd punish him. There's definitely a defiance there, but somehow that just makes his need for this all the sweeter.

"No, Maddie," he says. "No—don't make me do that." I love his choice of words.

"I've got to get downstairs, OK—so be good. I'll know if you did it, Gabe. You know I will."

"I can't go all day," he moans—almost a whine, in fact.

"Of course you can." I lean down and kiss him, softly. "I have total faith in you."

Though the truth is, I don't at all. I don't because as I'm leaving, I tell him I'll punish him if he fails. And this time he has to really struggle hard to keep the dirty furtive smile that threatens off his face.

—⁓—

It's more than difficult to keep myself downstairs. I almost go up at lunchtime, but somehow manage to resist. I really want to resist, because in the long run it'll make it sweeter. It's making it sweeter right now, as I serve a customer and think about him struggling not to masturbate.

While talking to Jeanette, I wonder if he's found my sex-toy drawer yet. There's lube in there, in case he wants to make himself extra slick for his greedy grasping hand. Or there's a selection of vibrators and butt plugs and dildos, all of which he could do very interesting things with, if he's feeling daring.

And then there's my slippery mess of underwear—stockings and flimsy nighties and that little corset thing I have that I've never worn for anyone. I think about him going through all of it, and all of my secret private things, and shiver hard enough for Jeanette to ask me if I'm OK.

"Sure," I say, but she definitely now knows more than she's letting on. I bet she heard last night, when Gabe called out my name. I bet she heard *me* call out *his* name, for God's sake. And tonight, she's probably going to hear way more stuff, too—like how much I want to pull his hair and make him wait and wait until he begs me for mercy.

It takes everything in me to wait until five. To keep myself calm and measured, as I turn the sign to closed and tidy various items. I guess somehow I thought he might break, and come down all dressed and normal, and the fact that he hasn't…it seems to be making my palms damp. My hands are shaking, just a little.

God knows what I expect to find. Certainly not a dark and silent apartment, with barely a sound coming from anywhere. A brief image comes to mind—him asleep, in my bed. Or maybe asleep, naked, in the bathtub.

But it gets brushed away fairly quickly by the faint buzz of the television coming from the bedroom.

At first I think it's just the news or maybe some weird thing that he likes to watch, like Making Toys for Dummies or Bad Things that Happened in History. Though maybe my body knows differently, because something sure makes me creep into the apartment, on tiptoe. Something makes me shut the door behind myself really quietly, in case it disturbs whatever fascinating thing he might be doing.

Like maybe dressing himself up in my underwear, or…I'll be honest. My mind doesn't really get past that one. It freezes me at the just cracked bedroom door, watching the colors from the television flicker against the sliver of wall I can see.

And then the sounds that only the DVDs I keep in my drawer can make.

Oh what a bad, bad boy he is. Such a bad boy! What am I going to do with him? What? I can barely think coherently, for all the things I'm going to do with him.

He's not even watching the sweet porn, with the occasional kiss and the nice lighting. No, he's watching the dirty threesome porn, with the cocks everywhere and the huge amount of filthy talk. I can hear it right now: *yeah, nail that arse. Do that pussy. Fuck that mouth.*

And many other variations thereof. In fact, it's one of my favorites because of that brick-headed dude with the potty mouth. He's not in any way attractive, but man, he sure can order a girl to do some disgusting things.

Something which Gabe seems to be very, very aware of when I wander into the bedroom. All casual-like, leaning back against the door I close, one foot crossing over the other.

He reacts on the door click. Which gives me a wonderful opportunity to see him up close and completely oblivious, getting stuck into some hardcore pornography. *While wearing my pajama bottoms.*

And OK, it's not my underwear. He didn't decide to do his makeup, or anything. But there's still something distinctly subversive and delicious about him wearing purple pajama bottoms that are clearly five sizes too short and just a little tight around the thigh. And the cock, of course.

When he fumbles for the remote and blusters things that are not words, delightfully panicked and oh so mussed, he kind of almost stands and I get a truly awesome view of his rock hard prick, stretching out the too-thin material.

It'd be a sight for a hardened sex veteran. I don't know what it is for me. He has exceeded my expectations, and then some. Hardcore porn while wearing my clothes and, oh my word, he seems to have attached a nipple clamp to just one of his nipples. Just one. As though maybe two would simply be beyond the pale.

My speechlessness tries to disguise itself as steely control. I think it succeeds, because boy does he look nervous. You don't get nervous if the person you're facing is clearly about to faint with lust.

"Oh, um, oh," he says. I want to tell him that those three things are no more words than his initial attempt was. And that you don't stop a DVD by hitting the volume control, so that suddenly MAKE ME COME BABY echoes off the walls.

"I was just..." he tries, as he searches the remote for the stop button. So good at finding things, usually! But then I guess it must be difficult when you're fumbling and flustered and stiff inside your girl-pants.

"Watching a dirty movie?" I offer, and he squirms harder. It doesn't make it any less sweet, though, that I think he's doing at least forty percent of it for my benefit.

"It was just there, in the drawer. You said I could do whatever I wanted!"

He finally manages to click it off, and his shoulders sag with relief. But his eyes are shining when they meet mine.

"You're right. I did say that, didn't I." He smiles, secret and furtive.

"I just wanted to see what it was like—I've never watched one before."

"Well, there's this thing now called the Internet..."

He makes a little noise, half kind of bashful, half amused. Looks down at his bare feet.

"I only just dared to send off for books. What if they found out it was me?"

"Who?"

He throws up his hands. Bless him.

"I don't know! The government!"

"Actually they called five minutes ago. You're wanted for crimes against good sense."

"Don't tease me, Maddie."

I can't resist raising an eyebrow at that. Showing some teeth too, maybe.

"I thought that's exactly what you wanted from me."

He frowns, still trying not to smile and squirm and a hundred different things at once.

"What?"

"Teasing."

His expression then becomes a perfect little *well, you got me there*. Head shrug to one side, as the corners of his mouth turn down. He's really getting cheeky, this one. And I'm sure I'm not supposed to love it.

"Though I can see you're already quite adept at doing it to yourself."

He clearly has no idea what I'm talking about, until I drop my gaze down and then up again, pointedly. You know, in the direction of the little silver thing he's still got attached to one of his nipples.

It can't be doing a good job of whatever it's supposed to do. Why, I think he's actually forgotten it's there!

He certainly snatches it off himself as though that's the case. And it would have been a really good attempt at hiding it rapidly, if it were not for the fact that he then winces and clutches at his injured nipple.

I don't mean to burst out laughing, really I don't. But he only makes it worse when he sucks a breath in over his teeth and says:

"Wow, you should never pull those things off fast. They don't tell you how much they *hurt*."

"Thought BDSM was all fun and orgasms, huh? No one ever cries for real in *Dark Passion* or *Whip Me Hard*, am I right?"

"At the very least, no one makes themselves cry with nipple clamps."

I step toward him, one foot slow in front of the other.

"Here, let me make it better," I say, and he stops rubbing the injured party. He drops his hand, without me having to tell him to.

Then I bend at the waist, and poke out my tongue.

"Is this the good part of BDSM?" he asks when I lick. Just a little. You can see the twin lines the clamp has made around the tiny red point his nipple has become, as though he's been wearing it for a while.

"Does it feel like the good part?"

"Yes."

His voice wobbles. His body pitches toward me.

"Did you have a good day at work?"

"I don't think we're going to talk about me, Gabe. Why don't you tell me about *your* day? Let's start with why you wanted to experiment with pain."

"I didn't—I don't—oh, that's nice. Lick…lick the other one."

I do it, just because he dared to ask me.

"Which feels better?" I ask, and then he does his little half-laugh and says *OK, OK, maybe you're right. Maybe I just wanted to see what it did to me.*

I stand up straight and he sighs, full of disappointment. But he can just go on being disappointed, because we've not even got to the crux of my issue. He seems to have forgotten something very important—or else done so on purpose, thrillingly—and now…well.

"Don't worry, honey," I say. "You're going to find out so much more about what things do to you, very soon."

He licks his lips and leans forward, just ever so slightly. As though going for a kiss, maybe.

"I've been good all day," he tells me, in such a gorgeous, lust-husky voice. "I've been waiting all day and I've been so good. I'm so hard, Maddie."

"I'll bet you are. Did you enjoy watching my porn?"

His warm, moist breath gusts over my cheek as he gets even closer.

"I'm like them," he says, and I close my eyes. I know exactly what he means before he explains; of course I do.

"I'm like the men in it, with their hairy bodies and their big dicks. Made me feel almost normal—especially that one where the two girls make that one guy do stuff, you know, and he kind of doesn't want to but they force him by sucking him and rubbing him and rubbing their bodies all over him…"

He trails off. Probably into the same dazed place I've just gone into. Did he really just say all that stuff?

"That got me really excited. I almost gave in."

He kisses my cheek—really wetly. His hands are trembling, so close to moving over my waist or my breasts or somewhere, somewhere.

"But you didn't, did you."

"I didn't. Feels like I haven't come for days."

"That's good, baby. That's really good. And I would reward you—I really would…"

I put a hand flat to his chest, and push him all the way back. He's oblivious enough to look confused—I think he really hasn't guessed what he's done wrong. It could be that he truly did forget.

"But you seem to have put on clothes, and what was it I asked you to do again?"

I snap the waistband of *my* pajama bottoms, for emphasis. He looks first startled, then appalled. I really think he forgot! It makes me want to clap my hands together.

"Oh—no but I—" he starts out, before he realizes there's nowhere to go with that *but*. "Damn. I didn't mean to leave them on. I was going to take them off before you came up, I was. I didn't even wear anything when I went to the bathroom—or when I made breakfast! I ate at your kitchen table, while naked!"

He's so earnest. Sometimes I wonder how he manages it, with those giant angry-looking eyebrows—though in truth I think they just add to his big, innocent expressions. They exaggerate him to the point of funny.

"Maddie, really—I didn't mean to not do it. I meant to be good. I just wanted to…" He seems to wrestle, visibly frustrated, with a certain word. Before it bursts out of him. "Fuck! I wanted to fuck. I want to fuck. Are you not going to fuck me, now?"

"That's a lot of F words, potty mouth."

And then he *apologizes*. The urge to clap my hands grows strong, again.

"But don't worry. We'll get to the fucking," I say, and he sinks down, relieved. Not so much, when I add, "After you've taken your punishment."

Then his shoulders snap back up again, all right. His eyes go big, just briefly. A little wider and then normal again—if clearly still charged with electricity. I think I zapped him with a Taser, without knowing it.

"No, don't."

It's the most deadpan, unenthusiastic refusal there has ever been since time began.

"Bend over and put your palms flat to the mattress, Gabe," I say, and am thrilled with the lack of wavering in my voice.

Though I'm more thrilled with the way he swallows, and shivers, and shakes his head almost as an afterthought. My sex swells, tight against the material of my underwear. It practically demands that I cup it through my skirt and my knickers—though it's only when I've done so that I realize what it looks like. Lewd, and somehow like a man.

Like a rough, dirty man, showing some slut what he's going to give to her.

And he sighs, just like said slut would. High and too aroused, not sure what to do next to get himself the maximum amount of pleasure allowable.

In the end, he goes with obeying me, exactly. He turns, jerkily, and bends over. Then plants his hands on the mattress, arms straight and strong. But it's the way he turns his head so that he can look at me, and mouths the tense muscle in his arm—almost like a wet, open kiss, but with a bit of a bite to it—that really makes me cream myself. His eyes, just over the line of his bicep, big and dark and lust-blown.

I stroke one shaking hand over the curve of his back, and he drops his head between his shoulders. He's panting, now.

"What are you going to do to me? Don't let it hurt too much,

OK? I don't think I'll tell you to stop. I think I like it too much, I'm sure I do. One time I sank my teeth into my hand so hard it bled—God. God. I can't believe the stuff I tell you, now."

He's babbling, and though I don't want him to stop I'm also sure I don't want to get anywhere near bleeding—no matter how much he might like it. Did he say he liked it? Lord, we're getting into some shaky territory here.

So I lean over his curved body, and whisper in his ear, *If you tell me to stop, I won't. If you say the word wicked, I will. Nod if you understand me.*

And he does, of course he does. He's read all the same books I have, and most of them have safe words. Even the ones that are only pretending to be BDSM, with silk scarves and ice-cubes.

I wonder if we're pretending or not. He certainly gasps when I kick his legs apart. And moans when I rip those ridiculous pajama bottoms down, all the way to his ankles. When I'm back standing behind his bare arse, I say, "Tell me what you did wrong, Gabe."

And at first, he doesn't respond. He's juddering all over, now—really going at it. When words finally come out, they're all over the place.

"I didn't stay naked," he says, then after a second blurts out, "And I almost made myself come, twice."

Though I don't think it's his conscience that makes him tell me.

"I see. Describe both instances to me."

He gives me a little frustrated whine in response. I think he might actually be wiggling his perfect firm arse for my approval.

"Uh…one time I was going through your things, and—"

"What things?"

Another frustrated sound.

"The toys. Your toys. And then I thought about what you did with them, like putting them on your clit or inside your pussy or your…other things and—"

"What other things?"

"Your arse, OK? Your arse! And then I almost came all over everything."

I stroke my hand over his hip, as a reward. He backs right into my touch, but his palms never leave the mattress.

"And the second time was when the guy…and the two girls…oh God. I thought I was going to come without touching myself. It felt like I was going to come—but I didn't. I promise I didn't do that."

His voice goes right up at the end of that last sentence. Mainly because right when he hits the word *didn't*, I bring my hand down hard on his arse.

It's amazing. He jerks forward, and the sound that comes out of him is like a shocked gasp—only it's deep, and guttural. And when I smack again before he can recover, he actually tells me *no*.

Though not because he wants me to stop. Not even because he fake-wants me to stop! No, he says it, then follows it with *this*:

"No, don't, Maddie, don't, I think I'm going to come!"

And I've no idea why that turns me on so much, I really don't. But I have to push my skirt up and shove my hand inside my knickers, all the same. Or at least I do so until he says in a weirdly much less out of control voice, "No, let me do it after. I want to lick you, after."

At which point I understand how a person might come without a hand on them. A great surge of pleasure goes through me, taking any sense I had with it. I crack my hand down on his already pink right cheek, and then the other, and then both and then hard hard hard until he's letting out all of these sharp little cries.

I can tell, too, when he presses his lips together to hold them in. Each one then ends on a *mmpf*, or some other kind of desperate noise—and all the while his arse grows hot and my palm gets even hotter, and sweat pools in the hollow of his back.

He's rocking his hips, now—but not away from me. Toward my hand, every time it lands. And I think…I think he spreads his legs wider, so that occasionally one of my smacks will land right over the seam between. Almost lower, too, over the just visible shape of his balls.

"You really love it, don't you, slut," I say, and he whines and tells me no, no. So I torment him a little more, just a little more. "If you hate it, I'll do it softer. I'll just tap your pretty little arse, in a polite sort of—"

"No!" He sobs, as the admission falls out of him. "Do it hard, OK? Use something on me, do it hard, please."

I think about paddles, belts, crops. Instead of palm marks on his arse—stripes. Red as anything, lining his perfect pale skin.

But we don't get anywhere near that far, because some kind of mad urge grabs hold of me and I grasp his hip tight in my hand, then jerk him back against the slap of my palm every time I bring it down. And good God, does that ever have the desired effect. I've no idea what the desired effect even is, but it makes me scorching hot inside my too-tight clothes and my mind goes blank and Jesus, I can feel how wet my knickers are, I can feel it.

And all while he *uh uh uhs* and finally tells me that he's definitely going to come, now. Definitely. He even warns me that he's going to make a real mess of my sheets.

Just before his body locks up and he twists under my grip and he can't even seem to make a noise, under pressure of intense insane orgasmic bliss. I think he stops breathing. I have to tell him to start again and then he gobbles up air like a crazy person.

Though I don't know what I'm doing, giving him advice. I'm the one with my nails digging into his hip and my face like a shell-shocked sex war survivor. I can't move, not at all, and I'm sort of frightened that he's going to ask me to because he's recovered already and I've forgotten what day it is.

"That was much better than I expected it to be," he says, after a long, long moment. As though he's been considering things like this for so long. Whereas I…well. I don't think I've ever fantasized about spanking someone until they came on my sheets. Not ever.

"Are you OK, Maddie?" he asks. "Can I take my palms off the bed?"

White noise buzzes in my ears. I think maybe I say yes, because he stands really slow and all awkward, as though oh, I don't know. Something on his arse is burning? And yet somehow, it's him who's putting an arm around me. He sort of hugs me, and starts unbuttoning the jacket I'm still wearing.

Man, no wonder I'm hot! I thank him for being considerate enough to remind me of my extreme hotness. But he just laughs and says—*why are* you *thanking* me? Then he gets all blushy and flustered when he has to start stripping the sheets off the bed.

Of course I try to stop him, because honestly I don't give a shit. They're probably already sticky with our bodily fluids anyway, so what does it matter? But then he smooths on new ones and starts taking off the rest of my clothes, and I'm glad that it mattered to him.

"You're really quiet," he says, as he unbuttons my shirt. "Did you not…like that?"

I try to smile, but it doesn't sit well on my face.

"I think I liked it a little too much."

"If you liked it too much, then what did I do?"

"You ran away to Las Vegas and married it."

He presses his face into the skirt he's knelt to unzip and tug down my legs. I think he says an embarrassed sorry against the material.

So I touch his hair.

"Don't be sorry," I say. "Don't ever be sorry."

I'm just in my knickers and bra, now. And then his cheek is brushing against the soft mound beneath the material, like he can feel the fur underneath. He works up to the press of his mouth against me, almost like he's trying to do it by stealth—though he must know that I'm never going to refuse.

Not when the sudden hot, wet feel of his parted lips through my knickers makes me gasp. He licks me through them, at first—just with me stood up, legs almost together. The moist stuttering drag of his tongue over the material making my underwear slide and tease over my pouting lips.

But that quickly ends. He just nudges me toward the bed and suddenly I'm sprawled across it, soft kisses all over my belly as he works my knickers down one-handed.

He licks, before he explores with his fingers. Just one lick over the apex of my slit, and then greedy probing fingers everywhere, and that drowning look on his face when he feels how wet I am, and oh—the sight of him squirming his free hand down over his stomach, so he can fondle himself at the same time.

I almost jerk right out of my own body, when the phone rings right in the middle. Though—weirdly—Gabe doesn't seem to mind. The intrusion of the real world doesn't put him off his stride at all, and even as it continues to shriek, he just keeps right on mapping out my clit with the flat of his tongue.

So slow. Too slow. The phone dies and then starts wailing again in a way that makes me want to throw something at it. Doesn't it know that I need this, that I've waited patiently for this, for God's sake—

"Answer it," he says, in between soft touches of his tongue to my clit. The syrupy slide of his fingers into my cunt. He parts them, gently, once they're in there, and I'm sure I've misheard him amidst all the gushing pleasure.

"You want me to answer the phone while you're going down on me?" I ask, but he just looks at me above the curve of my sex, mouth still intent on its task.

"What if it's your next door neighbor, Gabe?"

I think his eyebrow lifts a little. It's hard to tell while he's eating my pussy.

"What if it's my Great-Aunt Petunia?"

He licks harder, for that one. Ah, my Gabe. Always ready for a little lavender-scented humiliation—though it does make me wonder who exactly he's wanting to receive the humiliation. Maybe it's payback time?

I answer halfway down the bed, legs still spread. Gabe buries his face deeper before I've even got to the *who is it* part.

Though I've got to say, I don't think there's going to be deep enough when he figures out who's on the end of the line. I expected Jeanette, which would have been extremely amusing. But of course it's Andy, of *course* it is Andy—with his perfect sense of timing!

"Hey babe," he says, as I wonder about his psychic abilities. Born with, or learned?

Though in all honesty, at what intervals could he have called where we were *not* having sex? It was just a matter of time.

"You busy?"

He's not only good with timing. He's also great at choosing his words.

"You could say that."

"Ah, right. In the middle of fucking that pansy, huh?"

And at playing guessing games. I wonder if he can hear the wet lap of Gabe's tongue. The slick-clicking of my monumentally juicy pussy.

"No. We're not fucking."

Gabe stops briefly, then—just enough to fully meet my gaze with questioning eyes. Though I kind of think he already knows, if I'm here talking about the F word.

"He's touching you in a dirty way though, right? What's he doing? You got him fingering you?"

"I have to go, Andy. Stop calling," I say, only then…then I guess Gabe doesn't approve of that idea. I sense definite disapproval in the minute shake of his head. The way he kisses the groove between my pussy and my thigh, suddenly, and spans one big hand over my hip.

Andy interrupts when I ask Gabe a question. As though I was

talking to him, not Gabe. But then he falls silent, I think, when the picture becomes clear.

Gabe doesn't answer, however. He just squeezes my hip, and licks faster.

"He's a kinky fucker," Andy says, and I won't disagree with that assessment. Suddenly I'm trailing behind Gabe in a world of desires he won't *quite* voice, but that are clear and thrilling, nonetheless.

"So come on then. What's he doing to you?"

I have no idea who's telling who to do what. But I answer, anyway.

"Licking me."

Andy groans, still gruff even when it's down the tinny phone line.

"He's eating your pussy?"

"Yes. He's got two fingers inside me, too."

"Just the two?"

"Yeah, just two."

Gabe squirms against me, insistent, probing—and then it's three. Not as full as when he's fucking me with his cock, but still blissful.

"How hard is he doing it?"

"Not hard at all. Slow and firm, and right up against my G-spot."

"Good, babe?"

"No, I hate it. What the fuck's the matter with you?"

But Andy just laughs. I can hear the jangle of a belt being unbuckled, the rasp of a zipper.

"Think I'm going to come, soon. My thighs are trembling like mad," I say, and this time I get a sigh of pleasure. Though I've no idea if it's for the words, or because he's now got hold of his cock.

"Tell me what else he's doing."

"Licking my clit."

"Uh, yeah."

"He's amazing at it. Really amazing."

"Now you're just trying to make me feel bad."

"No—he really is. Oh yeah—right there. Lick me there, baby—yes."

I can hear him masturbating, now. One boy between my legs, the other at the end of a phone line, jerking to the beat of my pleasure. I'm sure life does actually get better than this, but I'd be hard-pressed to think of how.

"You're lying," he says suddenly, so I let him know all the ways in which I'm not.

"His tongue is so long and pointed, and he just kind of...oh... flicks it over my clit—you know, right on the underside, right where it's sensitive. But not too much, not too much. And then he licks in these *circles*, Jesus it feels so good."

"Yeah? Yeah?"

"He just...slides around the exact shape of my clit. All the way around it and—ah, yes. He's pinching my nipples, now, with slippery fingers. And when he's not doing that, he's stroking himself."

"Fuck."

"He's really hard again even though he only came a little while ago. He can get so hard so quickly, and the noises he makes when I'm sucking him and fucking him..."

I'm not sure who I'm supposed to be humiliating, now. But either way I can hear Andy really groaning and Gabe's almost humping the mattress and I'm definitely almost there. It's just too much for me to take.

"You dirty bitch. You dirty little slut—are you going to come? Come, baby."

"Ladies first," I say, and he grunts and curses at me down the phone line.

I think he just about makes it before I do. Though I'm sure he enjoys my jagged moans and gasps, all the same—not to mention the way I cry out *I'm coming, I'm coming*, as Gabe's tongue hits it just right and that warm tightness in my chest spreads down, through my belly, through my clenching, swelling sex.

I think I vaguely hear him mutter that he's come all over himself, before I tell him I've got to go. I've got to go, because Gabe is knelt over me, mouth wet, eyes dark and close to angry—though he doesn't say anything like what his expression would seem to suggest.

Instead, he blurts out, "Next time, I want to fuck you while you talk to him."

Chapter Thirteen

IT'S PROBABLY A TERRIBLE, terrible idea. Even I know that, and I'm the insane person who's spending her days ordering around a guy she's too crazy about, while another guy invites himself around for a cup of tea.

Because that's what Andy does. He invites himself around for a cup of tea, and Gabe says *maybe I'll make a Victoria sponge* and I think God, what world am I living in?

But I let it all happen, anyway. Mainly because just sitting in my living room with Andy sprawled on the couch like an arrogant arse, and Gabe not knowing where to look as though we're at tea with the Queen…yeah. That was worth the price of admission alone.

"So, how've you been, babe?" Andy says. Because now is definitely time for small talk. Unfortunately, however, even small talk seems gargantuan and loaded—when he asks, I think of exactly how I've been, in great and explicit detail.

I think of Gabe telling me how much being with me means to him. I think of the words I wanted to say to his back, with the sound turned down. I think of the way he'd excitedly shafted me, after saying how much he wanted to fuck me while I talked to another man.

Or perhaps more aptly, while another man watched us. Because that's what it boils down to, isn't it? He likes being watched, and told what to do, and I'm pretty sure he'd also enjoy Andy saying mean things to him while his cock stuttered in and out of my pussy.

I try to send him mind waves. Is that what you want, Gabe? Or do you just want to show off what a good lay you are, to the guy who's kind of looking at you with this mocking, knowing smile on his handsome face?

He just stares back at me, eyes burning behind the glasses. Even now, you wouldn't know what he's like, to look at him. I wouldn't know, and I've spanked him until he came all over my sheets.

"How about you, Gabe? That's your name, right?"

Lord.

"Yes. And I've been great. Thanks for asking."

I adore the way he says those words. Absolutely adore it. He kicks some real condescension into his tone—so much so that Andy looks peeved, briefly. Andy might think that he's tougher than Gabe, and better-looking—but he's not smarter. He'll never be smarter.

"Would you like some cake?"

I swear to God, he says it like he's offering Andy some pussy. And it's not just my imagination, either.

"You been getting all the cake you can eat, huh?"

Andy folds his arms over his chest. Gabe shrugs, but can't keep his smile all the way down.

I'm in the middle of a mud-wrestling match, and didn't even know it. Though all things considered, it's probably best that I don't think about mud wrestling. Both of them slick and stripped to their underwear is something my libido could probably do without.

"And what exactly do you think you've got that I don't?" God, he's an arsehole. They're both acting like arseholes. Only then Gabe answers, and all the hairs on the back of my neck stand up.

"Obedience."

"Yeah? You think you're obedient? Crawl on your knees to her, then."

WARNING. WARNING. WARNING.

"I didn't say I was obedient to you."

Why has my body decided to paralyze itself, just as the alarm goes off in my brain? It did this the last time this happened, too—though I have to say it's only got itself to blame. Letting him come around for a cup of tea and a slice of Victoria sponge! What by God did I think was going to happen?

They're like rutting bulls, only one bull's got the other one's number and enjoys exploiting it.

"Yeah, but seriously, mate. Why else would she have invited me over?" Andy laughs and looks at me like—what's this guy's malfunction? But it's OK, because Gabe answers neatly for me.

"Because I asked her to."

Andy doesn't say anything for a long, long moment after that. He stares at Gabe, and Gabe stares back, and the air feels prickly and charged and for a good portion of that long moment, I'm sure they're going to snog.

Finally, the brain of Britain comes up with, "*Really.*"

He isn't asking, however. Just commenting on the many interesting qualities Gabe's statement seems to have. I mean, it could have any number of connotations. It could suggest that Gabe fancies having a cock in his mouth—who knows?

I wonder if Andy fancies having Gabe's cock in his mouth. Though I don't think my question's going to be answered any time soon. They're still having an eye fight at the OK Corral.

"So maybe you want to do what I tell you to more than that little prickly stick up your butt denial suggests. How about it, chief?"

Gabe doesn't say anything. He's hard, though—I can tell he is. He's hunched over just a little bit in the armchair—in order to hide what would otherwise be obvious in those thin gray trousers. And he's squirming, minutely. If you didn't know him, you probably couldn't tell.

But I do know him. He's aroused, and working himself against it.

"I'll do whatever Maddie wants," he says, after a moment.

"Maddie doesn't know what she wants. Isn't that right, babe?"

I'm sure I do. I do, right?

"She needs a firm hand, the same way you do. She wants to just sit there, and let me take all the responsibility—she wants me to do all the talking. Don't you think?"

Gabe looks vaguely…worried? Like he doesn't know the answer, at the very least. But that's OK, Gabe, because I don't know the answer either. I just know that I'm wet and already wriggling on my chair the way that you are. And when Andy says *crawl across the floor on your hands and knees to her*, this time, Gabe obeys him.

It's not the fact that he does so, however, that blooms pleasure through me. It's him taking off his glasses, first, and putting them on the coffee table neatly. That's what does it. I think, weirdly: *like Clark Kent, turning into Superman*.

And then he prowls across my carpet, eyes on me, that dip to his back making him look like something dark and exotic and animalistic. A panther, I think, like a panther—but by that point I'm too breathless to process anything real or sane.

"Now show me what you got, mate," Andy says, and some of that intense uncomfortable sense of his arseholery melts away. He just sounds so genuinely curious and sort of leftover impressed from the night before.

Plus he's squeezing the bulge between his jeans-clad legs. Apparently I'll forgive a lot for that.

Gabe looks up at me, dark eyes pupil-less and glinting with a ferocious…something. But I don't tell him anything, or give him a word of reassurance. It could well be because Andy's got the reins, but there's also the fact that Gabe doesn't *need* my reassurance. He doesn't need anything. He uncrosses my legs, all on his own.

And there's something about him doing so that I don't mind *at all*. Dear God, no. He just slides one leg off the other like I'm a life-sized doll, and then splays his fingers over my bare thighs in order to effectively spread them.

And when that's not enough, he hooks his hands underneath my knees and *drags* me, suddenly, to the end of the seat cushion—so much so that my butt almost comes all the way off, and my skirt ruffles most of the way up my thighs.

Of course I'm not wearing any knickers. But the pair of them moan when they catch a glimpse of what's between my legs.

"She's got a nice pussy, huh?" Andy says, and oh Lord—is it OK if him talking like I'm not here turns me on? Especially when Gabe answers *yeah*, and his warm breath stirs over my already slick cunt.

"You like eating her out?"

"I love it. I love licking pussy."

He hesitates over the word pussy. But he gets it out in the end, all hoarse and kind of up and down.

"Yeah? How come?"

I can see Gabe considering—eyes far off and likely imagining something good and dirty—while he strokes just the edge of one knuckle over the fluff of hair at the curving edge of my slit. It's definitely not enough contact to do anything for me, but I shiver, anyway.

"The noises she makes. They're really dirty when I'm going down on her. And the way she moves, and the feel of her all wet against my face. She likes it when I lick fast just where her clit swells upwards—I could make her come really quickly, I think, but I like drawing it out and hearing her get louder and louder. If you do it for a long time, she'll say things and ask for things she wouldn't usually."

Wow. And not just for how much him talking about licking fast turns me on. He's dead on the money, even though he's only done this, like, what? Twice? But he's utterly right—wind me up and I'll go as mindless as I am right now.

"So come on then, man. What're you waiting for, if you know what you're doing that much?" Andy says, and Gabe flashes feral teeth at him.

"I *do* know what I'm doing. I could do this blindfolded."

This time it's Andy's turn to give the feral grin.

"That right?" he says, in a way that makes Gabe's grin drop, just a little. I think I know what Andy's going to suggest before the words come out. "Maybe we should test that out then, what do you say, mate? Think you can make her all fuck-happy blindfolded?"

He glances at me, then—a little harried-looking. I've no idea what he thinks of sense deprivation or anything like that, so it's hard to judge his expression. Is he just tense because Andy's calling the shots, or is it just the suggestion, the idea of going without sight?

Either way, I let Andy go first when he starts nudging us in the direction of the bedroom—all casual, *come on, kids*—and then when he's beyond the door I take Gabe's arm and remind him. There's a word he can say if he wants to stop. He can stop any time if anything makes him uncomfortable.

But he just kisses me, fiercely—as fierce as Andy probably would—before we follow him in.

Of course, he's stripped himself completely naked in the time it took to have a chat and a snog. And I won't lie—he looks *good* sprawled out on my bed. He looks golden and solid and edible, and so much so that Gabe seems almost startled by it. He lingers in the doorway, while Andy tells me to *get those fucking clothes off.*

Though for all I know, he could be talking to Gabe. In fact, I think Gabe believes that's the case, because he stutters beneath the hand I've still got on his arm. And then he shivers when I start unbuckling his belt and unbuttoning his tweedy trousers.

"Is this the way it usually goes?" Andy says. He's lazily jerking off while he does so. "You undress him?"

There's a sardonic twist to his words that makes Gabe flush, but his cock jerks against my unfastening hands, at the same time. He's left a wet spot on the material, too, and when I tug the whole lot down to his ankles, he looks hard enough to hammer nails.

Which is also something Andy wants to comment on, apparently.

"Christ, mate. That cock of yours. Does it ever go down?"

When Gabe answers no, he does so with a wry smile on his face. Shortly before he rips his shirt and jumper over his head and off, all by himself.

"Got to be honest. I can't wait to see you fuck her with that thing. You like that in you, Maddie?"

"What do you think?" I say, then rub my hand over and around it, just for emphasis.

Gabe's thighs tremble. But he's got himself under enough control to start undressing me before I explode from the heat and the wanting and all of this fucked-up-ness that's just about making me crazy.

"Oh yeah," Andy says. "Turn her around. Show me her tits."

Which is insanely hot, I have to say—though even hotter is Gabe getting his hand around my body to grope said body parts, while Andy looks on with molten eyes. He pinches my nipples and I squirm against his mostly naked body, the heated bar of his cock brushing over my lower back to excellent effect.

He groans, loudly, and Andy follows suit like we're a chemical reaction—add the acid and everything fizzes over. He's stopped jerking off, now, and I think I know why. In fact, it's obvious why—it's too much. It's just too much. I'm thinking *tell him what to do again, tell me what to do again*—it has to be too much.

"Touch her pussy, now," he says, while my legs turn to water. "Show me how you do it to her."

And Gabe just braces me against his front, and does as he's told. Two fingers sliding slickly through my slit, then parting them to spread me open on the way back up.

"That's good," Andy says. "So good. Get her over here."

I go without Gabe doing anything at all. He just follows me, crawling on the bed after me, hands all over my arse and between my legs. There's not even a hint of pushing me toward anything, until Andy sort of leans forward and indicates that he's going to kiss me.

While his eyes remain on Gabe.

It's weirdly the first time I've felt as though Andy is asking something like permission, and I have to say—as much as I like Gabe suddenly and definitely nudging me toward Andy's mouth, there's definitely a little stomach drop, at the same time. The backs of my knees go weak, and my clit jumps, and when Gabe actually *holds* me with my mouth on Andy's, everything inside me tangles together in a big confused mess.

I understand why he enjoys this. I do. I do. I understand why I enjoy it, too.

And yet. Just say if you don't want me to, Gabriel. Just say.

But he doesn't say anything at all. I feel his hand leave my back when the kiss deepens, Andy's strong masculine smell filling me up and the feel of his tongue thrusting like a hard fuck into my mouth and…oh. It's good, and even better when they both turn me onto my back with gentle and rough hands, and then there's Gabe's hot, eager mouth between my legs.

I stuff my hand into Andy's ever-so-slightly curling hair, and he growls his approval into my mouth. He gets a handful of my right breast in a way Gabe would never—firm, almost too hard, grip, biting at the nipple on every squeeze—but the contrast is incredible. Like being punished and rewarded, all at the same time. Hard pressure, then quick, slippery laps at my clit—Christ.

Suddenly I can't imagine why we didn't do this sooner. Why choose, when you can have the best of both worlds? Even if your stomach does occasionally bottom out.

Andy pulls away and I expect him to look smug, somehow—but he's the opposite. His mouth is wet and slack, and his eyes trail down my body as though he's waited and waited for this, before they settle on Gabe's dark head, working between my legs.

"You teach him everything he knows? Or is he just a natural?" he says, so I guess it's Gabe's turn to be absent from the conversation. Doesn't seem to matter any, to my libido. I cream over it either way.

"Natural," I say, and I'm sure I feel Gabe grin against my over-heated flesh.

"Yeah. Yeah. He licks your pussy so good."

I don't think I've ever heard anyone talk the way Andy does, outside of *Hot Cunts 4*.

"But you know—he did promise us that he'd be just as good blindfolded, am I right? Yeah—I think I'd like to see that. How about it, mate?"

Gabe looks up suddenly, dazed and slick-mouthed. But he soon comes to when Andy grabs the silly stripy winter scarf I've thrown over the chair in the corner of my room. It's going to look absolutely ridiculous over Gabe's eyes—though if I'm honest, I'm not sure we're going to get to that part.

Gabe gets up onto his knees, wiping his mouth self-consciously as he goes. He looks suddenly fumbly and not like I've ever seen him—this is definitely a different level of discomfort. And when Andy sort of lunges toward him, he almost backs right off the bed.

"Come on, man," Andy laughs. "You're not scared, are you? I'm pretty sure you and the boss lady here have a safe word. Am I right?"

When Gabe doesn't answer, Andy cocks a brilliantly incredulous look at me. Mouths: *you do, right?* And in that moment, I have to love him. He's the arsehole arrogant dom who cares! Find him in the phone book, kids.

I nod, and Andy starts toward Gabe, again. Tells him something that starts with *so it's not like…* before it tails off into nowhere.

But Gabe still backs off, and fumbles some words that may be about him not liking his eyes covered up. I think he means that he doesn't like the dark, but obviously saying so might make him seem unmanly or some other wretched idea like that, so I step in.

I take the scarf from Andy, and there's definitely a different look in Gabe's eyes when he glances back to me. *Trust*, I think, *trust*, and then feel something expand in my chest.

I wrap my fists around it, and pull the material taut.

"You don't have to, if you don't want to," I tell him, as he eyes that tight length of scarf. Licks his lips, in this quick little hungry sort of way. "I don't care whether you do or not, so just say the word."

I'm knelt up, and very close to him, now. He's breathing hard, but what's weirder is that I can tell Andy has held his. I can hear that silence, even over the grate of Gabe's breath going in and out.

And then he lets it go when Gabe puts his hands over mine and draws them up to his face.

"Babe," Andy says, and he sounds…I don't know. Turned on? I think it's turned on, but it's mixed with something else that I can't identify. It makes me think of Gabe's voice, sometimes, when he's all worked up and just waiting for me to tell him something dirtier to do, but I'm not sure why.

When I smooth the scarf over Gabe's eyes, and tie it at the back of his head—loosely, just in case he needs to shrug it off—Andy runs one firm hand the length of my bare back. And then between my legs, like he's allowed to, now, because Gabe isn't watching.

I move back over the bed when he urges me to. Though Gabe holds onto my arms, to any part of me, as long as he can—before he's cut adrift, unseeing, at the end of the bed.

Then it's just the sound of my voice that he responds to, hands out, fumbling for the feel of me.

"That's it," I tell him. "Come to me, baby."

And then thrill, when one of his blindly searching hands connects with that soft sensitive place behind my knee. He maps it out immediately with his fingertips, and I have to say—that kind of touch definitely beats out the one Andy's currently got on my breasts. There's just something about the care he takes, swiftly followed by a sure and confident grope, that's intensely arousing.

Plus there's that ever-thrilling possibility of a mistake. As I believe Andy knows only too well.

Before Gabe's got anywhere near my upper thigh, Andy kind of…spreads his own legs. Just so that one of them lies almost over the top of mine. You know, all innocent-like. He even raises one extremely pure and virtuous eyebrow at me as he performs this guileless task and, I think, waits for my approval.

But fortunately, Gabe's on hand to give his—or otherwise. Because his hand brushes against something that's definitely not a vagina, and he jerks away, as though stung.

Before going back for further confirmation.

He has one hand on Andy's leg and another on mine, and I watch him squeeze both of them. Andy looks confused—but of course, I understand perfectly. And my understanding fills me with such delight, I can hardly bear it.

He's testing both of them, to see if they really belong on different people. He's working his way through the flesh jumble to see what's what. And then his right hand goes directly between the correct set of legs to my pussy, while his left…his left can't seem to decide what to do.

But it definitely remains very high up, on Andy's leg.

"Christ, jerk me off, babe," Andy demands—and obviously he's saying it to me. Obviously. But I don't know, there's just something about the tone and the space into which he pushes those words… it's like he's saying, *If you want to, mate. Go on, I don't mind. If you feel like it.*

It's like he's jamming down hard on whatever limits Gabe might have, and although Gabe is biting his lip while really shoving two fingers into my slippery pussy, he's also rutting against my leg and getting very close with his cock to the knee Andy has crooked over me.

And he doesn't object in any way whatsoever when I link my fingers through his. When I guide his hand up, up.

Instead, he lets out this wavering gasp, and wraps his hand tight around mine the moment I circle Andy's heavy cock. I watch him watch what we're doing with sightless eyes, mouth open, red all over his cheeks and down his throat.

But it's me who really reacts when he moves first. I think I almost come, because dear God I know exactly what he's doing. I know it without having to be told and before Andy's reaction.

He's showing me what to do. He wraps his hand around mine, and jerks Andy off in a manner far tighter and quicker than I would ever have done—or could probably manage. But it has the desired effect—Andy's head goes back, and he calls out something dirty, and bucks up into our fists—and Gabe's expression is…

Smug. Of course it is. He's a natural. He's always knows exactly what to do and how to do it, and even more so, I guess, when it's something he's got, too.

But it's weird, and even weirder when I realize that he's blindfolded, and a total submissive, and yet he's on his knees over us, making us writhe like out of control idiots, too stunned by their own pleasure to do anything but.

Andy even calls out his name. Tells him more, more. Things only grind to a halt when he gets back some semblance of sense and orders Gabe to fuck my pussy while he carries on jerking him.

He groans in reply. Though I think more because Andy's actually named what it is he's doing right now, right with his fist around a rock-hard cock, than because he's being ordered to fuck me.

Until we're actually fumbling one-handed with a condom, and he's panting all high and tight. Then I know he just wants to be in my slippery pussy, and Andy's words about said activity don't make it any easier on him.

"Yeah, you want to shaft that cunt?" Andy says, and Gabe

almost loses his grip on the rubber that he's holding, as I try to roll it all the way down to the root of his cock. It's a tough thing to manage with two hands from separate people, but desperation can work miracles, apparently.

As can the disturbingly too-arousing handjob you're giving on the left-hand side.

Andy reaches over my body and our limbs tangle, briefly, but he gets it under control long enough to do something that makes me ache and ache and ache. He pushes my right leg further out then up, so that I'm spread wide open.

So that he can really see, when Gabe blindly feels his way toward my pussy and slides all the way in. Slow, slow—like he's putting on a show. And Andy seems to think so, too, because he moans something about how small I look, and how big Gabe looks, and although I can't see past the back of Andy's head, I know he's close enough to stick out his tongue and lick.

I know because I can feel his hot breath all over my sex.

By this point, Gabe has long since lost his grip on Andy's cock. Mainly—I think—because I have too, due to his body crushing my arm. But that's OK, because now there seem to be new objectives, other boundaries-pushing objectives, like licking someone's clit while another man fucks her pussy.

And I don't mind that at all. I don't mind it so much that I cry out Gabe's name, and rock myself over his prick, and beg him to do it harder, harder, go on, let go.

At which point Andy stops licking me. I don't open my eyes, but I feel him sit up at my side. And his voice is dark and syrupy when he says, after a moment:

"Yeah, go on, mate. Fuck her hard. Why are you holding back? She clearly needs that cock of yours reaming her out. Go on and do it."

Gabe makes a strangled sound in reply. His hands go to my hips, but not to do what I expect—he doesn't yank me down the bed onto him. He holds me fast, and stops me squirming and fucking myself and when I struggle he makes the oddest frustrated sound.

Which gets louder, when Andy says:

"You want to try her from behind?"

I think I actually blurt out the words: yes please! But Gabe just groans and fumbles for me when I'm suddenly manipulated over and up—like I'm just a doll, and Andy's my puppeteer. He arranges me sideways across the bed, unsteady on all fours, elbows flat to the mattress so that my arse sticks up nice and high and lewd in the air.

Then he says:

"Go on then. Feel for her."

And Gabe lets out this little sob that simultaneously thrills right through me, and makes me want to check that he's OK. Though the hot hard brand his cock leaves on my side as he shuffles around is a bit of a giveaway. His cock slides against my skin and at first he jerks away—thinking he's touching Andy, I'm sure—but then he forgets to care, and leaves me marked from ribs to the curve of my hip. And all the while he pants and gropes for me.

When his hand goes suddenly and roughly between my awkwardly spread legs, I lunge forward right into Andy's groin. He's arranged things so wonderfully and neatly—it's just that easy! And especially so when he tells Gabe that he's going to fuck my mouth, now. He's going to fuck my mouth while Gabe fucks my pussy, and that way everybody will be happy.

Especially me. Oh God, I'm so very happy when Gabe finally finds himself kneeling behind me, and runs his cock up and down my slit, up and down. I can feel him trembling, but he doesn't push in right away—instead he searches with the blunt head of his cock, fitting it to my waiting hole gently, so gently.

No matter what Andy says, there's definitely something to be said for the slow and steady approach. Though the feel of Andy's hand in my hair, and his cock shoving into my mouth—yeah, there's something to be said for that, too.

He doesn't go too brutal. I don't gag. But Lord, he's just rough enough to contrast deliciously with the slow rock of Gabe's prick in my pussy. And the harder he goes and the more I *mmpf* and try to breathe around the thick press of flesh against my tongue, the more Gabe measures his pace and holds my hips firm.

His moans of pleasure are getting steadily more frantic, however. And when he asks me if I'm OK, if Andy is really fucking my mouth—and Andy, of course, has to reply—he cries out, brokenly.

"She's taking it from both of us. Fuck—she gives good head. Bet it's even sweeter when she's not busy concentrating on a cock in her pussy. How's she feel? Good?"

To my surprise, Gabe answers.

"Tight. She feels tight."

"I bet she feels tight around that beast you've got. Plus she's got to be all swollen 'cause she's so turned on—think she's going to come soon?"

"Ask her, just ask *her*, God, God!" Gabe babbles, but of course Andy ignores him. Of course he does. He knows he's making me come with the absolutely tremendous feeling of being used alone.

"I'm surprised she doesn't let you bareback her. I mean, you must have been a first-timer, am I right? And I can just imagine unloading in her sweet little pussy, then watching it run down her thighs when—"

"Oh Jesus *Christ* I'm coming, I'm coming—I'm sorry, Maddie, I'm sorry, oh!"

But he really doesn't need to apologize. I stopped sucking Andy's cock about five seconds ago, because the moment he started talking about Gabe fucking me without a condom my entire body seized like I'd been electrocuted.

And it keeps going—all these glorious jolts of pleasure, from the root of my clit to God knows where—all the way through Gabe's orgasm, and right into Andy's.

I think Gabe rips off his blindfold just in time to see Andy coming all over my face. I think so. Because he definitely tells Andy to mind my eyes when he does a thing like that.

Chapter Fourteen

I DON'T KNOW WHAT time it is. Gabe has covered me with himself, and I can't see the digital read-out on my alarm clock. And if I squirm, I'll knock Andy, who's snoring on the other side of me with his back turned. I'm trapped, by my own threesome.

When I try to lift my head just a little, Gabe lets me know he's not asleep. Of course he's not asleep. I'm surprised he isn't up, pacing the living room, while maybe also beating himself with a wire brush.

I go to say something to him—along the lines of *sorry* or something else similarly guilty—but he pulls me up short before I can get there.

"Are you OK?"

That's right. He asks me if *I'm* OK. I wonder if he thinks *I'm* about to get out the wire brush.

"Why would you think I wasn't?" I ask back, as low as I can get it. The last thing I want is Andy waking up in the middle of…whatever sort of raw emotional discussion this is going to be. Because I can just tell it's going to be. When the sex stops, this is where we're up to.

Feelings.

But he just stays silent for a long, long time, and strokes a gentle hand through my hair. So simple and unconsciously done, and yet it turns my bones to syrup. And then, after a while, he says in a faint faraway voice, "He was pretty rough. He pulled your hair."

I can feel my brain trying to run away with the processing of his concern. Other stuff is occurring to me, like maybe all of this is just code for him not being OK. He's asking me because he isn't, because he can't say he isn't, because secretly he's dying inside.

In the end, I press down on all of that bullshit and go with, "Don't worry—I won't let him pull yours."

But it doesn't come out lighthearted. It comes up all mixed around, like the way I feel. And it just gets worse, under the pressure of what he says next.

"It's different for me." Pause. "I like it."

"What makes you think I don't?" I ask, and this time I miss lighthearted by a country mile. It comes out sullen, and bullish.

But he doesn't answer, no matter how forceful I didn't intend to be. He sidesteps the question I suddenly really want him to answer, and goes with something else entirely—how exciting it was, to not be able to see.

"Like anything could happen," he says, and his voice sounds even odder and more faraway. It makes me shiver to think about how far we could push him. How far *I* could push him. How much he liked it, and isn't afraid to admit that he did.

"What made you hesitate, then, at first?" I ask. Andy snorts loudly at the same time, and I feel Gabe go suddenly rigid against me. He only resumes stroking and being relaxed when Andy continues snoring, and sleeping like the dead.

"I don't know. It wasn't exactly what I had imagined—plus I'm not a fan of the dark."

Knew it.

"What were you imagining?"

I'm genuinely curious, I have to say. I mean, I think I understand. It's obvious he likes being in some way…humiliated. But even so, I'm sure he's having…you know. Feelings for me too. And I don't know many men who'd like to see their partner in feelings getting fucked by another man.

"Something I could watch," he says with such a wry twist to his words it slays me. I fumble out his mouth in the darkness, just for that. Just to be close to him for a second and taste mint on his breath—because he just had to get up and shower and clean his teeth afterward—and show him that I can.

And he presses closer right back at me. I feel his erection skim over my belly, prodding briefly but not getting into any kind of rubbing motion. He doesn't seem that bothered by it, to be honest—though I suppose other things are on his mind.

Like cuddling. He can do these things, all of these delicious detached sex things, and then cuddle. And kiss me. And murmurs things into my hair. I try to squirm away, but I don't think he's going to let me.

And then he says, "Do you not want me to hold you? You can go and hug Andy, if you want to. I don't mind."

What's worse is—I can't tell if he genuinely means it or not. But I know he means it when I remain right where I am, and don't say anything or do anything, and he quite suddenly decides to say words I know already, I do know.

"I love you," he tells me.

―――

When I get down to the shop—though in all honesty, I'm not sure how I even manage to walk in straight lines and negotiate stairs—Jeanette is at the door, waiting. Which I'm certain is not a good thing. And she looks excited, which is probably even less of a good thing.

She's so chipper that I might accidentally blurt out that I'm madly in love with Gabe, absolutely madly stupidly in love and oh my God he said he loved me last night squee squee Jesus have I really turned into this person? She's going to love the new me.

The new me worries, however, that I didn't say anything back to him. I just couldn't, OK? I went over and over my options, but "deep affection" simply sounded too patronizing, and "really like" too high school. There's just no in-between term—apparently it's either love, or nothing. I mean, why in God's name has no one invented an in-between term for people who are emotionally stunted or not sure what they want?

I'm thinking…blurn would be a good word. I really, really blurn you, Gabe.

Luckily I open the door before these thoughts get any more insane, and she bursts in like a hurricane. I pray that the two sleeping giants remain that way and upstairs throughout the entirety of whatever exchange this is going to be.

She leads off with, "What. Were. You *doing*. Last night?"

And that's probably when I brace myself.

"I've never heard sounds like the sounds that have been coming from your apartment! I almost called the police!"

Were we really that loud? Lord, I think *Andy* was. And I can almost see it in her eyes that she knows I had more than one man up there.

"It was…nothing," I say, which sounds even lamer than all the responses I imagined saying to Gabe's I love you. Is it weird that I'm thinking about those three words more than I'm thinking about an actual threesome that went on around me last night?

"You can't do that, Maddie," she says, and dear God she sounds really fierce. Is she *actually* going to call the police on me? I'm suddenly seeing the people of York carrying torches and other things to smoke out the massive whore.

Until she stamps her little foot, and puts her hands on her hips, and says, "Spill. I'm living vicariously through you—now come on."

I cease pretending I'm re-organizing books on the shelves for that. She deserves having me turn around, completely mouth-stopped for the second time in a very small amount of hours. Because she just used the word vicariously, and she's looking at me in this odd way that I don't think I've ever seen a woman look at me before, and it occurs to me for the first time:

I'm the crazy best friend.

I'm not the cool and collected heroine; I'm the *sidekick* to the heroine, who persuades the square girl to explore her freaky-deaky side. I mean, I'm sure that in most romance novels the threesomes are much less full of emotional minefields, but even so. I'm all backwards and upside down and I have absolutely no idea what to tell her.

Apart from: do it now. Don't live through me, don't wait for me to tell you exciting stories before you go for it. You don't need someone to persuade you into exploring everything there is about yourself, and even if it scares you…even if you're terrified—and probably about all of the wrong things—it's still more bliss than whatever nothing you were living before.

All the things I've done with Gabe, all the things I've done with Andy, the things that both experiences have taught me about myself…I wouldn't take it back. And it's a relief to actually realize and understand that—it really is.

When Andy strolls down, as louche and pleased with himself as anyone could expect him to be, I don't even flinch. Not a flicker. He cuts into Jeanette's babble about all the things she suspects I'm doing and how *bad* I am and how *awesome* that is, with nothing more than a *hey*.

Before he sticks out his hand and introduces himself.

Jeanette shakes, but looks at him like he's a rock star as she does so.

"Call me, babe," he says, before letting himself out. And then I wait for Jeanette to explode.

"You're doing it with *him*, too?!" she squeaks, as soon as the door goes. I see Andy glance through the window, smug, and know that he's heard her.

"It's…complicated."

Boy, is it ever. In erotica, the dirty sidekick almost never gets close to the world of caring. It's all just hot sex and mad escapades, while love is reserved for the semi-pure and half-decent heroine.

Though I have to say—I don't care how half-decent I am, or whether I'm only semi-pure or not. In fact, I suspect I may well be not pure at all, and that thought sure does make me grin with every inch of my body.

"Well, whatever it is, me and Derek—" She stops mid-sentence, suddenly bright red and looking for her own books to reorganize.

"You and Derek…?" I say, and when she resists, I poke her. I'm definitely supposed to do that as the dirty sidekick, after all. "Come on—you've just worked out all my naughty secrets. Now it's your turn."

She bursts it all out, in one big rush.

"We had the wildest sex *ever*. Well—I *made* him have the wildest sex ever. I think! I don't know. Anyway—we did it on the kitchen table. The kitchen table! Can you believe that?"

I can believe that I adore Jeanette in that moment. And I'm so happy to have her as some sort of friend. I'm happy to be the dirty sidekick to her semi-pure and half-decent heroine.

He's in the shower when I come upstairs—though I notice that the apartment has been tidied. Of course, that could have happened any time. He's been staying over a lot, and it's entirely possible that he cleans in the middle of the night. Puts magazines in a rack I didn't know I had, stacks books on shelves that hadn't seemed previously empty.

And there's something cooking in the oven. I peer in, just to check it isn't heat that's simply baking the encrusted food on the oven door. But no—he's made something and it smells like heaven and I think God, I might actually tell him that I feel the same way tonight.

Perhaps after I've fucked his arse through a wall. And talked to him about the ridiculous amount of showers.

He flinches when I just walk right into the bathroom. Though I can partially understand why, given that he's combing his hair into a neat side parting, while totally naked. He isn't wearing his glasses and he's turned sideways, facing the mirror above the sink, and I'm struck yet again by how handsome he is.

And how slender. I think I'm going to have to give him most of whatever pasta thing is baking in the oven. Maybe as a reward for how he instinctively covers his groin with one hand, and then kind of relaxes all over when he sees it's me.

"Experimenting with hairstyles?" I ask, and he gets the joke. Turns back to the mirror, half-smiling.

"I was thinking—straight up in the air, Billy Idol style."

"A little more like this would be good, I think," I say, and then he lets me turn him and rake the comb through his hair. "Just a hint of body."

"You think it will make me look more handsome?"

"I think I'd be hard-pressed to do that."

He touches his tongue to his upper teeth in that way he has— the one that says: don't be silly.

"You are good-looking, you know."

I smooth his hair up, up, to make an attractive and almost ridiculous-looking bow that sweeps over his forehead. It's easy enough to do—his hair is so thick.

"Not like Andy," he says, but he doesn't sound cross or resentful. A little wistful, maybe. But I'm not even fan of that, so I make my *don't be silly* signal. I cup his cock with my free hand, and kiss his still-damp-from-the-shower mouth.

When I pull away, he looks breathless and happy. But the question he next asks has nothing to do with sex things, and he turns back to the mirror and away from my hand in order to inspect his new hairdo.

"Did you have a good day at work?" I don't think he's all that impressed with my styling attempts. "I was going to come down, but then I heard Jeanette's voice and I knew that she'd probably seen Andy…so…"

"She had. She grilled me about it."

My voice sounds oddly pleased. I won't go into that too deeply.

"What did you tell her?"

I shrug.

"Nothing. She made her own assumptions."

"Can I ask what they were?"

"Of course you can. You can ask me anything. She just assumed that I'd been fucking both of you."

"She didn't think Andy was your new boyfriend?"

"No. Why would she?"

He turns to me then, and fishes his glasses from the edge of the sink, at the same time. Starts putting on his clothes real slow, like he's waiting for me to say something else. But in truth I'm just not sure what would be best, and so I let him continue into shaky territory.

"I don't know. I don't know. Andy just kind of looks like the sort of boyfriend women like to have, maybe."

And I know, I *know* I should have said to him then that I loved him—far more than anything I even vaguely feel for Andy, and perhaps more than I've ever loved any man.

But I didn't.

Chapter Fifteen

THEY'RE IN THE SHOP'S kitchen when I get back. Together, just talking, as though I don't know—they can do that, now, apparently. The atmosphere is tense, but not unpleasant, and when Gabe sees me in the doorway he smiles with all of his teeth.

I knew I shouldn't have left him in the shop alone, for Andy to pounce like a lion on a gazelle. But things needed to be bought and further thoughts about feelings needed to be had, and unfortunately the end result is me dying to ask what they've been talking about.

"Bought yourself anything nice, babe?" Andy says, as he leans back in his chair. He makes an almost comical contrast with Gabe, who remains all ramrod straight and clasped hands.

"The usual. Magazines, chocolate, fur-lined handcuffs."

Gabe looks as though he's happy about all three. Andy bares his teeth.

"We were just having a chat about all the things we'd like to do. And we came to some totally awesome agreements."

"Oh really," I say, making sure I don't let it slide into a question. .

"If you want to, though—only if you want to," Gabe adds, though his expression tells me I'm going to like whatever it is.

"I think she'll want to. You want me to fuck you, don't you, babe?"

I glance at Gabe, but he's gone unreadable, again. I get the feeling they've talked about more than Andy just fucking me, but hey, if they've decided—who am I to say no?

But I go to Gabe, first, and kiss him long and deep. Soon he's back in his chair almost as far as Andy is in his, but I use it as an opportunity for something non-sexy, too. I pull away just as he's starting to relax, and look him in the eye, and ask him if he's sure.

He barely hesitates at all before he answers. And he's already got his hands on the buttons of my shirt, and his leg between my thighs—what else could I read but enthusiasm?

Though said hands do falter, a little, when Andy comes up behind me. Runs his hands all over my back, and demands I tell him I want him. *Tell me how much*, he says, before I've even got anywhere near the answering part—but then, that's Andy. Just so sure that I long for him and desire him.

Gabe, on the other hand, watches as Andy snakes his hands around my middle, and starts unbuttoning my shirt. He takes right up where Gabe left off, and soon I'm standing in the kitchen, in just my skirt and bra.

"Upstairs," Andy says, and Gabe obeys immediately.

But I've decided I'd like to take my time. I think I'm not far off from exerting a little of my own control over the pair of them.

Not that Andy has any idea about such a thing, as he divests me of every item of clothing, and tells me to crawl over Gabe's sprawled-out-over-the-bed body, and give him a good long kiss.

Of course I do it, but more because Gabe is already flushed and breathing hard and palming the stiff shape of his cock through his trousers. His hands immediately roam all over my naked body, and he moans into my mouth when I return the favor.

He feels boiling hot beneath the neat tuck of his shirt and his tank top.

"You should see the view from here," Andy crows, so I spread my legs wider to let him get a better look.

Naturally, he takes that as his cue. Before I've even managed to wrangle off Gabe's many layers, Andy's stark naked behind me, one finger just trailing between my legs. And Gabe knows it, too, because he's had the same idea. He's less bold about it than Andy, of course, and he doesn't simply thrust his fingers into all the juiciest areas first.

But I feel their hands briefly meet, just the same—one underneath, and one from behind.

I think that's more exciting than the actual touching. In fact, I know it is, when Andy definitely grabs a hold of Gabe's hand and tugs it all the way through my slippery slit.

Beneath me, Gabe's eyes flutter closed. He says something that might be *oh you're so wet, you're always so wet,* just before sinking what I think are two of his fingers all the way into my pussy.

Behind me, Andy says:

"Describe what she feels like."

Probably because he's got some of the same kinks as me, and knows by this point that hearing Gabe dirty talk is the equivalent of a hot wet tongue between your legs. However, he doesn't say what I expect—not by a long shot.

"She feels beautiful. She's always beautiful."

And Andy goes with something even more jolting.

"Yeah. She feels real nice here, too," he says. Before pressing what feels like his thumb right over my completely exposed arsehole.

I jerk forward so vigorously that Gabe grabs my hips, as though he's afraid I'm going to shoot through the headboard or something. Unfortunately, this just means that I'm caught in position, with Andy's thumb pressing and worrying right over the place I've never had anything other than an accidental finger of my own.

And my fingers are *small.*

Andy's thumb is not. It presses and presses until I think I'm going to scream from the pressure, and when it moves away it's almost a relief. *Almost.* There's also this sense of shivering absence left behind by it, and I'm not ashamed to admit that I moan at the feel of something different but the same pressing back there.

Different because it's slippery when it returns. The same because it still seems huge and exciting and awful, all at the same time.

Gabe eyes me, all big and dark and concerned, then whisper-asks me what Andy's doing. I think he knows, however, because he still has two slowly working fingers in my pussy, and the distance between him and Andy can't be that great.

Plus every time Andy pushes his slippery thumb hard against me, I rock forward.

"He's trying to put something in my arse," I say, and I don't whisper it at all. I like the little conspiratorial thing we've got going, and I like being this close to him, but oh, it feels good to say something so dirty out loud.

And it feels even better to see Gabe frown and shiver, at the same time. Now it's his turn to ask what something is like. To get someone to describe something that makes them feel naughty and wrong.

"Thick," I tell him. "Too heavy and thick."

It's not the sexiest way to describe something like this, I'm sure, but the hand I slide between our bodies and pass over his still clothed cock—I'm pretty certain that helps the overall effect.

He makes a little *uh* sound, then tells me how he wants Andy to do it harder, press harder, fuck my arse. I ask him if that's what they talked about, but he doesn't respond. He's turned his head to one side, into the pillow, and his fingers stir fitfully in my creaming pussy.

"Don't you want to fuck my arse?" I ask, though more because I'm surprised he's expressed such a desire at all than because it's odd that he would want Andy to do it, not him.

But apparently the latter is not the case, because he pants a hot, moist *yes* into the press of my mouth, just as Andy's thumb slides suddenly and shockingly into my clenching arsehole.

It happens just like that—one moment I'm sure it's never going to fit, the next I'm so full of something it feels like I'm bursting. He's not going to actually try this with his cock, is he? Because I'm not sure I can take it and I'm definitely sure I can't take Gabe—though God, is it OK if I'd like to try?

He's rutting up against my palm, now, more frantic than I've ever seen him, and when Andy slides that digit back and forth—just a little—he whines, high and tight. Words spilling out amongst the sound, like: *he's doing it, isn't he.*

I tell him yes, and feel his cock kick up against my palm—a heavy, dull jerk. Almost as heavy and dull as the feeling of Andy fucking my arse with his thumb.

"Has he lubed his finger?" Gabe asks me suddenly amidst all of this fuck-up, so I calm his obviously frazzled nerves. I tell him yes, that it feels slippery and much more sensitive than I would have imagined.

But that I wish it was him fucking me there.

I think he flashes me a smile for that. Though it gets somewhat lost beneath his sudden moan—the one he gives because I squeeze, instead of rubbing. It pushes him over into leaving my pussy behind, so that he can get at his belt and his zipper and other things in the way of me stroking his cock.

"I'll get her ready for you, mate," Andy says—a sentiment that makes my clit jump. I imagine them talking in hushed, filthy tones about how they're going to lube me up and prep me, stretch my arse wide so that Gabe can fuck me there—God.

However, Andy's not quite so magnanimous as all that. Oh no no no. No—he's happy to prep me, but by prep he actually means *fuck you first, before your boyfriend gets a turn.*

And he's not lying, either. His thumb disappears and then all I can hear is him rolling on a condom, louder than a gong, while beneath me Gabe barely dares to touch his own freed cock.

His eyes are full of wonder and something like shame, and he leans in to tell me that he thinks he's going to come—so soon and so without anything happening to him at all. Though I feel I should probably point out to him—lying beneath your girlfriend while she strokes you off and someone else prepares to fuck her arse…I'm not sure that qualifies as "without anything happening at all."

In fact, it feels more like something really slippery and solid, easing its way into my yielding arsehole.

I slap my hands down onto the pillow on either side of Gabe's head. I'm also pretty sure that I tell Andy to stop, no, I can't take it. But he just holds my hips and surges forward, while Gabe examines every nuance of expression on my probably sweaty and very red face.

I can feel his hand, fluttering against my belly. But he still doesn't touch his leaking, too-hard cock.

"Does that feel good?" he asks. "Is that what you've been wanting?"

But Andy answers for me.

"You bet it is," he says, and then shoves into me hard enough to make me lose my balance. I fall to the side of Gabe, face first in the pillow. Of course, on the downslide my belly grazes Gabe's hard cock, and I'm pretty sure that's why he makes a sound of protest.

Though he makes a far, far louder one when Andy says, "Your turn, bud."

Only, you know. I don't think he means *now you fuck her arse*. And I think Gabe knows he doesn't mean that, because his gaze shoots up to Andy, somewhere over my shoulder, and he looks startled and almost angry.

But he waits for Andy to confirm.

"Come on. Fuck her pussy while I fuck her arse."

This is definitely not what they discussed. I can see it all over Gabe, and in Andy's slightly mocking tone, and through my body, which seizes up while my mind floats off to a higher place. Lord, wait until I tell Jeanette *this* story.

I feel Gabe's clammy hands slide over my rib cage, as Andy slows to a gentle rock in and out. Barely anything at all, really. It still makes nerve endings I didn't know I had shiver and shake, and I can still feel lube trickling down the crack of my arse in an utterly obscene sort of way, but now everything is calm, and not too pressing.

Though I can hear in Andy's voice how turned on he is.

"What are you waiting for? Come on, Nancy. She'll love it."

I kiss Gabe's open mouth, and reassure him that that's sort of the case. But Gabe still hovers on the edge of doing this, hands not wanting to take the condom Andy fumbles off the bed and passes to him, eyes wandering all over me in consideration.

I hover on the edge, too, sure that he's not going to. Andy calls him Nancy again and he flinches, so I knock my body back at Andy and tell Gabe it's OK, it's OK. Nothing that he doesn't want to do, right? And I like it. I do like it. He doesn't have to worry.

But he still hesitates. Even after he's wriggled and squirmed and somehow managed to get the condom on—while Andy and I hold our breaths and alternately clench and thrust in minute increments—he hesitates.

And then he says, "Are you sure?"

With worried eyes, and I'm pretty certain that no one in the history of the world has ever loved someone so fierce and sudden in the middle of almost double penetration. Pretty certain.

"Fuck me," I say, and it comes out much more like a sob than I intend.

I shake more than I intend to, too—and especially when Gabe searches out my wet hole with the head of his cock, and it's so obvious that this is just not going to fit until it does, and I bunch the pillows into my fists.

I've no idea what kind of sound I make. It must be something like the cry someone lets out when they're being strangled—a sort of choked gasp. But it's appropriate, because that's definitely how my pussy and my arse feel—like they're being choked. I feel utterly filled and completely wiped by it, as though somehow everything on my body is being touched by the two cocks trying to work their way inside me.

I barely hear Gabe tell Andy to stop, though I know he does. Mainly because it comes directly after the sound I make, and his hands clamp down hard on my hips—but not for the same purpose as Andy's.

He holds me away from the blissful sinking feeling of the two of them, not thrusting in any further while Andy tries desperately to do just that. It creates a delicious push-pull sensation that makes my clit throb, but Gabe insists again.

"No. We're hurting her."

I try to reassure him, but Andy's kind of laughing and ignoring him and thrusting oh God he's thrusting and it's so...unlike anything else I've ever experienced. All of which combines to make me unable to say anything but *oh, oh, oh* and maybe a *Jesus, yes—fill me up*.

Somewhere in between I'm sure I manage to tell him that I'm OK, I'm OK, please just do it, but his face is tense and tight when I finally lay blurry eyes on it. His fingers are pressing into my hips, and when Andy rocks, his concern gives way to a wavering cry of pleasure.

"He can feel my cock," Andy says, so full of evil delight that I really wish his words didn't turn me on. But they do, and I ask him for more, and soon he's fucking against both of us in these stiff little jerks, until I know I'm about to come.

I'd tell him, but all I can get out are inarticulate gasps of pleasure. My toes curl, my hands squeeze too hard into cotton and cushion—and then it comes. It blooms right through me, this immense spread of sensation, so intense that my entire body jitters.

I'm not aware of anything for a full minute, I'm sure. Which is unfortunate, because Gabe is definitely trying to tell Andy to stop, in no uncertain terms. And he's trying to escape, too, but I guess that's really hard when your immense cock is jammed tight in someone's pussy, and her body is all over you like a drowning person.

"No, no," he says, as he struggles—and he really has to struggle, because Andy is moaning that he can feel me coming and it's making him come and I don't think he could let go now if he tried.

But Gabe definitely wants him to because he repeats his concerns about hurting me, then puts a hand over his face, despairing. Before moaning, brokenly, that he can't remember the safe word.

This time when Andy tells him to *man up, pansy*, I slap back at him so hard he stumbles back, and I almost come right off the bed with him.

"Hey!" he cries out, but he can go on protesting forever. All I want to do is what I should have done ten minutes ago—reassure Gabe that I'm OK and that he hasn't hurt me and that we're stopping. We're stopping, now.

But as soon as I lift myself away from him just a little, he squirms free and pushes out from underneath me. Andy slides out of me, too—both of them no longer hard, but obviously for completely different reasons.

I've never wished so fervently in all my life for an orgasm glow to dissipate—my limbs are all loose and lax, and Gabe's wound tighter than a spring so he escapes me easily. My efforts at following him off the bed and out of the room amount to me sprawling over the bed in a liquid daze.

I think I shout his name. But it sounds a lot like *lane*, coming out.

I do, however, manage to tell Andy to shut up when he asks what Gabe's problem is. To his credit he then says that he didn't mean to upset the guy—but I'm not sure what difference that's going to make, now.

I think I can hear the shower running.

—◦◦◦—

Andy gives me this look when the first thing I do on regaining use of my body is throw on a robe, and make for the bathroom. But surprisingly, it's not so much a *really—for this wet pansy*? sort of look. It's much more like a *yeah, OK, I get it* sort of look.

I appreciate him a lot more than I did for that.

And then I've got to enter the bathroom of doom, and find out how much psychological damage I've visited on Gabe. Have I really visited psychological damage on him? Please say I haven't.

He isn't crying, at least. Though I can see him through the shower door, forehead against the tiles, spray on full blast.

I shut and lock the door behind me, just in case Andy should decide he wants to take a piss or maybe taunt some more. Though I've got to say, somehow I doubt it. It's all just games—he doesn't mean any of it. This isn't real for him, I'm sure.

"Gabe—are you OK?"

He starts, as though he hadn't even heard the door shut. Then he makes a bit of a show of washing himself busily, as though he just wanted to take a quick shower before we tried putting a ball gag in my mouth.

But when I open the shower door, he backs up against the wall and sort of…I don't know. Rolls his eyes at himself? As though his reaction was too much, but he just couldn't help it. Any of it.

"Honey—you weren't hurting me. I would have said if I wasn't OK—"

"I know," he says. "I know—I just didn't—"

Then his voice kind of breaks in a way that kills me, and he turns his face into the spray. He's got it so hot that it almost burns my skin, when I climb in with him. Robe and all.

"I'm sorry, Maddie—I just didn't want to. I didn't like it—I'm sorry."

Lord have mercy. Is that what this is about? Is that why he looks so mortified and torn up—because he didn't want to do something?

I take his face in my hands, and he calms, somewhat.

"It's not what I want," he says, softer. Softer yet when I kiss him, sweet and slow. "I like how things were before too much."

"You don't have to prove anything to me, honey. You don't. I like what you like, OK? I do—more than I ever thought I would. Don't worry so much."

"I couldn't remember the safe word, either—that's terrible."

He laughs a little when I laugh. It's a comfort. It's a bigger one when he puts his arms around me, and I find it easy to put my own around him.

"I overreacted, didn't I?" he says, after a moment—but I just squeeze him tighter.

"Listen—we can do whatever you want. It doesn't have to be Andy calling the shots—it doesn't have to be Andy at all. Whatever you want, OK—tell me what you want. You remember how much I liked that, right?"

He snorts another laugh into my shoulder.

"Yes. Yeah—I remember."

"So tell me what you want," I say. "And I can see, by the way, that you're wanting again."

"Really? I thought my erection had turned invisible."

It warms my heart to hear him snark. Thank God no irrevocable psychological damage has taken place. Go us!

"You can fuck me up against the shower wall, if you want. I'll be walking funny tomorrow, but I figure that's a given, anyway."

It's only been a few minutes of hugging and feelings, but he's already progressed to the point of bottom stroking. I can't blame him—the material feels amazing, wet. It's really soothing, after the whole filled-to-capacity thing.

"Are you sure you're OK?" he says, and I tell him his concern is touching.

It really is, too—I guess because it's so sincere. He's not trying to protect me or act manly or anything like that. He just is, he just cares for me, I just love him. I do. In fact, I actually almost blurt the words out, in that moment.

But unfortunately he gets there before me. And not with sappy words of love.

"I know what I want," he says, voice suddenly dark and syrupy. That ever-buoyant erection of his, brushing against the equally clingy and delicious material at the front of my robe.

"What's that, baby?" I ask, and he replies:

"I want you to tell Andy what to do, the way you do me."

Chapter Sixteen

AFTER I'VE TOWELED MYSELF off, and toweled Gabe off, too—much to his delight—I come out of the bathroom to find Andy in front of the fridge. Of course he's starkers, but that's not the most disconcerting part. He's also eating leftover pasta direct from its Pyrex dish, with his fingers.

It's like...I don't know. Maybe he wanted to make it easy for me. In all likelihood, he's just a slob. But either way I find it very simple to lean against the counter in the little black slip I've put on—the one that Gabe likes so much he sometimes just rubs it all over his face and body—and say to Andy:

"What a dirty disgusting boy you are."

Gabe doesn't come into the kitchen, but I know he hasn't made it to the bedroom yet, either. I told him to go in and make himself comfortable, but he's lingering and listening, I know. He asked me in a feverish sort of voice what I was going to do, and I told him honestly—I have no idea. Mainly because I'm not sure how Andy is going to respond to this.

But, as ever, he's quick off the mark. Good old predictable Andy.

"Oh right—so I've been bad, have I?"

He smirks and scoops up another mouthful of the meal.

Gabe cooked only yesterday.

"I'm pretty sure that you're always bad."

"But in that way you like, huh, babe?"

"Oh yes. I like it *very* much. And especially because the

badder someone is, the greater the punishment they deserve. Don't you think?"

He puts the pasta dish down in this very deliberate, eyebrows raised with the maximum allowable amount of curiosity sort of way. Licks sauce off his thumb and forefinger, all devilish and cheeky.

That's Andy, all right. Up for anything.

"You think you've got the chops to punish me, babe?" he says, and I'll admit—there's definitely a moment when I doubt myself. Partially, I think, because he's just so much more solid than Gabe. I feel like Gabe could just slip through my fingers, if I'm not watching closely enough.

"Why don't you try me?"

He grins broadly at that. Takes an almost predatory step toward me—though I stand my ground.

"And what am I going to be punished for, exactly?"

I narrow just one eye at him. He knows, all right. He knows.

"Let's call it…impugning the masculinity of another man. A man that I really like a lot."

"Oh-ho-ho! *Impugning*. OK, babe, all right. Tell you what— why don't we go in the bedroom, and you give it your best shot."

He strolls past me cocky as anything, while I don't say what comes to mind to his back. They're words that burn in me almost as strongly as the ones I wanted to say to Gabe, but for completely different giddy reasons.

You are really *not going to be able to handle my best shot, Andy Yarrow.*

⸺⁓⸺

He makes a complete rookie mistake, right off the bat. He lets me handcuff his hands to the headboard above his head. And he does so all sure of himself and like it's not a big deal, so when I tell him *no, face down*, he can't exactly refuse. He can't really worm out of it without looking like a...what was it he called Gabe, again?

Oh yeah. *Nancy.*

So that's how I get him, crouched awkwardly on his knees with his hands attached to my bed. And I guess that's kind of undignified enough, but somehow I don't really like how he's still got his head held high, and there's a grin all over his face that needs wiping off.

So I say to Gabe, who's just hovering, patiently, by the bed:

"Grab his legs and yank, until he's facedown in the mattress."

Gabe glances at me, quick and sharp—like maybe he hadn't even considered that this was the turn I'd take. And of course I know that I could do the action myself—Andy's solid, but he's not that solid.

However, it's nice to have a big strong man to do it for me.

"You want me to..." Gabe starts, but doesn't finish. He doesn't even wait for me to say yes, either. He just steps in front of me at the bottom of the bed, reaches forward and grasps Andy's ankles, then yanks.

Before Andy can get out the little *hang on a second.*

But I pay attention to it, I do. I would never say that I'm the kind of woman who doesn't listen to her men. I like to be fair, I know that much, and there's always the matter of safety to consider, isn't there?

So I tell him—while he's still flailing on the mattress, looking suddenly wide-eyed:

"Don't worry, Andy. If we do anything you don't like, you can just use the safe word, OK?" He stares back at me, over his shoulder. Actually waiting for it, I think. "The safe word is..."

I feel I make a good show of thinking one up. Even though I know what I'm going to name it already.

"The safe word is...*Nancy.* How does that sound?"

He looks madder than fuck, suddenly—but it's the strangest thing. He doesn't say a goddamned word.

Not even when Gabe tries to contain his smile, and his thick eyebrows go up and up, and then he waits—both of them do—to see what I'm going to do next.

Of course I have absolutely no idea. Until the actual words come out of my mouth.

"That's *very* nice—and so pretty," I tell him, because he's kind of struggling to get up on all fours and his butt is just as big and round as a ripe peach. I want to bite it almost as hard as I usually want to bite Gabe's constantly.

But I refrain. For now.

Instead, I pat him there with just enough pressure that he stops squirming, a little, and behind me I hear Gabe's intake of breath. It's not a surprise at all when I turn back to him, and see his hand splayed on his belly, just above his erection.

"So you're going to spank me," Andy says, in a tone that deeply suggests *how original.* "Come on then, babe—do it, if it gets you off."

But I just continue my sometimes prodding, sometimes patting exploration of his arse, and ask my already breathlessly excited partner-in-crime:

"I don't know. Do you think I should spank him, Gabe?"

"Yes, yes," he moans, before I've barely got the words out. He sounds so turned on that my pussy tingles and grows slippery in sympathy—but then, he hasn't had one go-around yet, has he? Me and Andy—we've got one orgasm in the bank.

While Gabe's just stuffed to the brim with unfulfilled pleasure, waiting and wanting and sighing with desire at the slightest thing. And so of course I don't deny him the hand he's got on his cock. I just tell him to stand at the side of the bed, so that I can watch him jerk off as I play with my new toy.

He does it slow, and far too close to Andy's turned-to-one-side face. And Andy doesn't flinch at all, he doesn't—why would he, he didn't complain when Gabe's hand was on his cock—but he *does* do something when I run one sly finger between the cheeks of his arse.

"Or maybe I should try out what I've been meaning to do to you, Gabe, for what seems like *weeks.*"

Andy immediately lurches forward and away. Gabe, on the other hand, goes a brilliant, perfect red, and stills the hand on his already dripping cock. I watch him lay it palm flat to his thigh, as though he needs the firm presence of an entirely different part of himself to keep him from jerking off.

"Would you like that, baby? You want my finger in your ass?"

Andy is the one who answers, however. Gabe's eyes just close, those too-long eyelashes making this lovely sooty semi-circle beneath them that I've never noticed before.

"No!" he yelps, and I have to admit—I'm kind of surprised. *That's* his limit? Something in his ass?

"How *provincial* of you, Andy," I say, and then I laugh, and I'm pretty sure Gabe would laugh too—if he weren't kind of squirming on the spot.

Because of course he's imagining it. I know he's imagining it. I even see him pass a hand very close to one smooth round arse cheek, as though working up the daring to touch himself there all on his own.

But then, I'm pretty sure Gabe's done something like it before—maybe with his pretty little pink vibrator. Whereas Andy…

Well. He's just a regular scrunch your face and bury your head in the sand sort of guy. The kind of guy who whimpers when I hold him fast with one hand at his hip, and slide my finger between, again.

"Don't be a baby," I tell him. "I did this just fine, not so long ago. And I hear that girls have hardly any nerve endings in there at all, while guys…"

I press down hard on the locked up tight pucker of his arsehole. He jerks forward as though struck.

And it's the first time he moans, too. His hands are clenching and unclenching straining against the cuffs, and I just can't believe it's really this easy to take someone apart. To have them writhing and gasping and panting no.

While the safe word goes completely untouched.

"Pass me the lube, Gabe," I say, and he does so gingerly. It's still on the bed, and almost underneath Andy's body, so when he leans forward to grab it his cock gets very close to brushing a whole bunch of stuff.

I don't think he can take the slightest pressure on it. Especially not any pressure that involves Andy's skin.

But once he's passed me the small tube, he does lay a sudden and inexplicable hand on Andy's curved back. Tells him: *feels good, doesn't it?* It's somehow the sweetest gesture, and Andy doesn't say a word in reply.

But he does come very close to pressing back against my slick finger, when I slide it back between the cheeks of his arse. And Gabe glances up at me, those sharp little lower teeth bared, and says in this wondering voice:

"He's really hard. Really hard."

"How many do you think I should fuck him with? One?" I can't tell you how thrilled Gabe looks to be consulted.

"No—no. Two. Use two."

"Is that what you want me to do to you, baby? Do you want me to fuck your sweet arse like this?"

I circle Andy's fluttering hole, and hear his breathing roughen.

"No," Gabe says.

Strangely, it's *his* denial that makes me pause. And almost giggle, when Andy clearly backs into me for a little more of that stroking action. I don't blame him—no matter what I said about girls and nerve endings and what the fuck, having your arsehole circled with a slippery mess of lube is just…glorious.

"No—I want you to…I want you to bend me over and fuck me with something. I want you to really fuck me—I do. Like in *Boss Lady*—like in that."

He doesn't even look mortified about saying it, either. It comes out all in a rush, but only because he's semi-touching himself as he says it.

I hardly notice Andy's arse giving, to let one of my fingers slide smooth and slow inside. I'm too busy growing jelly-legged and so swollen and slippery between my legs, it's painful. I fuck in and out of Andy almost absentmindedly, because I'm too busy thinking of Gabe's lithe body spread out beneath mine.

I'm too busy watching him rub and then tighten his hand around his cock. Rub and then tighten, rub and then tighten. His thighs are trembling.

"He feels so silky—I didn't even think," I tell Gabe, and both men give these little shocked cries of pleasure.

"What else?" Gabe asks, and I thrust in deeper, harder.

"I can feel his arse clenching around my finger, and if I twist just a little, like this—" I do so. "—you can see him reacting to it, even when he's trying not to."

Andy shudders—though in all honesty, I don't think he's trying not to, anymore. He's rocking back against my slowly thrusting finger, and when I add a second one, he mumbles something that might be *so good*.

"I didn't think he'd like it so much," Gabe says, with a little frown that comes and then goes as soon as it appeared, but Andy doesn't even argue with him. He's too far gone, now, and I'm pretty sure I'm hitting his prostate on every stroke. It's much more distinct than I would have imagined, in both feel and its effect.

"You know what I think he'd like even more?" I say, while Andy moans *fuck no, no*. I wouldn't be surprised if he'd guessed before I finish what I'm bashing on about. "I'd bet he'd love your cock in his arse, Gabe. I bet he'd love that so much, getting filled and fucked with that great big thing of yours. Don't you think, baby?"

Andy strains against the leash, snaps his head around, and spits out a *no, no, you're* not *doing that, Maddie, fuck*!

But yet again, he doesn't say the safe word. I mean, it's entirely possible that he's forgotten it. Or maybe I was just too cruel in the choosing of it, and now he's all emasculated and messed up inside.

Only he goes right back to moaning when I stroke and rub my finger over that neat little bump inside him.

And Gabe is just a shuddering, dissolving mess. I think he knows more than Andy that I'm not serious, but he's sweating just the same, and when I tell him to lay a hand on Andy's arse, he obeys me. I tell him to slap down hard while I fuck in and out, and he comes close enough to trail the tip of his cock along Andy's side.

"Would you like that, baby?" I whisper to him, and he kisses me—long and wet. He only pulls away so that he can slap Andy's arse again, and this time he really gives no quarter. He brings his hand down so hard it leaves a red print, and Andy calls us both fuckers, absolute fuckers.

"I'd do anything for you," Gabe says, and though I think he's doing it to tease Andy, I think he really would. He honestly would. So I tell him, in reply:

"No, baby. I'd do anything for *you*. Anything you want, just say the word. Anything."

"Really?" he says. "Really?"

"I promise—just tell me."

He hesitates, and lets his gaze trail over Andy's curved and gleaming back. And when he speaks it's shy, like it was before when he asked for the same thing. But I give it to him—I want to give it to him.

We go through to the living room and make love on the couch, while from the bedroom Andy calls us every name his extremely inventive brain can think of.

He's as mad as hell when we finally get back to him. I won't lie—I did a lot of it for show. But then again, Gabe makes it extremely easy to cry out *oh, it's never been like this before* and *do it harder, God, harder, yes—now, now!*

At which, Gabe actually giggled. Like he understood exactly why I was doing it, and found the whole thing hilarious—especially Andy's angry cursing. And when he came inside me, juddering all over and digging red marks into my hips, he said those words again.

But it's OK, this time, it's OK because I actually said—I do too. I said I do too! I am as giddy as all hell and standing on some sort of precipice when we saunter back into the bedroom, but it's OK. Because I really don't think the drop is all that high from up here.

"Did you enjoy that?" Andy says, in this sneery sort of voice. But I can hear the frustration underneath it—it's raw and broken up, and he seems to have come very close to rutting himself against the mattress. And there are weird red lines all over his wrists, as though he's tried to do some pretty spectacular contortions in order to either (a) get free or (b) jerk himself off.

On all counts he's definitely failed, however, because I can see his stiff prick from here. It looks as angry as he is.

"Aw, what's the matter, honey? Don't like waiting for it? You know—Gabe *loves* waiting for it. You're just coming up short, I'm afraid."

Gabe smiles with the whole of his mouth—though said smile falters just a little bit, when Andy snaps back, "I can wait. I've waited, haven't I? I could have done something to fuck myself and didn't, so fuck you."

"Language, Andy. Really—you're upsetting my guy."

I was going to go with boyfriend, but really. I'm a grown woman. Wait until he's my husband, and then we'll talk about epithets.

"Just—please, OK? I get it, you're torturing me. It's awesome, but please—he can fuck my arse, you can stick whatever you like up there, just get me off. All right? Please."

I step toward him, and run a hand over one still hand-printed arse cheek. He actually whimpers in response.

"You beg so prettily, Andy, really. Almost as prettily as Gabe."

"I can be as pretty as you fucking want. I'll dress up in girl's clothes and a wig, if that's your thing. Please, Maddie."

I glance at Gabe, who oddly still looks…what? Concerned? I have the urge to reassure him, but seeing to Andy's well-being would kind of shatter the whole illusion. I mean—he knows that it's an illusion, right? Andy can say the word anytime he likes, and do himself until the top of his head comes off. He can fuck me through a wall—if it's OK with Gabe.

But then, maybe that's it. Gabe knows that things are different, now. He knows that I don't want Andy to fuck me through a wall—that I want him, and him only.

"What do you think I should do to him?" I ask Gabe, but he doesn't answer. He just watches, as I lean over Andy and wrap my hand tight around his straining cock. Andy pants *yes, yes, oh Maddie I love you, you crazy bitch*, but again Gabe doesn't say anything when I ask him if I should show Andy mercy.

However, I do so anyway. I give one rough little tug, and that's all it takes. He comes, copiously, all over my sheets—just like Gabe did.

Chapter Seventeen

WHEN I WAKE UP, both boys are gone. I let Andy stay over—as shaken up and handsy as he was—but I told Gabe that it was going to be the last time. And found it kind of disturbing how non-excited Gabe seemed at that idea.

It has occurred to me that perhaps Gabe truly does enjoy the whole ménage dynamic, and didn't want it to end. And yet when I come in to an empty bed, I feel somewhat uneasy about the whole thing. His troubled expressions play on a loop in my head, and as I tug on a robe and try to convince myself that he'll just be out there, eating breakfast, I keep going over possible explanations.

Like maybe he's realized he's actually gay. Or possibly he can't function outside of weird humiliation games. Or some other daft thing that's thrown him that I can't possibly even imagine.

Maybe I shouldn't have said *I do, too*. It just sounds stupid, now, in my head. And even more so when there's just Andy out there, sitting on my couch, eating cereal.

At least he's wearing pants, I suppose.

"Christ—you slept like the dead," is the first thing he says, and for some reason that sounds even more ominous than all the irrational thoughts that are currently flooding my brain. I resist the urge to ask him where Gabe is.

I mean, it's a Sunday—but Gabe could still be downstairs. Or in the shower I don't hear.

"I thought you'd be gone," I say, though it doesn't come out as dismissive as I intend. I appreciate Andy a whole lot more for the hug he gave me last night, and the little *that was awesome*. I think I appreciate any guy who's willing to bend in many different ways.

"Why would I be gone, now that I've got you all to myself?"

To his credit, he doesn't look happy about this fact. He looks more disturbed than anything else. But that's OK, because I think that means we now have matching expressions.

"I was going to come and wake you, but he seemed pretty stressed out. Thought I should just let him go and then, you know. You can be the hero, running after the damsel in distress."

I knew something was wrong, I knew it. I think I actually stamp my foot at him.

"*Don't* call him a damsel, you shit!"

Andy's immediate contriteness is not a comfort. I want him to be an arsehole again, so that I can fucking punish him.

"What did you say to him? No—don't stand up. Don't. What did you say to him; tell me now."

The level of discomfort on Andy's face is also unwelcome. It doesn't bode well, for all the rational, calming thoughts I'm trying to have, such as—he'll just be a bit freaked out, like in the shower. He'll have gone back to his apartment, and locked himself in some flagellation closet he's got in there somewhere, and I can just talk him down again.

As soon as I find out what exactly has been said, and what crazy ideas Gabe has jammed into that brain of his. Because God, I know that's what he's done. All the little things he's been saying and saying—they're trying to eat *my* brain, currently.

"Look—I've got no idea what that guy's going on about most of the time! I didn't mean to upset him or anything, for Christ's sake!"

Lord. Lord. Lord. Just don't put your face in your hands, Madison, don't put your face in your hands—because God knows you'll never get it back out again.

"I told him I had fun, he went all tense. That was it!"

"You must have said something else, Andy—Jesus, all your pansy talk, I mean, what the fuck is wrong with you?"

Andy throws up his hands.

"Come on, Maddie—you know I never meant it to fuck with him this much. But I swear—I never said anything like that to him. I said you were really fond of him, for fuck's sake!"

I think my shoulders sag through the ground. Of course, I genuinely feel he meant well. I do. But *fond*? Like the way I feel about my elderly grandmother?

"You seriously said that?"

"I said you liked him more than me, too! But he didn't seem to believe that. He didn't believe it before when we were talking in the kitchen."

It takes every effort in my body not to hurl myself at Andy and claw the answers out of him. Stopping myself requires thinking intensively about Gabe being there, in his apartment, just waiting for me to calm him down. That's what's going to happen. Everything is fine.

"What. Exactly. Did you talk about. In the kitchen."

Despite my best efforts, my voice comes out like a maniac's. And I think Andy believes so too, judging by his terror-filled expression.

"He said you liked me more, and he could prove it."

Oh no. Oh no.

"That I could do things his way, but he couldn't do things my way."

Oh my God, I'm too stupid to live. Why didn't I just ask Gabe what they'd talked about? Though even as I'm thinking it, I'm guessing Gabe would have lied. He's set me up in some sort of...I don't even know. Some bizarre neurotic trap.

But I told him I loved him! I did!

Only no wait, I didn't. I said something stupid and cop-out like

I do too, and in the face of glaring me-loving-Andy evidence, that probably sounded like cracking icing sugar. Like something made of nothing.

"And then we talked this morning and he said that I'd be better for you. That girls like guys more like me, you know—and I swear to God, Maddie, I tried to tell him. I mean, Jeez, even I can see you're mad about him. It pisses me off, but hey—you win some, you lose some. I'm man enough to admit when I've lost."

I don't know why, but I break down crying when he says that last bit. Whatever anger I was storing up toward him gushes away and out of me, and then I'm just a mess. A mess that blubbers out *I love Gabe*, when I've never even properly said the words to him.

"Oh. Oh," Andy says. "I'm sorry about all this, then, babe. Really am. I thought he kind of knew that he'd won last night—swear to God. When you were out here fucking his brains out I wanted to deck him one."

Is he trying to say stuff that makes me cry harder?

"But this morning he was all…I dunno. And I told him he should let you make your own choices, but I think he felt you'd made it, you know?"

I don't even flinch when Andy gets up and steers me toward a chair. I even let him make me a cup of coffee, though I don't drink it. People who've made total messes of things don't deserve coffee.

"You all right now?" he asks, but I can't answer that. Instead I just ask him if Gabe went back to his apartment—at which Andy doesn't look as positive as I could have hoped. In fact, he looks downright grim.

"Uh, I don't think so."

"Please don't tell me he's flown to Brazil. I'm not an exotic billionaire—I can't chase my pregnant mistress halfway around the world."

Andy laughs. Makes me wonder if he's been reading some of my stock lately.

"No, no! I don't think he's taken the first flight out of here, or anything. He just said…" Andy makes a sound best described as an awkward *eh*. "…that he was going away for a couple of days. And he kind of…handed his notice in."

"Save the best for last, huh, Andy?"

At least he looks like he's swallowed something bitter, when he passes me a little white envelope—one of the ones I use for the shop. I'd say *how dramatic*, but really it just seems woeful and sad. I'm probably going to start crying, again.

Of course I don't open it expecting a fond farewell and some love hearts on the bottom. But even so it turns my stomach to see *Dear Ms. Morris* at the top. He's even put his address in there, and my address, and a *yours sincerely* at the bottom.

God, he's such a fool.

"Does it say where he's decided to flit off to?" Andy asks, and I just shake my head. I'm crying again, even though I know he'll have to come back to his apartment at some point. He will, won't he? And then I can just camp out on his doorstep and shake him until he knows he's an idiot and say in a big outside voice, I love you, Gabe, I love you.

Even though I know it's never that easy in romance novels.

—⁂—

The first place I go is to his apartment. Of course it is. Though when I get there, I wish I hadn't. When my guy follows his own insane reasoning, he follows it all the way and one hundred percent. I'm starting to suspect that romance novels have poisoned his brain, because he's only gone and given up his apartment.

An old lady even comes out and tells me, when she gets tired of me banging on the door and trying to peer through the peephole. He's gone, she tells me—moved out yesterday. As though I'm actually trapped in some awful horror movie in which Gabe never existed and he was really the ghost of a nineteenth-century priest trapped on earth by his need for sex.

I ask the old lady from a horror novel how he could have possibly moved out in, like, hours, but she tells me no. He's been moving out for the better part of two weeks. Not only that, but his landlord tells me he left no forwarding address.

And, I have to say, I hate Gabriel Kauffman in that moment. I hate me for not spelling things out for him, but I hate him for not asking, not telling, not being clearer. All the little cryptic hints he gave me—the frowns and the little *did she think Andy was your boyfriends* and all that bullshit.

And now disappearing like this!

Gah, I could just kill him. I'm going to kill him, when I find him. And I know where to start, too, so he needn't think he can hide from me. Unless he's hiding from me because he's started seeing someone else—probably a man—in which he case he can go on hiding forever.

Though I know that's not true. I know, even though it makes it worse, somehow. I can hate him when I just think of him as a cheating liar. But he didn't really lie at all, and now I'm standing on the pavement outside what used to be his parents' toy museum, trying to glean something of him from what is now a very upmarket jewelers.

It's in a prime location, too. Suddenly I'm starting to see his lack of previous job experience with different eyes—because if he sold this place he'll have made a pretty packet from it, no matter how rundown it was. There's that parking lot near the Minster not far from it, and the center of town only ten seconds away.

But all I can really think about is—I wish I'd talked to him about it more. I wish I'd asked him what it was like, back when it had toys in the window and *Kauffman's Clockworks* over the door.

Because that's what it was called. It was a museum, but they sold things, too—little clockwork toys and wooden puppets, colorful things that delight children of all ages. And I know because I googled Kauffman, York, and all of this is what came up. They weren't totally bonkers once, I guess.

And I hope they were kind enough to leave a forwarding address with the man behind the counter of Naughton's the Jewelers.

I'm still not sure what my plan is, as the taxi pulls up outside The Grove. That's the name of his old home, his family's home—The Grove! As though he truly did grow up trapped in some sort of bizarre fairytale like The Twits, and I really am going to find out soon that he was never real.

Maybe I should just put on an old wedding dress now, and sit inside his old house and rot with the rest of it, waiting for him to visit. That's a perfectly sane plan, isn't it?

None of this feels sane when I'm standing by the frankly massive and completely decrepit gate outside his house. And it *is* still his house. He didn't sell it, like the toy museum—and I know because Mr. Naughton was very kind and told me that Gabe still visits, occasionally.

Is it OK if I feel unbearably sad about that? I can just see him wandering around all the display cases, lingering over things shiny and new, lost in a world of faceless puppets and dolls that move.

Also: I'm really starting to creep myself out, now. And though the just-starting-to-push-into-summer-sunshine is pouring down, and the overgrown garden beyond looks lost in a haze of heat and green, it does nothing to ease that sense of creepiness.

I wonder if I'll go in there and never come back out again. I'll probably end up lost in the nineteenth century. But I push open the gate—which wails, ominously—and start up the gravelly, overgrown drive, anyway.

I think of Gabe's comment about Gray Gardens again, as I go.

Maybe his parents aren't dead and I'm going to find them some-where, dressed in their swimming costumes and carrying raccoons.

However, when I get up close, I can see the house is empty. The windows are boarded up, and most of it has been taken over by creeping plants of all kinds—in fact, I think I can see a tree starting to poke out of the boards over one of the upper windows.

But it's a massive and beautiful old thing. A real country house, gray-bricked and squat and sprawling, surrounded by so much grassy overgrown British countryside it's unreal. And when I peer through the cracks in the boards, I can just about make out a kitchen with an Aga stove and all of that nonsense.

His childhood would have really been idyllic, if his parents weren't insane. There's even a huge old apple tree in what might be the back garden—it's hard to tell, amidst all the vast grounds—and it has the remains of a rope swing attached.

Bees drone lazily through the overgrown grass and the ten-feet-tall dandelions. The grove of trees that lies at the bottom of an almost not there path whisper when the breeze hits them, and everything is still and summery and lovely, even with this film of dust all over everything.

I follow the path down because I can't not, and there's a little stream that dwindles off into nowhere. The water glistens beneath the shards of light that make it through the canopy of leaves, and I think of all the children that could have had wild Enid Blyton adventures here if their parents just. Weren't. Crazy.

But they were and this is it, and oh my heart just aches for him. I hope you were happy with me, my Gabe, even if it was only for a little while. I hope I made you happy.

However, when I turn and he's just standing there, and he asks me in this really surprised sort of voice why I'm crying, I just want to kill him all over again. I'm relieved to see him and he looks so good and not full of despair, but I just want to kill kill kill him for making me all ridiculous and dramatic like this.

Instead, I stumble in my stupid strappy sandals over to him, and throw my arms around his shoulders, and generally behave like a big sappy idiot. Thank God, thank God he didn't move to Brazil.

Thank God he hugs me back.

"What's the matter?" he asks, like a moron. "What's the matter, Maddie? Is it Andy?"

Lord, what is the *matter* with *him*? I do shake him, then, with my hands bunched in his shirt—a still dorky plaid thing, for some inexplicable reason—and my teeth all gritted and I must just look a mess. But I don't care.

"Why did you leave? Why? How could you just run off like that?"

I sound frighteningly high and not at all in control of myself. He tries to soothe me with his stupid big hands, but I'm having none of it, apparently.

"I thought that..." he starts, but I think it's already beginning to dawn on him that what he thought is totally ridiculous and so fucking wrong. "I thought it would be best."

I let go of him then, and try, fruitlessly, to compose myself. Which really just means I wipe my eyes and nose on the sleeve of the summer dress I thought it would be advisable to wear.

"You thought it would be best to stop me choosing for myself?"

His eyes go big at that. But then, I do pack an awful lot of mean and sullen into it.

"No, no! No, I just...I don't know. You want Andy, don't you?" Then smaller, in this almost sickly sounding voice: "You do want Andy, don't you? I mean, I just can't be like him, Maddie; I can't give you everything. I can't be in charge, I can't be in control, I can't."

He swallows around his words.

"I won't ever be the kind of man Andy is."

I think he intends the words to be loaded, and like a death knell or something. He actually does look despairing once they're out. But they just make me explode with stuff.

"Who says I care? Why would I care? You talk about how you'll never be the man he is, how you'll never be like him. But *he* won't ever be like *you*. He won't ever be kind, or funny, or smart, like you. He won't ever be able to do some of the things you do for me, not ever!"

Somehow, he gets the nerve to interject. In fact, he interjects pretty damned fiercely, for him.

"He did them for you the other night!"

I guess it's our first argument, because I can't stop myself from shouting right back, "But I don't *love* him!"

And then we're both quiet, for what seems like a long, long time. Gabe because he seems stunned and unable to process what I've said, me because I can't believe he's really stunned. I guess the *I do, too* was much more pathetic than I gave it credit for. I guess I'm much more pathetic than I gave me credit for.

"I love you, Gabe. I do. I've never loved anyone as much in my entire life as I love you. I've just spent the better part of two days searching for you—I mean, what did you think? That I just turned up here because I fancied a day out?"

His smile tries to emerge—oh, that lovely way his tongue touches to his upper teeth. So slyly happy!

"Go back to that other part, about the love," he says, and I could just punch him.

"You're an idiot, you know?" I say, but when he just nods I have the overwhelming urge to apologize. "I'm sorry I didn't tell you. I know I should have, I know—I've just never said it to anyone before. I've just never—"

I'm glad when he cuts me off with a kiss. Gladder yet, when it goes on for what seems like an age and gets deeper and deeper and oh, is that his tongue? Do I seriously crave him so much that it's only been two days, and a messy tear-streaked kiss is working me up?

Because it completely is.

When I grasp a handful of his arse, he stutters into my hair *oh, are we going to…*But all I can think about is the fact that he's wearing jeans. Ironed jeans, but jeans nonetheless. And his arse feels absolutely fantastic in them, so fantastic that I just have to squeeze.

"You know that I love you, too, Maddie," he says, but he's fondling me all over through the summer dress while he says it. I don't blame him—this is probably the thinnest item of outdoor clothing I've ever worn in his presence, and it takes next to nothing to get the front of it open and his mouth on my bare breasts.

All I can do is moan in relief and a crackling sort of happiness, reaching between us to pull and clasp at his clothes, as he does the same to mine. It doesn't take much to get the plaid shirt partially unbuttoned, the jeans unzipped, my dress up around my thighs—and then we're tangled together on the grassy embankment.

I look up and see the sun flickering through the leaves, as I sink my fingers deep into his thick, black hair. It feels warm on my upturned face, but his body feels warmer still—as urgent as ever and twice as greedy.

He runs sweating palms over the outside of my thighs, and groans when I do the same to him. I get feverish fingers under the waistband of his jeans, and scratch my nails all over his firm flesh, just delighting in the feel.

He delights right back at me. He squirms just like always beneath my touch, the familiarity triggering the hot gush of pleasure that goes through me, more than anything else. I'm actually familiar with someone, and that person's familiar with me, and that feels better than I ever thought it would.

Especially when he finds his way between our bodies, so that he can press the heel of his palm over my straining sex.

It feels good—like a relief. Like the pressure's being let out. But then I guess he always knows just where to touch and how to do it. He knows that when I arch into that firm press, it means I want him to kiss me open-mouthed and rub his stiff prick against my thigh.

And he knows that it's time to frantically search my handbag for condoms, while I lay back against the embankment, half-dazed—though not so out of it that I can't struggle out of my knickers.

I do it when he moves off me, briefly, and watch him grin to see me so desperate. He doesn't have to tell me that my eagerness is the thing that makes him happy, because I just know. I know it, and should probably feel embarrassed, but instead I'm busy telling him to fuck me, Gabe, fuck me.

His tongue touches to his upper teeth as he fiddles with the little square of foil, and I'm sure I know what he's going to say. It's there in his expression, that all-encompassing need, and sure enough he runs with it.

"Are you ordering me to?" he says, and I bubble over with laughter. I clasp him to me. *Yes,* I tell him, *yes—I'm always ordering you to.*

Just before his mouth finds mine again and his hand touches briefly between my legs in that soft, sweet, testing sort of way he has. His eyes shutter closed briefly, to feel my slipperiness and my heat—just like always. But this time he doesn't tell me what it feels like or go for the fuck or any of the things I expect.

Instead he tells me that he's glad I came to find him. That I should always come to find him. That if I were the one to run away from him, he'd have the guts to come and find me. He'd always come and find me.

So I kiss him and reach for his delicious curving cock, before he can see me getting all mushy, again.

"Fuck me," I say, against the side of his face. "And this time—I won't stand for sidetracking. Just get on and do it, right now."

I love his expression for folding inwards, as though I'd stuck with mushy without me knowing it. And I love it—and him—more for pushing my legs apart and getting right between them, when I grab a fistful of his arse and squeeze until it hurts.

I know it hurts, because he whines for me. Then pushes into my waiting pussy, smooth as silk.

His face goes slack over mine, but that's OK because I think my expression mirrors his. Play sex games for months and months, and fill your time with delicious pleasures, and suddenly two days without seems like forever. My body sings to feel it again—that roll and push of a good fuck, Gabe's eager body pressing into mine, the sound of his breath panted hot and tense against my cheek, my ear.

He starts off slow but that can't last—and I think that's in part due to where we are. It takes me a second to realize that we've just fallen to rabid fucking outdoors, where anyone could find us, but I think Gabe's been considering that idea all along.

I can see him flicking his gaze up the embankment as he rocks into me, as though he expects the posh neighbors from down the road to turn up at any second. To catch us rutting lewdly in the grass, my bare legs up around his waist and his arse largely exposed to the world.

Or maybe he's just thinking about where we are, exactly. About how many times he didn't come down here with a girl to make out or fumble with her, stickily, or just sit here, holding hands. Maybe he's thinking of his parents and their disapproving gaze, while we defile their property and moan and grunt and groan loud enough to send birds up from the trees.

However, his expression isn't half as tense as any such thoughts would demand. I'm sure it isn't. We get to some sort of blissful, shaking, halfway point, mouths all over each other and unable to come apart more than an inch, and then he suddenly rears up over me. Mouth wide and open in the broadest smile I think I've ever seen him give, breathing out in a way that almost seems to spill over into laughter.

He looks giddy, I think, and maybe if he were anyone else that would be kind of insulting. But it's Gabe and I understand that bursting feeling of something freeing, and newly discovered, and so I laugh back. I capture his face in my hands, and laugh back.

"I don't think I'll ever get over how good this feels," he tells me in between lurching, vigorous thrusts, and his hands suddenly dig in the grass on either side of my head. I see him bunch it into his fists, digging into the soil with greedy fingers as his hips churn against mine.

It makes me even more aware of our surroundings—little pebbles and the slippery twist of weeds and grass pressing into the bare flesh of my arse, the smell of summer and fertile heat surging through me with each ragged breath.

I can taste something green on my tongue. I can feel him, thick and hard and hot and strong.

"I love you, Gabe," I say, as my head goes back. "I love you."

And he laughs again, deliriously. Those dirty hands leave the soil and the grass and clutch at my hips in much the same way, so that this time when he fucks into me it hits hard against that sweet spot inside me.

I think I cry out. I probably shout that I love him, again. But that's OK, because he says it back before burying his mouth in mine, twisting our bodies until the world is spinning and suddenly I'm over him. I'm over him, all that mess of nature pressing into my knees instead of my butt, and his soil-streaked hands linked with mine as I push them up, up, over his head.

It feels good, and right, to hold them there. And it feels even better to shove down on that gorgeous thick cock, rocking until I get into that good good rhythm—the one that makes me shiver with pleasure and moan into his mouth.

On each surge upwards my clit brushes the jumping muscles of his almost-bare belly, but it hardly seems to matter. Just the feel of him and the taste of him and his cock shoving roughly into me as I press his hands to the grass—just those things are enough on their own. They make me ache and him say *oh God, yes, please fuck me, do me, do it*, as he grins wickedly—probably over his own unabashed lewdness.

When he jerkily asks me to get his shirt all the way open—yeah, then I know it's the lewdness. He wants to be filthy in this place, largely naked and rutting up against the slut queen he calls a girlfriend.

And I know this, because that's what he actually calls me. He actually calls me a slut queen while we're fucking.

Before looking naughty and caught and flustered, and bucking up at me all at the same time.

He needn't worry, however. I'm quite happy to accept my new title. In fact, I'll accept any regal epithets he chooses to give me, as long as we keep fucking while he says it. Anything, as long as we keep fucking. Or having sex. Or making love.

We're probably making love, even though it's on an embankment and we're a mess and people are likely spying on us from the farm across the way.

But the point is, I think—he doesn't seem to care. And I don't seem to care—not about anything. I just kiss him, and kiss him, and when he blurts out that he's going to come, I do too.

I watch him writhe beneath me, eyes burning dark and bright and mouth slack, and orgasm blooms in my belly, warm as anything. It pours through me, and pours through him, and all I can think is this: I would find you anywhere.

―――

We lie on the embankment, side by side—long enough to feel the day cooling around us. But the truth is that I only notice evening drawing in because he starts pulling his clothes all the way back on. He lay there that long, in comfortable silences and outdoors to boot, with his cock hanging out and his hairy chest on display and dammit, I should have teased him! I should have told him that someone was coming, and watched him scramble.

Instead I have to make do with marveling at the plaid and the jeans. Now that I can think straight, they're calling my attention, again.

I nudge him, as he fiddles with the buttons.

"What's with the outfit, Butch McBeeferson?"

He laughs—not giddy like before, but even so. And even better, he blushes—as though he's embarrassed about the getup.

"These are my—you know. *Dirty* clothes."

Of course I've got no idea what *that* means. But I'd certainly like to subscribe to its newsletter. Just where does one find these so-called dirty clothes, and what activities might one partake of while wearing them?

I'm hoping…more outdoor fun. Possibly with that swing included.

"No, Madison," he says, when he sees my look. He rolls his eyes at me, but on him rolling eyes is delightful. It suggests a new boldness that makes me all warm inside.

"Not *that* kind of dirty. I wear this for gardening and stuff like that. I tried to clear out the hundred-foot weeds while wearing tank tops, but it didn't work out well."

"You mean: *it hurt me to put holes in my good clothes*, don't you."

"Yes—all right, all right. I like things tidy. I keep things neat. I don't want my uniform getting all dirty because I'm a crazy clean freak."

He called it his uniform! By this point I think it's certain—we are definitely soul mates. Or at the very least, kind of meant to be together.

"And bad bad evil jeans just deserve everything they get, huh?"

He shows me those little pointed incisors. Looks so happy I could just bust with the delight all over him—never mind my own.

"Exactly. I had to go into The Gap to get them."

He says The Gap the way most people say *sewage works*.

"I'm mortified on your behalf."

"I know. I look like *Andy*. Next I'll be eating cold pasta right out of its baking dish."

He shudders—and gets a kiss on the cheek for that. Now that we're all hand holding and love and soul mates and whatever, I'm betting I'm going to see a lot more of funny Gabe—and this pleases me a great, great deal.

As does the feel of his fingers, lacing through mine.

"Do you really choose me, Maddie? In spite of the neatness, and weirdness and all the other things I probably haven't told you about myself?"

"Are you secretly a woman?"

"I'm serious, Madison!"

"Do you own a Simply Red album?"

"No—come on. Just—"

"For all I know, maybe *you* choose Andy."

He shakes the hand in his.

"You're just trying to be difficult now."

I glance at him, side on. Smiling wickedly, but meaning something else with my eyes. I know I mean something else with my eyes, because I can feel it trying to leak out of them, all warm and gooey and love-stuff.

"No, I'm not. You're just ridiculous, Gabe, absolutely ridiculous." Is it weird that he looks happy to hear it? "Of course I choose you. I've never chosen Andy—not even when in the middle of *fucking* Andy."

He closes his eyes, briefly, on the word fucking.

"I just thought it was what you wanted. You *told* me it was what you wanted."

"It was," he says, and I note the past tense. But that's OK, because it's past tense for me, too. Especially as it's kind of obvious why Gabe really and truly wanted to get into all of those shenanigans.

"And don't ever do anything again just to please me."

He frowns, and gets stuck between incredulous and protesting.

"I mean—don't ever do anything that hurts you, really hurts you, just because you think it's what I'm missing. That's not what it's about. You know it's not."

For a moment I think he's going to stick with the protesting, but then he lets out a big sighing breath. Rolls his head back against the grass.

"I know."

We lapse back into silence, after that—but again, there's nothing uncomfortable about it. Even after a conversation like that everything just feels lax and easy, and I could fall asleep, I really could.

Until he says:

"It's not so bad here, is it?"

He's staring up at that canopy of leaves, and at the way the light is starting to dim between—I suppose anything could look good from this angle.

And then it comes to me, in a rush.

"You're going to live here, aren't you?"

Of course he is. The jeans and the gardening and the apartment he's let go—God, I probably came here half-knowing it. He wants to come back to this strange and dusty place, and make it right again. Clear it out, and make it right again.

And then I think of my old house, down in the valley. The way my dad used to chase me around and around it, just in fun—because I was still little and not yet unwieldy, and confusing. How I used to long to go back there, back to that first home where everything was good and happy.

"I was thinking about it. I was thinking that it might be beautiful, if I just gave it a little work. Cleaned it up, and made it all right again."

I breathe out a laugh.

"Those are almost the words I was thinking, you know—make it right."

He squeezes my hand, and looks at me through what is now definitely evening light. His eyes, I think. God, those burning dark eyes.

"You could make it right with me, if you wanted to," he says. And I tell him I do. Always, I do.

About the Author

Charlotte Stein has written over thirty short stories, novellas, and novels, including entries in *The Mammoth Book of Hot Romance* and *Best New Erotica 10*. Her latest work, *Addicted*, was recently called salaciously steamy by *Dear Author*. When not writing salaciously steamy books, she can be found eating jelly turtles, watching terrible sitcoms, and occasionally lusting after hunks. For more on Charlotte, visit www.charlottestein.net.